DEFIANCE

Son of a Mermaid ~ Book Two

KATIE O'SULLIVAN

Wicked Whale
Publishing

First Edition: December 2015

(First published as Blood of a Mermaid by Crescent Moon Press, May 2014)

Cover Design: Cape Cod Scribe, K.R. Conway

Library of Congress Cataloging-in-Publication Data

O'Sullivan, Katie

Defiance/ by Katie O'Sullivan – First Edition.

Pages: 343

Summary: Now that fifteen-year-old Shea MacNamara knows he is the son of a mermaid princess, he finds having royal blood means making tough choices. When his girlfriend Kae is kidnapped by Zan the sorcerer, all three teens face life and death decisions, balanced precariously between doing what they are told and defying authority to do what is right.

Wicked Whale Publishing

P.O. Box 264

Sagamore Beach, MA 02562-9998

www.WickedWhalePublishing.com

ISBN: 978-0-9962789-2-8

Published in the United States of America

Dedication

For my Dad.

For your help and encouragement in my writing and in life,
and for introducing me to the wonders of the Atlantic Ocean,
so many years ago.

And for my Mom.

I love you and miss you every day.

DEFIANCE

Chapter One

Zan shivered as he felt his way along the uneven walls of stone, the cave as cold and black as a cloud of octopus ink. The message he'd received had been cryptic, but he was pretty sure he was in the right place.

"Right" being an extremely relative concept.

His eyes widened to their limits trying to see beyond the blackness of the murky Arctic cavern, but to no avail. *So much about this journey is wrong.* He flicked his tail and quickened his pace, thinking bitterly of the last year, doubting the path he'd chosen to swim. Or rather, the one he felt forced to choose. Choice was not a luxury afforded to one in his position.

In the span of a few short weeks, he'd gone from being the hunter to being hunted.

He exhaled heavily in the darkness as the tunnel led him downward, releasing the pressure building in his ears and feeling the bubbles stream from the gill slits underneath his now shaggy hair. He no longer looked the part of an Adluo soldier, but his altered appearance helped him blend as he passed through the small villages that dotted the floor of the Atlantic on his way north to this rendezvous point. Granted, the black hair billowing around his ears stood out, shining blue and green in the sunlight, but no one would connect him with the dark sorcerer of legends. In his years as Demyan's right hand merman, he'd kept his hair shorter than the dark stubble now sprouting from his jawline.

His eyes still straining against the darkness, Zan's mind wandered, thinking how close he and his comrades had been to accomplishing their mission and taking over the whole of the Atlantic.

After years of brutal and bloody battles, the Southern and Atlantic Oceans had finally come to an agreement. The end of war had been on the horizon, almost within reach, when he and the other Adluos made their way to Nantucket Sound for the final negotiations.

The oceans were now at peace with one another. But Zan was no longer a part of that peace.

He was an outlaw.

He'd been lucky to escape with his life, after being part of the plot to poison the Atlantic King at the Solstice Banquet. Assassination is not something ever taken lightly in the courts of Atlantis. Zan knew too well that the punishment for killing a member of the royal family is death. When he was young he'd made that mistake and had been paying the price ever since.

He'd left the Solstice celebration before Prince Demyan confessed to his own sins: poisoning the rightful Adluo heir as well as killing the boy's parents, the King and Queen of the Southern Ocean. Princess Brynneliana's drylander son miraculously appeared, bearing the Mark of Poseidon on his back and saving King Koios.

Zan had watched from afar, awaiting the signal to storm the castle with the rest of the soldiers. He saw the prince swim away, pursued by his own men after he killed the High Chancellor of Atlantis.

So why was Zan here now?

He shook his head in the darkness, trying to dispel the doubts. Why risk the potential for a quiet life in one of the small Atlantic villages, where he could raise crops and find a mate? Why was he now on the outer edge of the Arctic Ocean in these dark, subterranean tunnels? The answer was both simple and complex.

Zan owed Prince Demyan his life.

It was the prince who first noticed his innate magical abilities and saved him from a life in the dolphin stables – or worse. Demyan was the first to find Zan after the accident. Two young royals died that day, but instead of sending him to the High Court for judgment, Prince Demyan kept his secret. Demyan convinced the king to send Zan to the university to be trained as a sorcerer. Not only did Zan owe the prince his life for saving him that day, Zan's life would be forfeit still if the secret ever came out.

Now seventeen, Zan knew that while he was still a mere fry in the eyes of the elders, his magick was impressive, so strong that at times he still feared it might control him again rather than the other way around.

When the messenger arrived at the village where he'd been hiding, summoning him to this meeting, Zan had no choice but to obey. There was not a doubt in his mind. Which frightened him, and not only because Demyan knew exactly where to find him.

The message meant either the prince had gone completely insane with delusions of new powers, or succeeded in amassing a fresh army to continue his ongoing quest for underwater domination. Either way, it wouldn't have been prudent – or safe – to ignore the summons.

Up ahead in the blackness of the tunnel, Zan's eyes focused on a speck of glowing green. *A lantern! Finally!* His heart began to pound, knowing each flick of his tail brought him closer to Demyan. Closer to either his own death, or his redemption. He would soon find out which.

Emerging from the darkness, he entered a high-ceilinged cavern carved from the white marble rock. Lanterns glowing with luminescent sea creatures studded the walls at regular intervals. He raised one hand to shield his eyes from the sudden brightness, searching for signs of life.

Slabs of white and off-white marble lined the floor in a checkerboard pattern, reflecting the green light and making the room almost unbearably bright after the prolonged darkness of the tunnels. At the center of the chamber stood a tall, rounded table, also made of white marble, with twelve empty chairs surrounding it.

"Hello?" Zan's voice echoed from the rocky walls. "Is anyone here?" He waited silently. No one answered.

Exhaling his frustration, he moved forward, eyes darting around the bright chamber. Two places had been set out on the table as if for a meal, one on either side of the large circle. Facing each other.

"Hello?" Zan called again. A small mermaid with dark blue skin and long flowing hair that matched the color of the marble table emerged from a doorway on the opposite side of the chamber. In her hands a gleaming silver tray with a single clear bowl in the center caught the light, reflecting it around

the room in broken prisms. She placed the bowl in the middle of the table and a shudder ran down Zan's spine. The bowl was filled with small bluish-green berries, native only to the area around the Fiji Islands in the Pacific Ocean.

Eucheuma seeds.

"Zan! You got my message!" Prince Demyan's booming voice filled the entire cavern as the merman himself swam into the room. He stopped in front of Zan, folding his arms across his wide chest as the two mermen stared at each other. "You look like hell," he said with a wry smile. "What's with the long hair…and what's that growing on your chin? Is it black mold? Great Neptune's ghost, you even smell awful!"

Zan found his voice. "Thank you, Sire." He knew he looked frightful. He'd been on the run since the Solstice, not knowing where to go or who to trust.

Demyan, on the other hand, looked exactly the same as that Summer Solstice day when he'd almost accomplished his goal of taking over the Atlantic. How was such a thing possible? Zan opened his mouth to ask, then closed it again without saying a word. Such questions were not advisable, no matter how much the other merman smiled or joked. His was the smile of a sea snake, widening its mouth for the kill.

"But come, you must be famished." The prince gestured toward the waiting table. "Have a seat. Rest. Eat. There is much to be discussed as to my return."

"Your...return?" Zan said, his voice breaking roughly. "You're coming back to the Southern Ocean?"

Demyan laughed, his black eyes glittering coldly. "Hades help me, no. Brynn and her whelp are welcome to that barren wasteland." He took a handful of Eucheuma berries from the bowl and popped them into his mouth one by one as he continued. "No, the Southern Ocean isn't for me, Zan. It's so...limiting. I've developed a more global perspective, setting my sights on something bigger."

"Bigger? You mean like the whole Atlantic Ocean?"

"I mean all of it. The world." He pushed the bowl of seeds closer to Zan. "Have something to eat and I'll explain my vision for the future. Our future."

"Our future?" Zan repeated, feeling like an echo. "You...need my help?"

"Need is such a relative and transient term." The gleam returned to Demyan's black eyes. "I prefer to think of this as me offering you a position, but really more than that. I'm offering you a place in history! History that has yet to be written, but will be spoken of and remembered for centuries to come. Join me, Zan, and help me make my visions into reality, one ocean at a time."

"Are you offering me a choice?"

"No. Not really. I'm sorry if you don't feel up to the task of making history with me. You were always a good strategic

thinker, a good second in command for someone so young, as well as a truly powerful sorcerer. But everyone can be replaced." Demyan inclined his head to one side, his eyes shifting to something behind Zan.

Afraid of what lay behind him, he leaned forward. "I accept your offer."

"Good choice, my old friend." The wide smile returned to Demyan's face.

Turning in his chair, Zan saw two Arctic mermen swimming away, their snow white hair flowing behind them. One hefted a long steel blade and the other dragged a canvas sack secured at the top with a long length of blackened rope. The sack itself writhed furiously.

Zan took in a long, slow breath, glad he hadn't met them, and gladder still he didn't know what was in the sack. He felt certain if he knew the contents, he would already be dead. "Who are they?"

"Do you know the Arctic mermen have developed some quite innovative methods of…persuasion?" Demyan's smile widened even further. "I used to think we Adluos were the best fighters in any ocean, but I think the Arctic mermen are better."

"Better? How so?"

"More subtle. More precise with their movements, so as not to waste time or energy. It's fascinating to watch them

work, really." He grabbed another handful of the seeds. "Like artists, they are. The pity of the matter is they can also be quite overzealous. They keep going, and going, and going until really, you wish it would all just end."

Zan took in another long breath of the crisp Arctic water, grateful to know it was not to be his last. At least, not yet.

Chapter Two

Five aluminum soda cans covered in barnacles, three white plastic coffee cup lids, two empty water bottles, one pair of blue goggles with a cracked lens, one orange snorkel filled with sand, and a green plastic sand toy shaped like some kind of fish.

Shea MacNamara watched the early morning sun sparkle on the water, dancing like a million frenzied lightning bugs skimming the surface of the Atlantic. At low tide, the beach stretched on forever. Small waves lapped the edges of the sandbars while dozens of sea gulls circled overhead, taking turns diving for the green crabs exposed among the rocks below.

The black dog pranced along the shoreline, kicking up spray in his wake as he chased after the swooping birds. The salty breeze gusted along the sand, ruffling Lucky's fur and helping the gulls hover just out of his reach.

With one hand cupped over his eyes to shade them and the bag of trash dangling from the other, Shea stared intently across the water searching for signs of movement along the ocean's surface. He'd gotten so used to taking these morning walks alone that the voice at his shoulder made him jump.

"What're you looking for? Sea monsters?"

Shea tried to cover for his flinch by elbowing John in the side. "There's more to the ocean than meets the eye, Hansen." If he'd learned anything in the last month, it was that the Atlantic was filled with secrets. Not many of which he could share with his best friend. He glanced up at the taller boy. Now that the sun had bleached his hair, he and John looked more like brothers than friends. They'd even dressed alike this morning, in white t-shirts, dark jeans, and bare feet.

The only difference between them was the stone medallion hanging on a leather cord around Shea's neck. At least, that was the only difference anyone would see. The fact that Shea could transform his jeans-clad legs into a powerful mer-tail fell into that category of things he had no idea how to explain, even to his best friend.

He thought he knew what to say, but when he saw John at the airport last night all the practiced words flew right out of his head. Mermaids? Yeah, right. His friend would think Shea totally lost it. Instead, he let John do most of the talking, catching up on everything back in Oklahoma. Gramma gave

him the stink eye once or twice in the rearview mirror, but Shea decided to forget any talk of mermaid adventures. At least for now.

The dog trotted closer to where they stood, pink tongue lolling out one side of his smiling mouth. John bent to pick up a chunk of driftwood and threw it out into the waves. Lucky splashed after it and Shea smiled, reflecting on how much his life changed since coming to Cape Cod. In an incredibly short period of time, things went from boringly ho-hum-normal to anything but.

The problem was, he couldn't share any of his new life with John.

Last summer, his biggest problem had been how to get his father to take time off from work on their farm to drive into Oklahoma City to see a baseball game. That was before the tornado ripped the farm to shreds and he moved to Cape Cod. He absently brushed the spot behind his ear, fingers tracing along the soft slits that formed there the first time he fell into the ocean. Slits that covered his new gills. It was almost like the old Shea drowned that day, and this one emerged.

Lucky dropped the driftwood at his feet and barked, bringing him back to the present. "Guess it's my turn." He heaved the driftwood into the waves, not quite as far as John had thrown it but far enough not to be embarrassed. Lucky,

however, was not impressed and brought the piece of wood back to John instead.

Shea agreed that John could throw a lot farther. After all, his friend had played varsity baseball since freshman year and already had scouts looking at him. That was the first thing John told him about when he got off the plane at Logan Airport. The coach from Oklahoma State saw John pitch in the playoffs and practically guaranteed him a spot on the team. Shea grimaced. College was another thing that wouldn't be normal for him.

Nothing was normal anymore, not since the day he'd met his mother.

Finding his mother had been the best – and strangest – part of his new reality. Shea's grandfather, the King of the Atlantic, didn't approve of his only daughter marrying a human and approved even less of her pregnancy. By leaving Shea and his dad in Oklahoma, she'd been trying to protect him and give him a somewhat normal childhood. The birthmark on his back meant he would inherit the throne and rule the Atlantic Ocean, despite the fact he was half-human. But. The ocean was a treacherous place for a baby without gills.

As Shea found out earlier in the summer, his mother's undersea world still held dangers for him, even now that he had gills and the ability to transform.

Lucky gave a short, sharp bark, and pushed his nose against Shea's leg, interrupting his thoughts. Shea bent to scratch the scruff around his neck. "Okay, you're right. We should leave before the lifeguards get here. Or before Officer Tandy catches us again."

John's face scrunched in a lopsided frown while he wiped sandy, wet hands down the front of his shirt. "Officer Candy?"

"Tandy. Dogs aren't technically allowed on the beach." Shea clipped the leash to Lucky's collar. "We've already had more than our fair share of run-ins with the local cops."

A wide smile split John's face and he let out a deep belly laugh. "Don't tell me Mr. Do-The-Right-Thing is breaking a rule! You've changed, MacNamara."

If only he could tell John the truth about all the changes… but he didn't know where to start. Maybe he'd let his mother take the lead on what to say and not say when she stopped by the house for breakfast later. He shrugged his shoulders and smiled sheepishly. "It's a bad rule. I mean, look how happy this makes Lucky. Sometimes breaking the rules can be the right thing."

"Hey, I know that." John held up his hands defensively. "I just never thought I'd hear those words coming out of your mouth. You've always been so black and white about stuff."

Shea shrugged again. "Yeah, well, I guess I've discovered the world isn't a black and white kind of place."

The pair trudged up the beach toward the metal barrel sitting at the edge of the sand while Shea tied the top of his plastic bag of trash. The dog shook the last of the salt water from his fur, almost jerking the leash from John's hand, as a police cruiser pulled into the parking lot. A familiar face with mirrored glasses and a beaky nose leaned out of the driver's side window.

"Good morning, Mr. MacNamara," Officer Tandy said, slipping the sunglasses down his nose and peering over the top rim. "You weren't thinking of walking your dog down onto the beach, were you?"

"We took a walk and stopped here to throw out some garbage we collected along the way." Not a lie exactly, just not the whole truth. Shea tossed the bag into the barrel, the solid thunk reverberating in the morning air.

Tandy nodded. "I like to see a young man caring for the environment. Reminds me of myself at your age, you know, when I dated your mom." His eyes slid over Shea, landing on John. "Are you going to introduce me to your friend?"

Shea couldn't think past the "I dated your mom" crack. John stepped forward and stuck out a hand. "John Hansen, sir. I'm friends with Shea from back in Oklahoma. He was just showing me around."

Tandy narrowed his eyes. "Oklahoma, eh? Pretty far from home, aren't you?"

John shot a look over to Shea before answering. "Yes, sir? I'm here visiting, like I said."

"Staying with the MacNamaras?"

Shea finally found his voice. "Actually, we need to get going. Gramma will have breakfast on the table by now." He nudged John with his elbow, pushing him away from the policeman. "Nice to see you again, officer." The boys headed for the street.

"Say hi to your mother for me," Tandy called after them, getting back into his car.

"I will when I see her." Shea wondered yet again just how much the police officer knew about his mother, her family, and the underwater world in which she lived. He knew Tandy had been friends with his dad growing up, and had known both his mother and father when they were younger. But what else did Tandy really know? And did it matter? Because Shea was pretty sure the guy had no clue what had actually been going on this summer.

As the only daughter of the King of the Atlantic, and whose own mother had been a princess of the Southern Ocean's Adluo clan, Shea's mother Brynneliana had been declared Queen of the Southern Ocean soon after Prince Demyan fled the Summer Solstice gathering. Shea was proud of her for taking on the responsibility of helping the Southern Ocean recover from too many years of war and deprivation, but at the same time he resented the fact that she planned to leave him. Again. Kae would follow with the rest of the entourage, to help settle the new queen into her new responsibilities. And Shea would be stuck here on Cape Cod. Alone.

John punched his shoulder, reminding him he wasn't actually alone. "What was that crack about your mother?"

"Oh, man, I forgot to tell you! I found my mom here on Cape Cod, and she's pretty awesome."

John stopped in the middle of the street, a skeptical look on his face. "So awesome that she left you on your own for the first fifteen years of your life?"

"Totally not her fault. What is it they say? *Extenuating circumstances.*" Shea shook his head and waved a dismissive hand. "Anyway, she explained everything and it's all cool. I can't wait for you to meet her. She's looking forward to meeting you. Maybe she'll be at the house by the time we get back."

"Whatever." He fell back into step next to Shea. "I'm more interested in meeting this girlfriend of yours. Forgive me if I don't totally believe your over-the-top description of the royal hotness of your blonde beauty with the cute booty."

"She's not royal," Shea corrected, much to John's amusement.

"That's the only thing in my description you're going to object to? Man, you're more messed up than I thought." John chuckled and shook his head. "She must have you wound pretty tight around her little finger."

Shea felt the blood heating his cheeks and clenched his jaw shut before he said anything he'd regret. He and John had been friends for as long as he could remember and he didn't want to lose that. But there was no way he'd let John say anything bad to or about Kae. He took a deep breath, releasing it slowly. "Lay off, okay? Can't you just be happy I found some new friends here on the Cape? It was hard enough losing my dad, but then to be dragged away from you and the other guys too…"

"Hey, I didn't mean anything by it." John threw his arm around Shea's shoulders and gave him a kind of half-hug squeeze. "I missed you too. And you know I'm just kidding." They were almost at the MacNamara house. "Hey, no extra car in the driveway. Guess your mom isn't here yet."

The corner of Shea's mouth turned up in a grin. "Umm, she doesn't actually own a car. She would've walked."

John frowned, dropping his arm. "What, you mean like she lives around here? And she couldn't bother to let you know she was alive?" He stared at Shea for a long moment

before looking away. "Man, I don't think I'd be as forgiving as you."

Shea's mouth opened, but no words came out. He didn't know what to say, because he pretty much agreed with John. Except. His mom had good reasons – sound reasons – for letting Shea grow up on land, far away from ocean politics. It didn't make it hurt any less, but he understood and he'd forgiven her. Maybe he would've handled things differently, but then again, who knows what he'd do in a similar situation. He hoped he'd never have to find out.

Through the kitchen's screen door, Shea heard bacon sizzling in the frying pan and his grandmother humming to herself, but Shea didn't recognize the tune. After rinsing the sand from his feet and Lucky's paws, Shea handed the hose to John and peered through the screen door. "Is there a towel to dry Lucky, Gramma?"

Martha MacNamara appeared framed in the doorway a moment later, holding an old grey towel. She wore her usual faded housedress and an apron that was probably once some shade of blue. Her long, steely grey hair was pulled into a severe bun, giving her that no-nonsense air Shea had come to appreciate over the last month. The rising sun glinted on her half-moon spectacles as she pushed the door open and handed

the towel to her grandson. "You boys were up and out early today."

"I wanted to show John the beach at dawn," Shea said as he began to dry the dog. "You know it's my favorite time of day. Is Mom here yet?"

"No, Brynn hasn't yet graced us with her presence," Martha said with a grimace.

The sound of the doorbell chimed through the house and Shea threw down the towel. "Maybe that's her now!" He raced through the house to answer the front door and barely hid his disappointment. "Come on in, Hailey. Gramma's still cooking the bacon."

"You don't look very happy to see me. Are you sure you want to invite me in?" Hailey put her hands on her hips and didn't budge from the steps. She was dressed head-to-toe in black today, from her black t-shirt to her black Converse high tops. The only bit of color was the scorching yellow Batman logo on the front of her shirt.

He pasted a smile on his face, not wanting to hurt her feelings. "Come in already, you dork. Who else will eat all that bacon?"

Hailey's dark braids swung around her head and her brown eyes crinkled as she returned his smile. "Who else but me shows up on your doorstep at breakfast time?"

Shea sighed, closing the door behind her and wondering yet again how a girl could eat as much as she did and stay so thin. But Hailey was right. He should've expected it was her and not gotten his hopes up. He really wanted to introduce John to his mother, and show him that everything was okay. He drew in a deep breath. She was expected. She would be here soon.

In the kitchen, Martha was using tongs to pull the bacon out of the frying pan, laying it flat on the sheets of paper towel covering the countertop. "Good morning, Hailey," she said without looking up. "Would you like some breakfast? You haven't eaten yet, have you?"

"No, ma'am, not technically," Hailey answered, pulling out one of the metal chairs and seating herself at the Formica table as she unleashed a flood of complaints. It never failed to amaze Shea how fast the words could flow from her mouth. "My mom just discovered those breakfast shakes? You know, the kind that come in all the flavors that sound like they should taste amazing but they taste more like aluminum, which isn't surprising since they come in a can and all. She stocked up on tons of them in every conceivable flavor combination. Some have coffee flavoring, some have fruit, some are even plain vanilla. When I say she stocked up, she went all out. But somehow they figured out how to make even chocolate taste bad. Who would have guessed it?"

Martha shook her head and made sympathetic clucking noises. "You know you're welcome anytime, dear."

The screen door to the backyard opened and John stepped into the kitchen. "Is this a private conversation or can anyone join in?"

Hailey's eyes widened as she took in John's tall muscular frame. "Umm, Shea? There's like a Greek god in your doorway?"

Shea and John both laughed out loud. Shea finally caught his breath. "I know you're obsessed with Greek mythology, Hailey, but give me a break. John Hansen? A Norse god, maybe. On a good day. But he's no Zeus."

"Hey, I resent that, I think," John said, coming closer to punch Shea's shoulder.

Hailey stared. "Wait, so you're Shea's friend from Oklahoma, right? Oh my gods! It's so great to meet you!" She jumped from her seat and grabbed his right hand, pumping it in a frenetic handshake. "He, like, talks about you all the time, and how you're a baseball god for real! I'm so glad you're finally here!"

John's mouth quirked into a crooked grin as he shook her hand. "He talks about you all the time too, gorgeous, but I thought you were supposed to be blonde?"

Hailey froze, her eyes darting from John to Shea and back again. "Blonde?"

22

"Aren't you Shea's girlfriend?"

She dropped his hand like it was poison. "No. You must mean Kae." She hesitated for several seconds before plopping back into the chair, the cushion letting out a long sigh.

John had the good sense to be embarrassed, he cheeks and ears turning bright red almost immediately. "Hey, I'm so sorry. Shea told me his girlfriend was infinitely cuter than any of the girls back home and when I saw you, I assumed..."

It was Hailey's turn to blush, but she pulled herself together quickly. "With lines like that, how can I stay mad at you? How about we start over?" She stood and extended her right hand once again. "Hi, I'm Hailey Thompson. And you are?"

A goofy grin spread across John's face. "John Hansen. It's a real pleasure to meet you, Hailey."

"Likewise." Hailey's cheeks stayed pink as she sat back down and gestured at the empty seat between her and Shea. "Pull up a chair and tell me everything."

Shea rolled his eyes as John plunked into the empty seat. "Be careful, John. Hailey's a dangerous one. She almost drowned me the first time we went fishing."

Her mouth fell open again. "Really? You really wanna go there with me, Mr. MacNamara?"

"So Hailey, how is your brother Chip doing?" Martha asked, pointedly ignoring her grandson. She cracked another egg into the mixing bowl. "He seemed like such a nice young man."

Hailey turned her gaze toward Martha and snorted. "Yeah, he can certainly seem that way. All like, 'Yes, ma'am,' and 'No, ma'am,' and whatnot. To me he's just a royal pain in the butt." Her eyes slid toward Shea. "No offense."

He shrugged. "No big deal. I agree that your brother's pretty much a jerk, especially to girls," he said, thinking of the few times Chip tried to hit on Kae.

"Your brother's a jerk?" John asked, seemingly unable to take his eyes off Hailey.

Hailey dismissed his words with an excited wave of her hands. "Forget about him. There's something truly important I want to tell you. Like, knock your socks off, swallow your gum important."

John looked back and forth between Shea and Hailey. "Should I leave?"

Shea scrunched his eyebrows. "Why would you need to leave?"

John cleared his throat, looking uncomfortable. "Well, if it's important…"

Hailey threw her hands in the air. "Are all boys so stupid? Honestly! Okay, here's the scoop. Mom got a fab new decorating job, for this gazillionaire she knows from her New York days! You've heard of Monica Andreaopolous, right?

24

Well, the woman recently bought a new home – a total mansion, really – and hired Mom for all the interior design work! What a coup, right?"

John grabbed her hand with excitement. "That sounds awesome!"

Shea frowned. "How will she manage that from Cape Cod?"

"Oh, she so can't," Hailey agreed, smiling at John all the while. "She's gotta be on site, like 24/7. She's gonna to take Chip and I along with her! Isn't that cool? Like, uber-amazing and I'm so excited I can't stand it!"

Shea felt his world crumbling around the edges. "You're going back to New York City?"

Hailey seemed oblivious to Shea's misery. "Not New York at all! Would I be this excited for New York? Heck no. Andreaopolous is the Greek shipping heiress, you know, the one on the cover of *Vogue* magazine last month? Her family owns, like, most of Santorini for goodness sake!"

Shea shook his head, still not understanding. "Why would I read *Vogue*?"

"Are you even listening to me? I'm trying to tell you I'm flying to the Greek islands for the rest of the summer!"

Chapter Three

Shea stared at his friend, unable to process what she was saying. John, meanwhile, was letting out some kind of cheering whoop as if determined to puncture someone's ear drum.

"Can you believe it? You know my obsession with mythology. This is like a dream come true, for real!" Hailey grinned as Martha placed three full breakfast plates of steaming eggs and bacon on the table.

"Congratulations on your good news, young lady." Martha smiled at her, and looked over at her grandson. Shea stared at his plate like he wasn't sure what to do with the food, unable to meet anyone's eyes. "Shea? Aren't you going to eat?"

He picked up his fork, and pushed at the scrambled eggs until Martha turned away to wipe down the stovetop. As soon as she wasn't paying attention, he put the fork down and folded his arms over his chest. He narrowed his eyes at Hailey, who was happily crunching a slice of bacon. "When are you leaving?"

Her eyebrows shot up and she put her own fork down, swallowing the food in her mouth. John glanced between the two of them, obviously unsure whether to get in the middle of this argument. "I'm not sure. I think Mom's trying to arrange flights for next week." She paused to take a drink of her orange juice before adding, "I've always wanted to go to Greece. Ever since we studied mythology in school, back in New York."

Shea relented. "I'm happy for you, really, it's just going to be a lonely summer here without you."

John piped up. "What about me? You've got me here for the next few days, at least until I need to go back for baseball camp."

Shea snorted. "Three days. Out of a whole summer. Big deal."

"Ouch, dude. That's cold." John forked a pile of scrambled eggs into his mouth and chewed in silence.

"You've still got Kae, right?" Hailey's eyes locked on her juice glass as she lowered her voice. "You guys would be swimming off without me anyway, kissing and playing mermaid games and whatever."

John choked a bit on his eggs and started coughing. Shea flinched, knowing there would be questions to answer, but kept his eyes glued to Hailey. "What I have with Kae, what she and I share is…different, that's true. But you're still my friend."

She blew out a long breath before picking up her fork and stabbing at her scrambled eggs. "Friends. Right."

"Besides, she's leaving for the summer too." Shea thought about Kae swimming off with his mother for the Southern Ocean, leaving him behind. John was leaving in a few days for an intensive baseball training camp at the University of Michigan and with Hailey gone too, Cape Cod would be awfully lonely for the rest of the summer.

Hailey's laughter sounded bitter. "So, what? She's allowed to take a trip and I'm not? Some friend you are. You should be happy for me! Hello? I'm going to Greece, where all the gods and goddesses were practically invented! Besides, I always end up feeling left out when she's around."

Shea inhaled deeply and blew out a slow breath. "I'm sorry I snapped. I *am* happy for you, it just feels like I'm being left out while you all go off on cool adventures."

"You can always come to baseball camp with me," John chimed in. "You'd come back ready to be a baseball star at your new high school."

The doorbell rang and Martha's voice wafted up from the basement even as Shea rose from his seat. "Shea? Can you get that? Maybe it's your mother."

"On it." He ran to the front door but it wasn't his mother on the steps. He exclaimed happily, pulling Kae close for a hug. He buried his face in her mop of unruly blond curls, letting her fresh scent of sunshine and saltwater fill his senses. "I thought we were meeting on the beach this morning. I wanted to introduce you to John."

"I got held up by the...oophff! Shea, stop squeezing me so hard! I can't breathe!"

Shea relaxed his grip and took half a step back. She wore board shorts and her usual woven halter-top. Her transmutare medallion dangled from her neck, and reminded him of the gift he'd purchased for her. He dug into his pocket and pulled out the small box he'd carefully gift wrapped. He'd taken it to the beach that morning, and although one edge was slightly damp it seemed to be in perfect shape. "I bought this for you the other day when I was in Hyannis with Hailey. It reminded me of you."

Kae stared at the package in Shea's hand, but didn't reach for the gift. "Oh, it's pretty. And so shiny blue! Like the ocean's surface on a sunny day. But Shea, I don't think paper will last very long underwater."

Shea's face cracked into a wide grin and placed the box in her hand. "That's just the wrapping, silly. You need to look inside for the gift."

"I've never heard of wrapping paper." Kae turned the box slowly in her hands, the shine of the paper reflecting the light. "It's so pretty."

"You're supposed to rip it off." Sometimes he forgot that they came from such different worlds. He tore the edge of the paper to show her what he meant. It was a small package, and the paper came off fairly quickly.

She stared at the white box. "Oh, it's lovely. But Shea, cardboard is not much better than paper…"

He interrupted. "The box isn't the present."

She looked up at him, cocking her head to the side. "Then why did you give it to me? Why give me shiny paper to rip and a box that isn't a present? I don't understand. Isn't it wasteful?"

He shifted his weight from foot to foot, not quite knowing how to explain. "I don't know. It's how we give gifts. Just open the box, okay?"

Inside was a cuff bracelet of hammered silver, made of five thin distinct strands that rippled across like waves, looking like the undulating surface of the ocean. Kae stared, not saying anything.

"It reminded me of the stories our moms were telling about their journeys when they were our age, traveling the world," Shea stammered, unsure how to gauge her reaction. "You know, the five lines of silver flowing like water, like the

five oceans, and how soon it will be our turn..." His voice trailed off. "You don't like it?"

"It's beautiful," she whispered, her eyes looking watery.

"It's just a bracelet." He reached over to take it out of the box. "Let's see if it fits." He slipped the cuff over her wrist and gently squeezed so that it closed snugly against her skin. He trailed his fingers up to her elbow and leaned his forehead against hers. "It's so you don't forget me while we're apart. It's a long time until September when I see you again in Atlantis."

"Oh, Shea..." Her voice was still a mere whisper. "I won't forget you."

He suddenly straightened. "Speaking of forgetting! John and Hailey are in the kitchen. She just told me her family's leaving Cape Cod on a trip, too. Mom was supposed to be here for breakfast, but I guess she's running late."

Kae frowned. "You and I need to talk."

A slight flurry of panic twirling in his belly. Wasn't "we need to talk" girl-code for breaking up? They'd barely been dating for a month and she wanted to break up?

"There you are, Shea!" John clamped one arm around Shea's neck and scrubbed the other hand through his hair, turning it into a tangled mess. "I take it this isn't your mother at the door."

Shea struggled against the chokehold, quickly realizing the futility of the situation. "Quit messing around, John. This is my friend Kae, the girlfriend I told you about."

Her eyes widened, tipping her head back to meet John's friendly gaze. "It's a pleasure to meet you, John. I've heard so much about you, and yet Shea neglected to mention you were so much taller and stronger than him."

"Only a few inches," Shea protested as John finally released him, his laughter filling the hallway. Hailey wandered out of the kitchen to join them. "Hailey, help me out. These two are being cruel."

"I'm sure it's nothing more than you deserve," she retorted. "So why are we all standing in the hall with the door wide open? And where's your mom, Shea? I thought she was coming for breakfast today to meet John. And oh cool, you gave Kae the bracelet I helped you pick out in town the other day. Isn't it awesome? Don't you just love it? Like silver waves or something, right? I tried to talk him into earrings, but we couldn't remember if you have pierced ears or not, so a bracelet seemed like a good compromise. It was the only one like it or I would've gotten one for myself too and we could've been like twins."

When she paused to take a breath, John started laughing again. "Do you ever stop talking?"

"No, she doesn't," Kae muttered. "Listen, I came over with a message from your mom, Shea."

He grinned and wrapped an arm around her waist. "That she's going to miss breakfast? Because we already figured that one out. But we've got you here instead, so everything's okay. I know, why don't we all walk over to Harwich Port and show John the Cape Cod version of downtown?"

"Sounds good to me!" John grabbed Hailey's hand and spun her around. "Shall we hit the street and paint the town red?"

Confusion filled Kae's face. "The pavement here is solid and unyielding. It wouldn't be wise to hit it. And why do you need red paint?"

Hailey rolled her eyes and huffed out a breath. "They're just expressions, Kae. Honestly, you can be so remedial."

Shea threw up his hands. "Hailey, you're the one being impossible. Can't we all get along?" He looked from one girl to the other, noting that both of them were scowling. "Please?" He hated the whining note that had entered his voice, but he wanted things to feel normal. Or at least, as normal as his world was ever going to feel, now that it was filled with mermaids and magick.

At that moment Martha came up the stairs from the basement, arms loaded with damp towels to be hung on the clothesline. She glanced from one frowning face to the other, before focusing on the mermaid. "Kae, dear, it's so good to see you again. Your mother tells me you're headed to University this fall."

"University?" Hailey asked, the sarcasm in her voice replaced by curiosity. "I thought you were fifteen."

"It's when we start," Kae explained, glancing at Shea. He realized half a second too late that he was in trouble.

"We?" Hailey's head whipped in Shea's direction, her eyes narrowing into thin slits as she slapped his arm. "And you're upset with me for leaving for the summer? When were you going to tell me that you're headed off to private school in September?"

"That's different. I have no choice."

"Different, huh? So when we took the tour of Monomoy High School together last week, you knew the whole time you wouldn't be going there. Why didn't you tell me?"

Shea looked down at his feet. "It's complicated."

His grandmother spoke up. "Nothing is certain until it is certain." All four teens turned to stare at her. "Except laundry. If you children will excuse me. Shea, could you get the door?"

He went to open the screen door out to the backyard. When he returned, Hailey was already stomping out the front door and down the steps. "Hailey, wait!"

"I'll go after her," John volunteered. "You know girls, she probably just needs to blow off some steam." John jumped down the stairs, hustling to catch up with Hailey on the street.

Kae put a gentle hand on Shea's elbow. "Let them go for now. We still need to talk."

He turned to stare at her, noting the serious look in her eyes and feeling his stomach clench into a ball. There was that phrase again, the one that a boy never wants to hear from his girl since it never leads to anything good in books or movies. Or in real life, for that matter. His mind spun through the possibilities of subject matter, deciding her parents probably raised more objections to their relationship.

It was as if Kae could read his mind, and see the swirl of emotions wreaking havoc in his head. She smiled, her eyes glittering. "It's not *that* kind of talk." She leaned in and planted a soft kiss on his cheek. "I liked when that tall boy called me your girlfriend. And thank you for the bracelet. You have good taste in jewelry, even if you have strange taste in human friends."

Something unknotted in his stomach. Feelings were proving a trickier thing than learning to swim. "Okay, then," he said, still feeling slightly uncertain. "What is it we need to talk about?"

"Your mother."

The knots returned with a vengeance, his stomach churning as his breath stuck in his throat. "Is she alright? Did Demyan return?"

She smoothed a hand down his cheek, staring into his eyes. "Your mother is in good health, but she had to leave last night for the Southern Ocean. She was upset you were not here when she came to say goodbye."

"Gone?" He and Martha had been in Boston picking up John at the airport yesterday. He missed his last chance to see her. "I thought we had a few more weeks together before she left for her new position as Queen."

"There's been a lot going on that you don't know about, Shea. You haven't been around."

"Because she banned me from the ocean until they catch Demyan," he reminded her, his words clipped. "It's because of him, isn't it? He stirred up some kind of trouble and Mom had to go fix things."

"Something like that." She couldn't meet his eyes. "And there's something else. I'll be leaving too."

"Well, we both knew that was going to happen." Shea exhaled a long breath. "You go where the Queen goes. At least until school starts in the fall."

"I'm not going to the Southern Ocean. I'm headed to Atlantis now."

Chapter Four

Shea lay on his back, his eyebrows furrowed with frustration and anger as he stared at the ceiling over his bed. The "talk" with Kae hadn't been what he thought…it was worse. She was leaving Cape Cod in the morning. He'd been expecting goodbye. But not like this.

He didn't want her to go. It wasn't fair and he told her so. He understood how she had no choice in the matter, but he picked a fight anyway and almost made her cry. It was not how he'd pictured things going this summer. He didn't even get a goodbye kiss. Not that he deserved one after being such a jerk. He gave himself another mental kick, remembering how her shoulders drooped as she walked down the front steps and out of the yard. He knew it wasn't her fault, but he couldn't stop being angry.

John had dragged Hailey back to the house, passing Kae on the street as she stomped back toward the beach. Shea told them to go into Harwich Port without him, and John seemed to understand. They promised to be back before dinner, leaving him alone to wallow in his self-pity.

His eyes followed the tiny hairline cracks fingering their way along the edges of the room, showing where the old house settled over the years. Some type of small spider had taken up residence in the corner over the window, trapping the flies and gnats who tried to sneak in through a hole in the old screen. The spider moved back and forth slowly and methodically, repairing a damaged section of its web to prepare for another night of hunting. As he watched the rhythmic movements, Shea's breathing slowed to match the steady pace.

This was the same ceiling his dad had stared at when he was a boy. Back when the houses up along the ocean probably still looked a lot like the MacNamara house. Shea wondered if the same cracks were already there for his dad to trace with his eyes, and whether there were similar spiders intent on spinning similar webs.

It wasn't the first time Shea had thought about his dad, wishing he were still around to give advice. Plenty of questions piled up in the last two months. Entire topics of conversation that had never even occurred to Shea back on the farm in

Oklahoma. Like, how much did Tom MacNamara really know about the mermaid he married? How much did he understand about undersea politics, and the wars between the clans? Questions his father would never get the chance to discuss or answer.

Prince Demyan took that option away.

Shea still didn't fully comprehend how anyone could control the weather, or how mermaids could travel that far from the ocean without losing their magical abilities. When his parents made the plan to move inland, they obviously thought Oklahoma was far enough away from either coast to be safe from mermaid magick. Demyan and his sorcerers proved that idea wrong, conjuring a fierce and concentrated tornado to destroy the MacNamara farm.

Part of Shea still wished he'd stayed home from school that day. Maybe there would've been something he could've done to change things. To stay with his father.

"Demyan has to pay for what he did," Shea muttered. Someone knocked softly on the bedroom door. "Go away," Shea yelled. "I don't want to hear any more about *summer plans*."

"It's me, boy-o." His grandmother's voice sounded muffled through the door. "Let me in."

Shea swung his legs over the side and heaved himself off the bed to unlock the bedroom door. His grandmother wore the same faded housedress and apron, but she'd unpinned the tight bun. Thick grey hair hung down her back in a single long braid that swung side to side as she crossed the room to the window, looking down on the street below with her hands clasped behind her back. Lucky followed her, toenails clattering on the wooden floor.

Shea flopped back onto his single bed. "I'm gonna be stuck here alone all summer, while my friends go off on adventures. It's not fair. I'm the one who helped expose Demyan. I should be going to that hearing. Why does Kae get to go to Atlantis to give testimony while I'm forced to stay here on Cape Cod?"

Martha turned from the window, narrowing her eyes at her grandson. "And what makes you think you know better than King Koios?"

He threw an arm over his face to shield himself from her penetrating stare. "It's not that I think I'm smarter than the king. I'm just saying I should be going with Kae to Atlantis. I'm fifteen. I'm not a child."

"You're the heir to his throne. Perhaps the king doesn't feel it worth the risk for you to make the long journey when Demyan is still out there somewhere."

"So why are they having the trial already if they haven't even captured him?"

Martha shrugged. "The High Chancellor was killed. There needs to be a hearing."

Frustration consumed him, constricting the muscles in his throat and making it hard to choke out his words. "I was right there, Gramma. I saw him kill that old merman. He threatened me to my face, and slashed Kae with a knife while I stood there helpless. He poisoned the king and blackmailed my mother into almost marrying him. Demyan is totally evil and they need to capture him and put an end to his reign of terror, once and for all."

"In this regard, you and I are in full agreement," Martha said. "Demyan needs to pay for his crimes. But the courts of Atlantis must first determine which crimes he is truly guilty of before passing judgment. You must understand that the law is the law."

Shea's laughter sounded hollow even to his own ears. He was tired of her cryptic words and phrases. "You're just full of wisdom today, Gramma. 'Nothing is certain until it is certain,' and 'the law is the law.' Where did you dig up this new bag of tautologies? Say what you mean or don't bother."

She was silent for so long that Shea began to wonder if she'd left his bedroom. He lowered his arm to peek, and saw that she was back at the window, staring out into the sunshine again. Finally, she spoke. "Demyan caused the deaths of my husband and both of my sons. He should be held accountable

41

for those deaths, and all of his other crimes against humans and merfolk alike. Unfortunately, it's said the courts of Atlantis don't consider crimes committed above the water's surface."

Shea's eyes opened wider. "I'm sorry, Gramma. I almost forgot about Grandpa and Uncle Rick in that hurricane. That was Demyan messing about with the weather too? Like with the tornado back in Oklahoma?"

"They say the Adluo sorcerers are some of the most powerful under the seas. It's been rumored for a long time that they can manipulate the weather on a far grander scale than others have ever attempted. Demyan can not be allowed to harness that power."

He considered her words, letting them roll around in his head for a moment or two. "Gramma, what do you mean when you say the rumors have been around for a long time? How long have you known about the mermaid clans?"

She turned from the window, her blue eyes glittering. "I've known about the clashes between the Adluos and the Aequoreans for my whole life."

"But…how is that possible?"

Martha sat on the edge of Shea's bed, next to where his legs were stretched, and patted his knee. "Things are not always as they seem, you know. For instance, how old would you guess that I am, right at this very minute?"

Shea had no idea. He could tell by her grey hair that she was pretty old, but her exact age was one of those things he'd never quite worked out. His own dad had been pushing forty, so he figured his grandmother must be at least twenty years older than that. He decided to take a conservative guess. "Are you about sixty?"

"I'll be one hundred and forty seven come September," she said in a gentle voice. Shea's jaw dropped open in surprise. "I was born into a small eastern village of the Aequorean clan, back in a time when tall sailing ships commanded the seas and Queen Victoria still ruled the British Isles. I met your grandfather when I was a mere ninety-three and he was a sweet young U.S. Naval officer of nineteen."

"So Grandpa wasn't…"

"British? No, dear, he was an American," Martha said with a smile, a faraway look in her eyes.

"That's not what I meant, Gramma," Shea muttered, but she'd already started speaking, continuing her story as if he hadn't interrupted.

"I fell head over tail in love with that man the first time I saw him, I must say. He would tell you the same, that is, if he were still here to tell you. Sometimes you just know it, when you meet the person that you're destined to spend your life with. More's the pity that you never had the chance to get to know him. Given all that has happened, I don't doubt that your mother was right in sending you away, but now you'll never have the chance to know what a kind and decent sort your grandfather truly was." She patted his knee one last time and then folded her hands in her lap, waiting.

"So you're…" Shea couldn't finish the sentence.

"…a mermaid." Martha nodded her head as she spoke as if to confirm her words, but Shea couldn't believe what he was hearing. "I was born a mermaid, at least, many moons ago. I've been on dry land for so long now it's hard to know whether I'll even remember how to use the transformational magic."

"But, how? When? Why?" There was so much about this revelation that Shea just didn't understand. "What about my father?"

Martha sighed, smoothing out the front of her apron as she stood. "I'm headed downstairs to put the kettle on the stove. Why don't we finish this discussion in the kitchen, over a nice cup of hot tea while we wait for your friends to return from town?"

Chapter Five

It was certainly a risk for Zan to return to Nantucket Sound. Despite his changed appearance and the magick aura cloaking his journey, he felt exposed. *Why am I doing this?* As he rounded the tip of Cape Cod to head into the waters on the southern side of the land, he dove deeper toward the bottom, avoiding the tumultuous currents that raged near the surface around the volatile stretch of shoal. He wondered, for what felt like the millionth time, how he had let Demyan bully him into putting his life on the line yet again. *Is there no limit to what I must do for that merman?*

Was it fear of his own death that kept Zan from fleeing? For certainly, those Nerine forces currently working with Demyan would hunt Zan down and kill him if he dared to disobey Demyan's orders. And he never forgot that Demyan could turn him in for his childhood transgressions at any time, although Demyan wasn't likely to go to the authorities now that he was a wanted man himself.

But Zan's execution was almost a sure thing should he be captured on this mission. Death was a foregone conclusion no matter what path of action Zan chose.

Loyalty, then. Some twisted sense of devotion held him in Demyan's snare, and kept him on the path of revenge and resurrection the madman outlined in that Arctic cavern.

"I owe him my life several times over," Zan repeated to himself aloud. "He deserves my fealty." But as he repeated the phrase again in his head, he realized most of the times his life had been in jeopardy over the last ten years were a direct result of Demyan's actions. Demyan was the one to put him in harm's way, just as Demyan had been the one to save him.

Zan stopped swimming, resting his hand against a boulder to steady his body as his mind reeled with sudden realizations, feeling much older than his seventeen years. It was Demyan, after all, who discovered him covered in blood all those years ago and given him this second chance at life.

His parents hadn't known what to do with him. As he grew, odd things tended to happen around him, both good and bad, depending on his childish moods. In desperation, his

father made a deal with the castle's stable master and left Zan to live there with the dolphins at the age of six.

One day, some older boys were making fun of Zan, calling him names and poking him with sticks. He'd been scared, unable to protect himself from their jabs and prodding, until his frustration reached the point of anger and the current around him start to heat, unbridled magick swirling around him. The others didn't seem to notice the change in water temperature until it was too late. The two who were in closest proximity to Zan began bleeding from their ears and noses, their blood gushing in a steady stream joining the swirling eddy of magick that circled the smaller boy. The others fled the stables, screaming.

When Demyan and a second soldier arrived to investigate, the two older boys lay dead on the sandy floor. A dazed Zan hovered above them bathed in their thick blood and twitching like a seahorse's tail. Demyan quickly assessed the situation, seeing two of his royal cousins dead and realizing the potential of Zan's innate magical ability.

It was Demyan himself who covered up the crime, blaming another stable boy who was quickly put to death. It was Demyan who convinced the king to secure a place for Zan at the University of Atlantis to learn to harness his magick. As the king's only remaining nephew, Prince Demyan's word held some sway.

At the University, they taught Zan to control the magick. After several years, they sent him back to the Adluo Palace, no longer a stable boy but an accomplished sorcerer. Anything and everything he desired could be obtained with his magick. It wasn't his own desires he fulfilled, however, but those of the Adluo king who spared his life. And those of the king's cruel nephew, Prince Demyan. There were times when the magick still got the better of him and Zan lost control, but for the most part he was its master.

And Prince Demyan was, in turn, Zan's master.

At this point, he felt had no choices left. He'd tied his fate to Demyan's until one or both of them ended up as shark food. Or worse. There had been a small glimmer of hope on the night of the Summer Solstice, when he watched Demyan flee from his own soldiers after his schemes went horribly wrong. But that was then and this was now.

At the entrance to the courtyard, he paused to survey the surrounding gardens. He'd spent a week at this castle during the Solstice celebration, but had spent almost none of that time outside of the castle walls. He'd been too caught up with the machinations of getting Princess Winona to poison her own brother, too busy flattering both the old mermaid's vanity and her ambition to take much notice of his surroundings.

He could now see that the gardens were beautiful, the swaying greenery flowing gracefully with the current under the watchful eyes of a tall statue of Buddha, with the crossed legs of his human form. Just inside the archway, blue-haired servants were loading a wagon with several trunks, carrying them out from the main doors of the Great Hall. Stable hands secured a pair of dolphins to the front harness.

Obvious from their hair and skin tone, these servants were from the Pacific Ocean. Zan wondered if Prince Azul's body was in one of the trunks being loaded, and sighed heavily, the bubbles streaming from his gills. Although poisoning King Koios's Eucheuma seeds at the Solstice banquet had been part of his plan, he never in a million years considered that the king would share his private bowl with the other royals. The deaths of both the Pacific prince and the Southern Ocean's young king, Theo, were unexpected consequences of Aequorean hospitality.

Only King Koios was supposed to die that night. And he was the one who survived, thanks to that drylander bastard. *How did Shea figure out which antidote to administer?*

"Are you with the Pacific delegation?"

Zan whirled at the sound of the mermaid's voice, surprised to find he wasn't alone in the garden. He was face to face with the most beautiful mermaid he'd ever laid eyes on, her billowing blonde curls swirling around a heart-shaped face, with glittering green eyes like diamond-cut emeralds. A string of elegant pearls graced her slender neck and a delicate silver

bangle surrounded her wrist, both seemingly at odds with the rough hemp vest that he knew was in style among mermaids her age group. *My age*, he corrected himself. *She's only a year or two younger than I am.*

He quickly plastered on what he hoped looked like the youthful swagger and grin of a University student and rubbed his hand over his unshaven jaw. "Nope, I'm not from the Pacific, babe. Didn't you know their court frowns on facial hair? I'd be kicked out of Prince Azul's castle faster than you could say *jumping jellyfish.*"

Her eyes went wide as she rested a light hand on his arm. "Didn't you hear? Poor Prince Azul was poisoned at the banquet!" She nodded toward the wagon. "Those are his things they're loading now, taking them back for his father."

Zan was overly aware of the softness of the mermaid's touch, the slight pressure of her fingers on his arm sending shivers of electricity shooting through the length of his body. *Get a grip, Zan.* "I've been traveling home from Atlantis these last few weeks and seem to have missed all the gossip. Is there more you can share with a traveler?"

She nodded and gave him a shy smile that made his heart race. "Quite a bit more, actually. Come with me, traveler, and we'll find you something to eat and drink while I tell you the events of Summer Solstice."

His body tensed at her unexpected offer. Was she luring him into some kind of trap? "Why are you being so kind when you don't even know me?"

Her eyebrows shot up in surprise. "Is it not common courtesy in your village to welcome travelers with food? I thought that particular custom was pretty universal throughout the Atlantic." She smiled again, and his heart did another somersault. "But I'll admit to an ulterior motive, in that I leave soon for Atlantis and would love to hear first-hand details about both the journey and the University itself."

He'd almost blown his cover by not remembering the stupid Aequorean customs of hospitality. Of course she had to offer him food as soon as he said he was a "traveler." Lucky for him, she was more focused on hearing about Atlantis than noticing his discomfort. "So that's why I haven't seen you around campus, you haven't started University yet! And here I was, wondering how I could've possibly missed noticing someone as beautiful as you, Miss... Miss... I don't know your name, babe."

Bright spots of crimson bloomed on both of her cheeks. "You can call me Kae."

His eyes opened wide, realizing this intriguing mermaid was the one he'd traveled to find. The one Demyan sent him to kidnap. He tried to regain his composure. "What a pretty name for a pretty mermaid."

Her blush darkened. "And you are…?"

"Alexander," he told her honestly, although he hadn't used his full name in many years. Not since his father had sold him to the stable master who shortened it to Zan. But that name was too risky to use here, in this court, even with his current disguise. "You, however, can call me Xander, with an 'X'." Which was close enough to his real name that he should be able to remember it.

"Xander, with an 'X'," she repeated with her musical voice, and he felt a thrill go down his spine all the way to the tip of his tail. "Pretty cool name."

He shrugged, trying hard to be nonchalant and resisting a strong urge to throw his arms around her waist to pull her closer. Instead he reached for her hand and squeezed it. "You'll find I'm a pretty cool guy, babe. But I'm also a pretty hungry guy, and I think you mentioned food…"

Her expression changed as if she'd suddenly remembered something important. Slowly she pulled her fingers from his grip, putting more space between them, her voice losing some of its musical quality. "Of course. Follow me to the kitchens. I'm sure Marietta has food to spare for a traveler."

He touched her arm before she could turn her back on him. "Did I do something wrong?"

Kae shook her head, curls bouncing in the slight current as she shrugged away from his touch. "No, that was me. I didn't mean for you to think I was flirting," she said, lowering her eyes. "My mother always tells me I'm too naïve, and too casual with my words."

Zan reached out and put a finger under her chin to tilt her face back up. Their eyes met, and he was again struck by their glittering depths. "You're awfully young to be married, babe." She shook her head. "Not married, then. So, you're officially promised to another?"

"No, but there is someone special in my life."

An unexpected flare of jealousy filled Zan, even though he already knew of the mermaid's relationship with the half-drylander bastard. He cocked his head to the side. "Is he here? I'd like to meet the lucky fellow."

Her eyes darted toward the path through the gardens. "No. He's...away."

If you were mine I'd never leave you. The direction of his thoughts shocked him, but he indulged himself a moment longer by cupping his hand against the silky smoothness of her cheek. "You've done nothing wrong, babe. You offered food and friendship to a traveler."

She sighed, a stream of small bubble rising from her gills. "Thank you for understanding."

He took her hand again, and this time she didn't pull away. He closed his eyes and sent a slight current of magick out through his fingers and into her body. Not enough for her

to notice it consciously, but enough to send a happy vibe running through her. When he opened his eyes, she was smiling again. "Now, about that kitchen you were going to show me?"

"Follow me," she said with a grin, pulling him along. "But let's go around to the back, so we don't bother Prince Azul's servants."

Which served Zan's purposes just fine, although somewhere along the way the mission's priorities shifted in his head. No longer was he planning a day of sneaking through shadows to gather information before grabbing the hostage Demyan sent him to retrieve.

His new and improved plan was to get to know Kae. Maybe with some time, and maybe a bit more magick, he could convince her to come with him willingly. As he watched the undulating movement of her hips and tail as she swam, he wondered how deep her connection truly was to the drylander whelp. He saw the look on her face when she talked about Shea, feelings that went way beyond anything he could conjure or imitate through sorcery. How could he get her to look at him with that same love and longing?

For the first time in his life, Zan wanted something that he couldn't attain solely with his magick. And he wanted it bad.

CHAPTER SIX

Shea listened to his grandmother's footsteps receding down the short hallway and descending the stairs. Lucky jumped up on the bed taking Martha's place, staring into Shea's face as if the dog were trying to gauge his reaction to the news.

Shea wasn't sure quite what to think.

His grandmother, a mermaid? Who else knew about this? Did that mean Dad was more than a mere drylander? What about his mom...did she know her husband's heritage?

Lucky whined and rested one of his front paws on Shea's chest. "That's enough, boy," Shea told the dog, batting the paw away. "I'm okay. I've just got a lot to think about right now." The dog barked in response and jumped off the bed, turning to look back at him before dashing out of the bedroom door.

Shea pushed himself into a sitting position and swung his legs off the edge of the bed. He looked up at the shelves of dusty sci-fi paperbacks, swimming medals, and baseball trophies that lined the space over the dresser. The stuff his dad left behind when he moved to Oklahoma. None of it reminded him of the no-nonsense farmer. Nothing in the room gave Shea the first clue whether his dad knew his mother, Martha MacNamara, was a real live mermaid.

Or whether Dad himself ever swam far beneath the ocean's surface to the bottom of Nantucket Sound to meet his father-in-law, King Koios.

There was only one person who had the answers to the questions twirling through his mind. And she was waiting in the kitchen, making tea.

Steam rose in swirls from the mug in front of him. Shea sat across from his grandmother at the kitchen table, stirring slow circles with his spoon, waiting. In the few short months he'd lived on Cape Cod, he'd never seen her quite this…nervous? Was she nervous about telling him the truth?

She fidgeted with the sugar bowl, fussing over a small chip on the lid and mumbling to herself. She squeezed every last drop of liquid from her tea bag until it was nearly bone dry. At last she set it aside with her spoon and raised the mug to her lips, blowing across the hot surface.

Finally, Shea cleared his throat, tired of waiting for her to start the conversation. "So, you're a mermaid. And you're, like, a hundred and fifty years old."

"One hundred and forty six, if you please." Martha shook her head. "Let's not rush the aging process. The sun and air do the job fast enough, thank you very much."

"If you're a mermaid, what's with all the bleach? The 'keeping the ocean out of the house' stuff?"

"The scent of bleach helps mask my origins from others who might seek me out."

"Like Mr. Guenther?"

She nodded. "Yes, despite our long friendship, he never discerned my true nature. On the other hand, while I knew he was of merfolk descent, I had no idea he was sent here to spy on our family."

Shea thought about his for a moment. "What about my dad? And his twin, Uncle Rick?"

Martha smiled sadly. "Alas, not every child born with mermaid blood has the ability to transform. Both of my boys had a natural affinity for the water, but neither ever developed gills, and neither of them could use the *transmutare* stone to full advantage."

Shea reached up to touch the stone that hung from a cord around his neck, his own *transmutare*, given to him by his mother. He winced as he remembered that first painful time he'd fallen into the salt water of the Herring River, and the burning sensation caused by his first breaths of water through his newly formed gills.

"Twins are unheard of in my world, although your grandfather's MacNamara side of the family is filled with them," Martha continued. "I think the lack of transformational magick had something to do with their genes being split between the two of them. I'd see flashes of ability within each, but then no more. Take, for instance, your father's wonderful talents on the high school swimming team. He was the fastest swimmer the Cape had ever seen."

"I saw the medals in his room. If he was so good, why didn't he continue? Couldn't he have gotten a scholarship or something?"

Martha agreed. "Oh yes, there were colleges trying to recruit him. There was even an Olympic coach who came to watch him swim in the state tournament. But by then, Tom had already met your mother." She bit her bottom lip, frowning. "There's probably more to that story as well."

"You still haven't told me if Dad knew you were a mermaid, Gramma." Shea lifted his mug and took a sip, keeping his eyes glued to her the whole time. He watched as a range of emotions played across her face, from surprise to smiling to sadness, as she sifted through her thoughts.

"Your grandfather MacNamara never knew the whole truth about me," she started. "When we met, he was stationed on one of the few battleships that was patrolling the Atlantic at that time, and not mired in the wars of the East and the Pacific. The *U.S.S. Saratoga* was part of some NATO war games, where the commanders were practicing in the unlikely event of an attack by the Soviet Union. I met your grandfather when his ship was anchored near the British navy docks in Portsmouth, for refueling. He cut a dashing figure in his shore-leave whites."

"What were you doing on dry land?" As Shea understood things from Kae, it had long been forbidden for mermaids to co-mingle with humans.

Her eyes narrowed sharply. "Though some clans shun contact, Aequoreans have traditionally enjoyed a more symbiotic relationship. Over the years, there are certain things Aequoreans found it easier to purchase than to create for ourselves, such as the brass lanterns you must have noted at the king's castle."

Shea nodded, remembering the strange green glow of the luminescent sea creatures swimming within the confines of the glass globes. He hadn't really considered where the lanterns themselves might have come from, but this explanation made sense. He'd wondered about the fields of oysters under

cultivation at the bottom of Nantucket Sound. "Did you trade pearls for goods?"

Martha's eyebrows shot up, surprised by his question. "Among other things. Many times we posed as fisherman's wives or daughters and sold cockles and mussels on the piers. An old merman named Angus ran a fish and chips stand that was popular with the sailors. It was one sunny day while I was helping at the stand that I met your Grandfather MacNamara. Such sapphire blue eyes he had, like the deepest ocean…" Her voice trailed off for moment, until she shook her head and continued her tale.

"Naval forces from Britain, Canada, France, Norway, and Holland all joined together with the United States for these war games – hundreds of warships and hundreds more merchant vessels. My friends and I heard all the men talking about it and decided to watch the maneuverings for ourselves. I wanted to spy on your grandfather some more, because I couldn't get those few moments of flirting with him out of my head. We took a trip to the Norwegian Sea, almost into the Arctic Circle, to watch the events unfold. And it's a good thing that we did." She paused to take another sip of her tea.

"Why?" Shea had both elbows propped on the table, holding his face in his hands as he listened to her story, fascinated. There was a black and white photograph on the fireplace mantel of Martha at her wedding day, so he knew how beautiful she was in her youth. He could see her in his mind, a young thing wearing a long skirted apron, selling fish and chips and flirting with the foreign sailors. "Why was it a good thing you went to watch the war games? Did Grandpa fall overboard? Did you have to save him from drowning like a storybook mermaid would?"

Martha chuckled. "Your grandfather was far too good a sailor to simply fall into the ocean. No, the problem was not with the sailing men or their battleships, but more with the location they chose to hold their war games." She paused and cocked her head to the side. "How much do you know about the Norwegian Sea?"

Shea thought for a moment. "It's near Norway?"

"And?"

He frowned, scrunching his forehead in concentration. His exposure to coastal and world geography had been almost non-existent at his school back in Oklahoma. "It's connected to the Atlantic Ocean?"

It was Martha's turn to frown. "I'm glad you're headed to University soon. There is so much the drylander schools haven't taught you."

"Forget about my limited education for the moment, Gramma. What happened during the war games?"

"The Nerine happened." She stood suddenly, taking her mug with her to the stove and filling it from the kettle. As she

selected another teabag from the canister, she asked, "Do you know the basics about the different clans of merfolk?"

Shea nodded, pulling up the information in his mind. The fact that he had a perfect photographic memory for everything he read and learned had puzzled him when he was younger, but now he understood the importance of a good memory. Mermaids don't have reference books or internet service at the bottom of the ocean. The ability to retain information and retrieve it from memory is key to survival, although Shea still wondered about some of his other odd abilities.

"Kae told me there are mermaid clans in each of the five oceans, with villages scattered among practically every body of water on the planet. It sounds a little like medieval Europe, with the five kings – or queens like Mom – who rule the lesser lords of the various seas. And then the High Council in Atlantis rules over all. The Aequoreans are the largest clan, stretching across the whole of the Atlantic Ocean and all the Seas it touches, and the Adluos live in the cold Southern Ocean down around Antarctica."

"The Nerine are the clan that resides under the polar icecaps of the Arctic Ocean," Martha explained. "It's the smallest of the oceans and also the shallowest, but the ice keeps them safe from discovery. It also serves to keep the mermaids there isolated from most human contact." Martha

moved back to the table with her fresh cup of tea. "You won't find any examples of a Nerine falling in love with a human – such things are strictly forbidden in their culture. Their clan's antagonism toward drylanders is legendary around the globe, as are some of their other strange customs. You can tell just by looking at them that they're an unusual lot."

Shea thought back on the Summer Solstice gathering at the castle of King Koios, and all the different colors of hair and skin on the mermaids from around the globe. If blue and green hair and multi-hued skin were run-of-the-mill, what did mermaids consider unusual? Something else bothered him. "What about all the stuff Aequoreans do, like cultivating pearls or selling fish? Don't the Nerine need things they can't get in the Arctic?"

Martha pursed her lips before answering. "I think this conversation is veering off track. There are many things you will learn at University, from teachers far more knowledgeable than I am. You may even learn about the NATO incident in the Norwegian Sea, when the Nerine almost succeeded in starting a war with the humans. The Aequoreans intervened, and most of the sailors were none the wiser. Several witnessed things not easily explained and had to have their memories altered. I was assigned to follow up with a group of sailors from the *U.S.S. Saratoga,* and so I came to the Americas."

"Grandpa's ship," Shea whispered, remembering.

Martha smiled. "Even with his mind wiped, he remembered me from the docks in Portsmouth, and that I'd introduced myself to him as 'Martha.' We were married soon after he was released from his naval duties, and settled here, on his native Cape Cod."

He interrupted. "What do you mean he remembered you as Martha? Isn't that your name?"

She reached over and patted his arm. "It certainly is now, and has been for more than fifty years. 'Tis a solid drylander name, and one I've worn proudly. But no, your grandfather never knew me by another name or another form. If your father and uncle had been born differently, there might have been explaining to do. But that is now water well under the keel, so to speak." Tears filled her eyes. "In all our years together, your grandfather never questioned me, and never wavered in his love. I made my choices and have had no regrets. Until now."

He sat up in his chair. "What do you mean?"

Martha slowly wiped her fingers below her eye, catching the first salty tear that trickled down her cheek. "If I'd been more honest with your grandfather, and with Tom, then perhaps they wouldn't have succumbed to Demyan's forces. They might have been able to avoid…death. Demyan has much to answer for, but I blame myself for not giving my family knowledge that could have saved them."

Shea reached across the table and squeezed her hand. "Gramma, it's not your fault. There was nothing anyone could have done to prevent what happened, and knowing you're a mermaid wouldn't have saved Grandpa from the sudden hurricane." He shook his head, accepting for the first time that there was nothing he could have done to save his father, either. If he'd stayed home from school that fateful day, the freak tornado would have killed him as well as his dad. "From what I've seen and heard of Demyan, there is no way to stop him. He is pure evil."

Martha nodded. "Evil he is. But you are wrong about the other."

"The other what?"

"That he can't be stopped." Martha leaned across the table toward Shea. "Even evil has its limitations. We just need to discover Demyan's weakness."

He frowned. "We? Gramma, in case you forgot, you haven't transformed for a gazillion years. And no one knows where Demyan is even hiding. What can we do to help when I'm not supposed to even go into the ocean?"

She sat back in her chair, a smile spreading across her face. "We hold the key to something Demyan desperately desires."

"What key are you talking about?"

"You, Sheachnadh." She reached out and placed her hand over his. "Demyan will blame you for foiling his scheme and he will want revenge. He will come to us. And we will be ready for him."

Chapter Seven

Kae sat at a table in the corner of the castle's kitchen, across from the dark-haired stranger she now called friend. The customs of hospitality dictated that she offer him food and drink, but there was something about Xander that Kae actually liked. While he seemed all casual and confident on the outside, with that rakish scruff of beard and stories of Atlantis, she could sense the loneliness inside him, like a little boy who needed a hug.

It occurred to her briefly that Shea probably wouldn't like it if he found her hanging around with this cute merman, sharing sushi and laughter in a quiet corner. She frowned, thinking of all the times she knew Hailey shared meals with Shea or took long walks with him. They seemed to share a lot of common knowledge of things that she didn't understand, like *Xbox* and *comic books* and *wrapping paper*, although he always

insisted the pair were no more than friends. Well, she could make friends too, and let Shea be the one to feel left on the strandline.

"Is something troubling you, babe?"

She looked up to find concern in Xander's dark eyes, and realized she was frowning as she pictured Hailey and Shea riding those stupid two-wheeled machines he called bicycles. She made an effort to lighten her expression. "Nothing's wrong. Just remembering something silly."

A smile stretched across his face and she noticed he had a dimple on his left cheek but not his right, just visible above the line of his beard. It gave him a bit of a lopsided appearance, and for some reason made her think again of a lonely little boy, despite the muscles that rippled across his arms and bare chest. "Tell me your silly story," he pleaded, a devilish twinkle in his eye. "I've already told you too many from University. It must be your turn to embarrass yourself by now."

She returned the smile. "Well, although I haven't had nearly as many adventures as you have, Xander, there was one time I tried to master an evil contraption called a bicycle. It proved most tricky to escape, and I must admit my elbows ended up worse for the experience."

His eyes narrowed as his grin widened. "You? Mastering a bicycle? Hasn't contact with drylanders been forbidden in recent years because of the war? And here I was thinking you were a total rule-follower, little miss sweetness and light!"

Kae frowned again, her tail twitching with frustration at his teasing tone. "I'm not totally bound by the rules. And even if I were, you make it sound like a bad thing to follow the law."

He laughed, reaching across the table to lay his large hand on top of her smaller one. "It's not a bad thing to be a good girl, babe. I'm just having trouble picturing someone as sweet and beautiful as you sneaking out to play with drylanders."

There it was again. She felt a pulse flow through her body as his fingers pressed against hers, almost like an electrical charge. She'd felt it before, outside in the garden when he'd taken her hand so she could lead him to the kitchens. It was almost like the tingling sensations she felt when she and Shea kissed, that lightening shock that coursed through her body, head to tail, and made her want more.

Xander's touch was similar, but different. What passed between them felt familiar and intimate, like a warm Caribbean current flowing through her blood, heating her from the inside. But how? Why? She'd only just met him. She couldn't have feelings for him.

Besides, she reminded herself sternly as she glanced at her new bracelet, she loved Shea. Just the thought of him made her stomach tighten into delicious knots of anticipation. All this despite the fact that he had awful taste in human friends.

"You're frowning again, babe," Xander teased. Without letting go of her, he used his free hand to tuck a stray curl behind her ear, his fingers lingering to twirl themselves in her hair. "You have the most remarkable curls," he said, his dark, penetrating eyes focused on hers. "It looks like a tangled mess of seaweed, but feels like the softest anemone tentacles."

Kae felt a tremor of discomfort as his fingers pulled through her hair, followed by another pulse of warm feelings. Why was she drawn to him, when she knew her heart belonged only to Shea? Forcing herself to ignore the sudden attraction she felt, Kae pulled her hand away from his and snapped, "You're the one with eelgrass for hair, Xander. So dark and inky, like an octopus squirted all over you!"

His eyes widened before he threw back his head to laugh out loud. "My, but you're a feisty mermaid!"

"Don't forget, anemone tentacles can be poisonous," she said, softening her words with a mischievous grin. "Best be careful so you don't get stung."

Suddenly, Marietta was looming over their table. "What's this talk of poison in my kitchen? I'll have none of it, especially so soon after the unfortunate incidents of Solstice. There is no poison in my food now or ever, and I won't have you accusing me of such." Her right hand was planted firmly on her generous hip, while her butcher knife dangled menacingly from her left.

Kae held up both hands in protest. "My friend Xander and I spoke in jest, Marietta. He compared my hair to anemone tentacles!"

The older mermaid narrowed her gaze, lowering her bushy eyebrows until her eyes seemed to be mere slits. "Jest or no, there will be no more talk of poison. Now, finish your meal and be gone with you both." She whirled around and swam off in a flurry of bubbles.

Xander leaned forward across the table, lowering his voice. "Is it just me, or is she a little oversensitive about the whole *poisoned food* thing?" He waggled his eyebrows in an attempt at imitating Marietta's threatening stare and Kae barely stifled her giggles. "Come now," he said, smiling as he rose from the carved rock bench. "Why don't you show me more of that wonderful garden outside?"

He held out his hand and she took it, feeling again that pulse of warmth flow between them. This time it didn't disconcert her, as she'd already decided she could trust Xander. Maybe not as completely as she trusted Shea, but her feelings for Shea were as complicated as their situation.

He was, after all, the heir to the throne while she was a mere servant in his mother's household. And she wasn't going to be able to see him again until September, when they both arrived at University for their first semester in Atlantis. She wondered if Xander would be returning to Atlantis in the fall, and if they would be able to remain friends. It would serve Shea right to be the jealous one for a change!

As they meandered through the formal gardens, Kae named the different plants. She and her mother planted many of them over the years, so she knew much of the history and lore of the plant life both native and foreign to Nantucket Sound. Xander attended to her every word, asking questions and making her laugh at his jokes. He seemed to have a fair bit of knowledge of medicinal uses for some of the plants, which Kae found fascinating. The afternoon swam by at breakneck speed, and Kae knew the servants would soon be coming outside to light the various lanterns. Her parents would be looking for her to join them at the supper table.

Should she ask Xander to join her family for their evening meal? What would her father think of that? Would he think she was flirting with this cute merman? Is that what she was actually doing, or was she just hanging out with a friend? Kae was no longer certain.

Perhaps things would be easier if she'd fallen in love with another commoner in the first place, someone like Xander who was funny and charming, and handsome in a roguish sort of way. A merman who could anger her one moment and make her laugh the very next. Whose touch filled her with warm feelings of security and confidence, rather than the breathless exhilaration she felt in Shea's arms. Her life would certainly be simpler, less complicated.

If only she'd met Xander first.

But she hadn't. She'd met the boy on the beach first, and her life would never be the same. Despite the fact that she worked for his mother, who was now the queen of a foreign ocean, she knew she was totally and desperately in love with Shea, heir to the Atlantic throne. The boy at the center of her heart and her universe...but oddly enough, she barely mentioned him to Xander. Did her simple act of omission mean something?

Meeting Xander now didn't change the way she felt about Shea. It couldn't. Besides, she had to leave in the morning on her journey to Atlantis to testify before the court. She would have to say goodbye to Xander tonight, just as she'd said goodbye to Shea earlier in the morning.

From the corner of her eye, she saw the first of the servants coming out of the castle with a net full of luminous sea creatures. It was time to light the lanterns. Time to say goodnight and goodbye.

She stopped swimming, hovering next to Xander, watching his dark hair tossing gently with the current. "It's getting late. I think it's time to say good night."

He turned, a frown upon his face. "So soon? But you've only named half the plantings in the garden for me! Can you meet me here again tomorrow morning?"

"I leave tomorrow on a journey. I told you I was leaving for Atlantis soon."

A look of genuine surprise crossed Xander's face. "Atlantis? But it's only mid-summer. I thought you meant you'd be headed there for the fall semester."

Kae looked away, unable to meet his eyes. Her real reason for the journey was supposed to be secret, known only to her family and the king himself. And to Shea, of course, since she had no secrets from him. "My mother wants to accompany me, and we are going early to see the sites." Which was partly true. Her mother planned to swim with her on the journey as she was also called to testify. King Koios asked her father to stay and watch over Shea until Demyan was captured.

"So this is more than a mere good night," Xander said, swimming closer. "This is a goodbye as well." He took both of her hands in his, and she felt a much stronger pulse of electricity flow through her, drawing her closer. His dark eyes searched hers as he bit his bottom lip. Staring into their depths, she saw again the lonely boy who needed to be comforted and her heart ached for him. "Don't leave me.

We've only just met." Another surge of electricity shot through her body and her mind slowly began to cloud.

Kae struggled to retain control of her thoughts. "I must…get home. It's late and…and my parents will worry." She knew she should back away from Xander and leave the garden, but she couldn't make herself swim away. In fact, she found herself inching closer to his warm body, as if against her will, until his heat completely encircled her.

"Stay with me, Kae," he whispered, using her name for the first time. His words hovering in the water around her, echoing in her head.

"Okay," she heard herself agree, although she knew it was wrong. But she couldn't quite remember why it was wrong. She did know she didn't want to leave him, not when he needed her.

His words, *Stay with me*, seemed to have invaded her entire being, insinuating themselves into every fiber and muscle of her body, sapping her will power to make any decision other than to stay. A small part of her mind tried to disagree, but her body would not listen. She hovered in place, staring into Xander's dark, bottomless eyes, unable to move away.

* * *

Zan had not planned for this, and mind control wasn't his magical forte but he couldn't let her leave. Why in Neptune's name would she be heading for Atlantis tomorrow? He could not allow that to happen, not when Demyan ordered her capture. They'd never be able to take her once she reached the city of Atlantis, where it would be far too risky to attempt a kidnapping. He sent another wave of magick through their clasped hands, binding their minds together. They would have to leave for the Arctic tonight.

Demyan planned to use the mermaid to lure Shea into Nerine territory, and then use a captive Shea to negotiate with both King Koios and Queen Brynneliana. The Aequorean forces would be no match for the Nerine. Demyan and the Nerine would easily win, and then begin to work their way toward Atlantis. It wasn't Zan's place to point out the holes in Demyan's twisted logic, but only to fulfill his own small part of the plan: capture the mermaid who held Shea's heart.

It would be a faster journey if Kae could swim on her own, so controlling her mind seemed the most efficient option. He'd been using his magick sparingly up until now, gently sending trickles of warm feeling to make her trust him. It'd been so long since he'd met anyone so open and friendly, so innocent and good, that it felt wrong to use stronger magick on her. But there was no more time.

As he stared down into her wide, green eyes, the muscles in his jaw tensed. He realized he desperately wanted to kiss her, to taste her soft lips, but that would be wrong. Anything that happened between them now wouldn't be real. Magick can't make a person fall in love with you.

He wanted to get to know Kae better, her likes and dislikes, what made her laugh and smile. She was so very beautiful when she smiled, like a brilliant sunrise on a cloudless morning. He would never wish harm to such a sweet and trusting mermaid. What Demyan planned was so, so wrong.

Zan wanted the chance for Kae to know him not as the Adluo spy sent to capture her, but for who he was on the inside. Could she love a merman like him? Would she? Now he'd never know, because he'd run out of time. They needed to leave the castle grounds now, before anyone noted her absence. Before her parents missed her at the supper table.

Before he lost his nerve.

He released one of her hands and gently lifted her transmutare necklace over her head, letting it fall to the sand. "You won't be needing this where we're going," he murmured.

"But…my parents will worry…"

"Come now, Kae," he whispered. "You'll be safe with me. We have a journey of our own to make."

CHAPTER EIGHT

Four aluminum soda cans, two and a half white plastic coffee cup lids, one Styrofoam coffee cup with a bite mark out of the rim, a broken red shovel, a supermarket rewards card, and a faded pink flip flop.

Shea kicked another spray of sand into the oncoming surf. His usual two-mile walk had done nothing to alleviate the unsettled feeling swirling through his gut. Since saying good-bye to Kae the day before, nothing had felt right. Having John and Hailey around only exacerbated the strange premonitions that something bad was happening, even though everything seemed normal. Well, everything except for the fact that Kae left for Atlantis without him.

He hadn't waited for John to wake up this morning, slipping out of the house before dawn to try and shake the inexplicable panic washing through him like ocean waves. "I should be with Kae, keeping her safe." Logically, he knew his ranting was in vain. King Koios couldn't hear Shea yelling at the pounding surf as it curled onto the sand. And even if he could, it wouldn't change the king's decision to send Kae to the hearing but not send his grandson. "If the journey is too dangerous for me to undertake, how can it be okay for her?" Kae said her mother would be traveling with her, along with a contingent of guards, but that the king had ordered her father to stay in Nantucket Sound to guard Shea.

Martha's revelations gave him even more to worry about, but in the end, Shea decided that the stark choices his grandmother had been forced to make between love and her life undersea were also the fault of the Atlantic King. No one should ever be forced to choose between such things, to give up everything because they'd fallen in love with the "wrong" person. That wasn't fair.

Lying awake during the long, sleepless night, he'd wondered what Kae would have done if faced with a similar choice. If Shea had been a mere drylander, like his father and his Grandpa MacNamara, would Kae still love him? Would she have given up the mermaid life to live on dry land? His grandmother had chosen love.

His own mother had chosen differently.

Were the stakes different for his mother and father, because Brynn was a royal princess? Did that mean things would be different for him because of his own royal status?

Maybe King Koios already had a plan for Shea's future, one that didn't involve a happily-ever-after with Kae. Shea frowned, and kicked more sand into the ocean. There were too many questions roiling around in his head that had no easy answers. Besides, he was way too young to start thinking about marriage and forever just yet. He hadn't even finished high school. The curves of his mouth slowly turned upward as he realized the way things were going, he'd be skipping the rest of "regular" high school and headed straight to the mermaid University. With Kae. Where they'd have plenty of time together to figure out their future, whether King Koios liked it or not.

The sun was finally getting ready to peek out over the horizon, already turning the few clouds floating over the ocean to dusky pinks and purples. Sunrise was his favorite time along the shore, when even the wind seemed quiet and reverent in anticipation of the rising sun. The Native Americans once named Cape Cod the "Land of the First Light," since it jutted so far east into the Atlantic. The sands and the beaches were always shifting, always changing at the whims of the capricious ocean, but Cape Cod itself endured over time.

Since moving here in May, Shea had yet to experience a coastal storm like the one that had killed his Uncle Rick and Grandpa MacNamara, one with the strength to rip dunes apart and send houses and other structures tumbling into the ocean.

Now that he knew about the magick wielded undersea, he wondered how many of those storms were caused by Mother Nature and how many by vengeful mermaids. Surely storms like the tornado that killed Dad were the exception rather than the rule.

He scanned the beach, wondering how far Lucky had run chasing down early morning seagulls sleeping along the edge of the dunes. Movements far down along the water's edge caught his eye, and he watched as the figures walked in his direction. One was definitely Lucky, next to a tall figure of a man.

As they came closer, Shea recognized the long graying beard and wide shoulders of Kae's father, Lybio. He'd never seen the merman take human form before and was intimidated by how large and imposing Lybio looked. He stood more than six and a half feet tall, towering over the large black Lab prancing by his side.

"Greetings, my Prince," Lybio called as he drew near. "Are you alone?"

Shea smiled wryly as he nodded his assent. "Good thing I am, or you'd have some explaining to do with that 'prince' crack."

A look of consternation crossed the large merman's face, but his attitude remained decidedly unrepentant. "Forgive me, my Prince. I didn't think."

Shea dismissed the apology with a wave. "What brings you onto shore like this?"

"Actually, I was hoping to find my daughter with you. Have you seen Kae?"

Eyes wide, Shea shook his head. "Kae came to my house yesterday morning to say goodbye. I thought she left for Atlantis before dawn."

Lybio turned toward the horizon, the rising sun illuminating his stern face. "That was to be the plan. But she never returned to the cottage for supper last night, and we can't seem to get in touch with her. She must have taken off her medallion, or lost it again."

Shea squirmed, remembering the medallion he'd found washed ashore so many weeks ago. "Just so you know, sir, Kae means the world to me."

"I'm sure you think you believe that," Lybio said, turning his gaze on Shea. "But you are still very young, ignorant of the consequences of your actions. And the responsibilities of the kingdom are not yet yours to bear. Again, I must ask you, where is my daughter?"

Shea narrowed his eyes. "I really haven't seen her since before noon yesterday."

Lybio kept his gaze locked with Shea's. His eyes looked similar to his daughter's, large and deepest green, but with none of the sparkle that drew Shea to the girl. After a long pause, he asked, "Were you in the ocean yesterday?"

Shea narrowed his eyes, startled by the question. "Both you and my grandfather told me it was forbidden. The king made me promise not to swim without you by my side."

"You've been known to bend rules in the past." Lybio jammed his index finger toward the dog, lying in the sand at their feet. "You're breaking one even as we speak."

"Only rules that are meant to be broken. And I never break promises. What's going on? Why don't you trust me all of a sudden? Where is Kae?"

"I'd truly hoped she was with you." Lybio exhaled a long breath, some of the stern attitude leaving his face, replaced with worry. "She was seen holding hands and laughing with a young merman yesterday in the gardens. I assumed she was with you and that you'd run off together somewhere to spend time alone. Now I have no idea where she might be, or with whom."

"Holding hands?" Shea felt the green monster of jealousy rear up inside him and tried to stamp it back down. There must be a logical explanation. In spite of the disagreement they'd had the day before about her leaving for Atlantis without him, he knew she loved him. "Is that something she does with her friends, perhaps? Friends other than me?"

He shook his head. "She has no male friends in Nantucket Sound, except for you, my Prince. Neither is she loose with her affections, as you might be implying, my Prince."

"Would you quit it with the 'my Prince' stuff? You're driving me crazy." Shea clenched his hands into fists and rested them on his hips. "And I wasn't trying to imply anything, I'm just trying to figure out where she could be. Where did you say she was last seen?"

"In the castle's courtyard gardens. I questioned a servant of the Pacific clan who happened to be loading a wagon yesterday in front of the Great Hall. He recognized Kae from the kitchens, and said she was with a young merman, acting in a familiar manner. I assumed it had to have been you."

"Acting in a *familiar manner*?" Shea shook his head. "What exactly does that mean in mermaid-speak?"

"I would assume it means the same as it would for drylanders," Lybio retorted. "Acting like they were familiar with each other. Like they knew one another in a comfortable sort of way, my Prince."

It was not just the things the older merman was saying that made Shea angry. It was the way he was saying them. And the things left unsaid. "What is it I've done to make you think so little of me?"

Lybio's mouth pressed into a thin line. It was a full minute before he spoke. "She is my only daughter. I do not wish to see her heart broken."

"Why do you think I'm going to break her heart?"

Lybio didn't answer, turning again to face the horizon.

"I will never hurt Kae."

Lybio let out a long sigh, cursing under his breath. He turned his head to look at Shea. "It may not be your choice, my Prince. Royals are never free to marry whom they choose." He let his words sink in for a few moments before adding, "In the end, you, my Prince, will always need to do what's best for the clan."

Shea thought of his own mother, having to leave her husband and child behind. He took a deep breath and exhaled slowly. He would never let that happen to him. Royal or not, he wouldn't abandon the people he loved, not in a million years. He also knew there was no way to convince Lybio of that at the moment. "Let's not focus on what might happen in the future. Can we get back to the problem at hand? If Kae isn't on her way to Atlantis, where is she?"

"You're positive…"

Shea was tired of defending himself for things he knew he wasn't guilty of. Impulsively, Shea wrapped his fingers around the transmutare stone hanging from the cord around his neck. "Let's go talk to that servant who saw Kae in the

gardens yesterday. If she wasn't swimming with me, who was she with?" He looked down at the black Lab, still lying at his feet. "Lucky, go home. Off the beach."

Lucky jumped to attention and barked.

"Home," repeated Shea. The dog barked again, and trotted up in the direction of the boardwalk.

Shea watched him go and then turned to walk into the waves. For once, Lybio didn't argue with him. He fell in step beside him as they walked out into the deeper water, asking, "What about your grandmother?"

Shea checked the sunrise that was only now fully cresting the horizon. "Judging by the sun, it's only just 5:30. She's not even out of bed quite yet, and won't be looking for me for a few hours, not until she has breakfast ready." He dove under the next wave, with Lybio following by his side.

Chapter Nine

They swam quickly away from the shore, out into the deeper waters off the end of the rock jetty. It had been a while since Shea had used the transforming magic of the transmutare stone, and he felt slightly uncomfortable changing in front of Kae's father. But there was no other way.

He stopped swimming and planted his feet into a soft area of sand, pulling in a deep breath of saltwater to steady his nerves. He needed to help Lybio get to the bottom of this mystery. He desperately wanted to talk with the servant who saw Kae in the gardens, to hear for himself what that merman had seen. And, if he wanted to make it home in time for breakfast, he'd need to swim pretty fast. That definitely meant changing.

"*A pedibus usque ad caput mutatio.*" As he recited the last of the spell, a familiar heat bolted through his body, stemming from a spot right behind his bellybutton and shooting down all the way to the tips of his toes. He looked down at his legs, where tiny bubbles circled their way up, starting at the soles of his feet and swirling ever faster around his shins, his knees, and finally his thighs. Out of habit, he tried to wiggle his toes in the sand and found he couldn't move his legs at all. The paralysis doesn't last long, he reminded himself, trying to keep his anxiety in check.

This was always the hardest part, losing control of his body like someone or something else was taking over. It was the magick. It controlled the transformation, and controlled his body in the process. The water around him churned. The tingling moving further up his legs, each moment seeming like forever as the tiny bubbles zoomed around his body, binding his lower region together into what he knew would become one powerful tail.

After what seemed like hours but was in reality less than a minute, the bubbles stopped their frenetic movements and the froth began to dissipate, rising slowly past the rest of his body to the water's surface. He shut his eyes tightly as the rising bubbles swirled around his face, the surrounding water still warm from the transforming magick. Cracking one eyelid open, he glanced downward. There, where he usually had two separate legs, was now one big bright green fish tail with flecks of blue and gold scattered along its length.

Lybio's powerful tail was a deeper shade of emerald than Shea's, with even darker green scales scattered throughout. He turned to Shea. "Are you ready to swim, my Prince?"

"Quit calling me that already, would you? And yeah, I can swim." His voice projected more confidence than he felt. He hadn't been in the ocean for weeks now. King Koios had been quite clear about the restriction, but none of that mattered right now. Besides, Lybio was right beside him. Nothing bad was going to happen. It was Kae they were both worried about.

As they pushed ahead into deeper water, swimming side by side, Shea remembered the first time Kae helped him through the transformation process and taught him how to swim. She led him down to the river dock and they jumped into the deep water. He pictured the deep crimson blush on her cheeks when she transformed in front of him. He'd been awestruck by her sheer grace and beauty, how perfectly her tail undulated through the water as she swam, like an underwater wave rolling slowly up and down through the murky depths of the river. He remembered the salty sweet taste of her lips when they'd surfaced and she'd kissed him, like the sea salt caramels they sold at the Candy Manor in Chatham. Irresistible kisses with their sweetness tinged with salt, from an irresistible mermaid.

Although he thought he was used to the idea of swimming, each nuance of the shimmering tail that was now a part of him continued to fascinate and distract Shea. His senses threatened to overload from the sheer pleasure of the cool ocean caressing his body, like the ocean was running its fingers through his hair, welcoming him home. He wondered if he'd ever be able to get used to the feeling enough to ignore it completely.

The smell of the water as he breathed in through his nose and pushed it out through his gills was salty, but not in a bad way. He could taste the salt in his mouth too, and he couldn't help but think of Kae. He kicked his tail fin faster, the urgency of the errand growing in his mind with each passing moment.

He clenched his fists at his sides and kicked harder, swimming faster toward the bottom of Nantucket Sound. Something bad must have happened to Kae or she never would've disappeared without telling him where she was going. Maybe that servant misunderstood what he saw in the gardens. That other merman must have been holding onto her hand to drag her away from the castle grounds against her will.

The water around them began to lighten with the rising of the sun, even as they swam deeper into the ocean's depths. Sunlight filtered downward, illuminating the awakening sea creatures as Nantucket Sound began the cycle of another day. Shea could hear the cacophony of voices beginning to stir, some in greeting, some in warning, as the never-ending circle of life continued to turn throughout the undersea world. Being able to understand the voices of sea creatures had ultimately saved the life of King Koios, but at the moment Shea thought it might make him insane if he couldn't tune out the chaos in his head.

Why had it not bothered him so much the last time he'd been in the ocean? Were the abilities getting stronger, or was it the complete silence of his swimming companion that was leaving him vulnerable to the voices surrounding him? They passed a huge school of silvery minnows, and Shea felt overwhelmed by the sounds of a thousand tinkling voices all speaking at once in his head.

"Talk to me, Lybio," Shea finally pleaded. "I need to focus on something other than the sound of gossiping minnows or I'll go nuts!"

The larger merman scrunched his forehead, his eyebrows coming together to form one bushy line. "Nuts? Is that a place you want to go, my Prince?"

Shea blew out an exasperated breath, bubbles streaming behind him from his gills. He always forgot merfolk weren't very well acquainted with human slang and tended to speak more formally. He decided to ask a direct question instead. "How goes the search for Demyan? Any leads on tracking him down?"

The expression on Lybio's face darkened. "Our forces tracked him to the upper reaches of the Atlantic but then lost the trail. Although the king of the Nerine clan denies any knowledge of Demyan's whereabouts, I fear he has made an alliance of some sort with them."

Shea opened his mouth to tell Lybio he'd heard about the Nerine from his grandmother, but stopped before the words came out. Was Gramma's secret common knowledge among the Aequorean court? Did King Koios already know that his daughter's husband wasn't one hundred percent drylander? He couldn't be sure. And he certainly wasn't going to be the one to open that can of sea worms. Not today.

"Tell me more about the Nerine," Shea said. "I don't remember meeting any of their clan during the Solstice celebration."

Lybio snorted. "You would certainly remember if you did. They are distinctive in both looks and customs."

His grandmother had told him something very similar. "When your daughter and I watched the Solstice procession through the courtyard, it looked to me like mermaids come in every color, shape and size. What could be so distinctive about their clan in a race that already has so many variables?"

"Just as you observed, merfolk are a rainbow-hued race that thrives on variety, just as the humans are. Our hair and eye colors, our skin tones, even down to the scales on our tails

and the names we give to our children. Some clans favor one color over another, but there is always the diversity that comes from the intermingling of the clans, and from our interactions with drylanders. This is not the case with the Nerine."

"How so?"

"For them, there is no intermingling. They may attend gatherings, and they send a select few of their young to University, but they never marry outside of their own clan. Ever. And they have little, if any, contact with the human race. Their location under the thick Arctic ice helps to shield them from such temptations, but it is also strictly forbidden by both their king and culture."

"So they all look the same?"

Lybio nodded, kicking his tail a little harder to pick up the pace as if the subject angered him. "All Nerine have the same distinguishing features. White hair, dark blue skin and tails, and eyes of the palest blue with no pupils and no whites visible surrounding them."

A shudder ran down Shea's spine as he tried to picture eyes like the ones Lybio described. He might have seen a Nerine at Summer Solstice, because he certainly remembered blue skin and white hair amongst the multi-hued crowd. But he never noticed any creepy, unnatural-looking eyes. "And they all look just the same? Throughout the entire Arctic Circle?"

Lybio nodded. "There is rumored to be a second race of mermaids hidden in the Arctic, descended from the Gorgons of old, black of hair and heart, but perhaps those are but scary stories we tell our young ones in the dark of night to keep them from adventuring too far from the safety of home."

Something Kae had once told him echoed in Shea's head. "There is always some truth to every fairy tale. Assuming these other mermaids with the black hair do actually exist, who were the Gorgons? Part of the Nerine clan?"

A chuckle erupted from deep within Lybio's wide chest. "Is the education of drylanders really so limited? Do you no longer study the ancient gods and demons?" When Shea said nothing, Lybio exhaled a long breath. "I apologize, my Prince. I did not mean to insult. The Gorgons were children of the ancient sea god Phorcys, who is said to preside over the terrors of the deep."

"I thought merfolk descended from Poseidon, brother of Zeus and ruler of all the oceans?" Shea felt like he had to redeem himself in Lybio's eyes. He didn't want Kae's father thinking he was uneducated. After Hailey had told him about Poseidon, he'd found a book on Greek mythology and read it cover to cover. The author, however, hadn't covered mermaid lore.

Lybio nodded in agreement. "Yes, Poseidon and his descendents rule the seas, but the existence of mermaids and the various clans predates even Poseidon's take-over. Poseidon is the one who brought peace and balance to the oceans. He set his own children on the thrones of each of the five oceans, believing that if he bound the oceans together by blood it would end the fighting between the various clans. It is said that to this day, Poseidon himself decides which offspring should inherit the throne of their fathers, marking the heirs with the brand of his own trident."

At Lybio's words, Shea felt overly conscious of the birthmark on his own back, shaped unmistakably like a trident. It matched the ones on his mother and his grandfather, who now ruled the Southern and Atlantic Oceans. Shea found it hard to believe that Poseidon himself had decided to "mark" him, but then again, so much of his life had become unbelievable in the last two months.

The older merman continued speaking, unaware of Shea's discomfort. "The children of Phorcys were dangerous sea monsters, like Skylla who devoured passing sailors, Ekhidna the she-dragon, and the Gorgons with their hair of vipers."

"Like Medusa?" One of the tales in that book of mythology Shea read had been about Perseus, son of Zeus, who'd been given the impossible task of killing Medusa. Her head was a nest of snakes and her gaze could turn a man to

stone, but Perseus had help from the gods and succeeded in his mission.

Lybio agreed. "She was the most famous of the Gorgons, and perhaps the most misunderstood. After her death, her sisters fled, fearing for their lives. It is said they ended up hiding in the ice caves of the Arctic and that they found mates among the Nerine."

"I thought you said the Nerine didn't intermingle?"

"They don't," Lybio agreed. "Not willingly, at least."

The pair had almost reached the castle. From his previous visit, Shea recognized the fields of oysters and scallops that lined either side of what he now knew to be an underwater road. He stared at the hundreds of fluted shells sitting in neat horizontal lines along the ocean floor. On three sides of the bed were rows of large stones, covered with green, fingerlike branches of the soft codium weed stretching upwards three feet toward the surface, forming a waving green barrier. He was reminded again of Oklahoma, and the fields he used to tend with his father. The father who was no longer around because of Demyan and his minions.

After a few moments of silence, Lybio spoke. "When we get to the castle, do not mention our conversation about the Nerine, or the Gorgons. We are in search of my daughter and I don't want to confuse the issue in anyone's mind."

"Understood." Shea felt a clench of fear in his belly. "What if someone kidnapped Kae to keep her from testifying in Atlantis?"

"Impossible," Lybio said with absolute certainty. "Only King Koios and our immediate family knew of the summons. No one else in the castle was privy to the information, or knew why Kae and her mother were leaving today or where they were going."

"Why else would she have disappeared?"

Lybio had no answer. Soon Shea saw the elaborate marble archway that marked the entrance to the courtyard, as well as the tall statue of the Buddha along the edge of the formal gardens, the one that he and Kae hid behind to watch the Solstice procession. The castle itself was not a very imposing structure, built long and low to conform to the ocean's bottom, with long connecting hallways and clusters of suites that stretched over the span of a mile or so. Since Nantucket Sound is a fairly shallow body of water, the Aequoreans had built a modest summer retreat for their king, only one story high and made from the same local granite as the drylander's jetties. They'd allowed algae and seaweed to grow on the sides and roof, which served to further camouflage the building from any prying human eyes.

Kae had assured him this castle was modest in comparison to King Koios's Winter Palace down in the far depths of the Southern Atlantic. He'd also heard the Adluo Castle his mother now occupied had been built on a grandiose scale, comprised of the polished marble local to the Southern Ocean. At the moment, the granite structure that loomed ahead seemed imposing enough, with its myriad rooms and passageways and with so many servants at the king's beck and call. Shea had no hope of finding his way around the inside, having visited less than a handful of times. He was glad to have Lybio by his side.

Together they entered the Great Hall, and found King Koios waiting for them. His voice boomed across the hall, "Ah, there you are, my boy! So good to see you again!" He was seated on a tall throne that Shea hadn't noticed when he'd been in this room on the night of the Solstice celebration.

That night, the cavernous hall had been filled to capacity with guests from every ocean and sea around the globe. Round dining tables had filled every inch of space and long buffet tables lined the far walls, laden with all different manner of foods, some Shea recognized and some that looked completely alien. Kae had told him that everyone of age was welcome to partake in a Solstice feast, even all the servants, and none were ever turned away.

Now, Shea crossed the hall and approached his grandfather's throne, noting that the king looked fully recovered from his near-death experience. As if reading his mind, King Koios let out a belly laugh. "I can see you giving me the once over with those sharp eyes of yours. I'm fit as a fiddler crab, thanks to you, my boy."

"It's good to see you healthy, Sire." Shea bowed his head as he came to a halt in front of the throne before raising his eyes to meet his grandfather's deep blue ones. "Thank you for allowing me to help find Lybio's daughter."

The king chuckled again. "The moment he told me he was headed to Windmill Point, I knew I'd be seeing you this morning. I'm happy to know you have such compassion for your friends."

Shea's eyes darted over to where Lybio hovered in the water near him. *Didn't he tell him?* Had Lybio not been honest with the king about the nature of Shea's relationship to his daughter? Before he could say anything more, Lybio cleared his throat.

"You are wise, Sire. I could not stop him from coming to aid in the search. Is the Pacific servant still waiting here in the castle for us to question?"

King Koios gestured toward the swinging doors that led into the kitchens. "Marietta is placating him with food. He is worried he won't be able to catch up with the carriage and the rest of the Pacific entourage before it reaches Cape Horn. I tried to tell him the passage is no longer dangerous, now that my daughter leads the Adluo clan, but he is still as nervous as a sea robin, blustering on about treacherous conditions."

Lybio bowed his head. "Thank you for detaining him, Sire. Sheachnadh and I can question him in the kitchens if you like."

"Nonsense. Bring him out here and let's see what he has to say for himself." After Lybio swam out of the hall, the king turned back to look at Shea, narrowing his eyes and lowering his voice so that Shea had to lean forward to hear him. "I'm not sure how much Lybio has told you, but the mermaid was supposed to leave today to testify before the High Court in Atlantis. It is most troubling to me that she disappeared on the eve of her departure, but the nature of her journey is not a fact we want to share with the masses."

"I understand, Sire."

"I was hoping to avoid putting you in this position, but if we can not find the girl, and quickly, then I'm afraid I must ask you to take her place."

"Me?"

"You will travel to the High Court to give your testimony of the events on the night of Summer Solstice, regarding the poisoning plot, all that you and the girl overheard, and of course the slaying of the High Chancellor."

Shea felt instantly guilty that Kae's disappearance was giving him the opportunity for adventure he'd been hoping for. He wanted to testify in Atlantis, but right now finding Kae was more important. The kitchen doors swung open and Lybio swam back into the hall with an unfamiliar merman at his side. Shea noted his dark blue hair, reed thin arms and long, pale face. They came before the king and bowed their heads in respect.

The king dispensed with such niceties immediately. "Arise, both of you. We can waste no more time on the proper protocol of Court."

Lybio nodded brusquely. "Yes, Sire." He gestured to the blue-haired merman. "This is Riord. He was part of the Pacific delegation who traveled here with Prince Azul, and who have been tasked with bringing his body and belongings back to his father, the king."

Under the Atlantic king's direct scrutiny, Riord bowed even deeper, keeping his head down as he spoke. "Forgive me, Sire. I don't understand why I've been detained. I have done nothing wrong."

"No need to be nervous then, is there? We simply wanted to ask you a few questions." When Riord didn't raise his head, the king continued speaking. "I understand you saw one of my servants, a blonde mermaid girl, in the gardens yesterday afternoon."

"That is correct, Sire."

"Was she alone in the gardens or accompanied by another?"

"She was with her boyfriend, Sire."

Shea's eyes flew wide at the merman's choice of words and couldn't keep quiet. "What makes you think the merman was her boyfriend?"

Riord finally looked up at Shea and shrugged. "They were in the gardens quite a while talking and laughing, all the while we were packing up the covered carriage. I couldn't hear what was being said, but the tone sounded very genial. When the servants came out to light the lanterns in the courtyard, I happened to look over and see them face-to-face, quietly holding hands, before swimming away together into the dark. I assumed…"

The king interrupted. "Before you finish that sentence, you should know that the merman by your side is the girl's father. Choose your words with care."

Riord glanced quickly at Lybio. "I meant no disrespect to your daughter. I'm just telling you what I saw."

Shea's heart felt tight in his chest, like a vise had been clamped around it with some unseen hand turning the screw. "What did this merman look like?"

Riord closed his eyes for a moment. "Dark hair with matching scruff around his jawbone so I knew at a glance he wasn't one of our company from the Pacific. His scales were darkish green, but they were too far for me to see his eyes."

Seeing the look of surprise on Lybio's face, Shea turned to him and asked, "Does that description sound familiar?"

"Not at all, and that confuses me. I thought I knew all of Kae's friends on the staff."

"I doubt he's part of the staff," Riord interrupted. He seemed more at ease in the king's presence and his tongue had loosened somewhat. "We've been here for a few weeks now and I'd never seen him before yesterday. He had a strange blue tint to his hair I'm sure I would've remembered. I've noticed the blonde around quite a bit, though. In the kitchens, in the halls, she's hard to miss. That's one beauty of a mermaid, a *syren* in training if you ask me."

The king had been oddly quiet as he listened to the questioning. He finally spoke up, asking, "How long was the merman's hair?"

Riord cocked his head to one side. "A strange question, Sire. How do you mean?

"I don't need the exact measurements, just an assessment of his appearance. Did he have the short hair of a guard or soldier, or longer, like my grandson here?"

The Pacific merman's eyes swept over Shea. "More like him than a soldier. Honestly, when my eyes strayed in their direction, I was more smitten by the mermaid than her mate."

The word "mate" had Shea's stomach churning again, but this time he held his tongue. His fists clenched by his sides in frustration, wanting to defend Kae's honor but that wasn't his place. He needed to remain silent and allow Lybio to defend his daughter. Which he did, with a resounding cuff to the side of the head, sending the blue-haired idiot reeling backward. "Do not speak of my daughter in those tones, sir. I will not have it."

Riord rubbed his head, staying where he'd landed a few paces behind Lybio. "Forgive my wagging tongue. It's been a long, exhausting few weeks and I know not what I'm saying."

King Koios rose from his throne. Ignoring the altercation that had just taken place, he thanked Riord for his information. "And now you are free to go join the rest of your entourage. If you hurry, you will catch up with them easily before they even reach the equator."

Riord bowed deeply, and swam from the Great Hall without another glance at either Lybio or Shea.

Shea wanted to reach out to stop him. "Why are you allowing him to leave, Sire? If he was the last person to see Kae…"

The king chuckled, cutting him off. "I see you have no qualms about questioning the motives of your king. Which will make you a fine leader someday, if a poor subject."

Heat blazed into his cheeks. "Sorry. I didn't mean to be rude, Sire."

"Not to worry." The king looked sharply at Lybio. "As your king, I could not allow you to further manhandle a foreign guest in my presence. I understand a father's feelings, but put them aside for the moment. Did his description trigger any cogent thoughts?"

Lybio shook his head. "I know of no one in the castle with hair as he described, nor has my daughter ever mentioned such a merman. My daughter is also not one to wander away with a stranger without informing her mother or myself. I'm beginning to agree with your grandson that Kae was indeed kidnapped."

CHAPTER TEN

Shea blinked rapidly as he looked from Lybio to the king and back again. It was one thing for him to worry that Kae had been kidnapped. It was an entirely different thing for everyone to reach the same conclusion. The blood pounded in his ears, making it hard to listen to what was being said. Lybio and King Koios discussed possibilities, but Shea's mind reeled off in its own direction.

Kidnapped! Who would really do such a thing? If no one knew of the secret hearing in Atlantis, who would even have motive to take her? Who would want to harm her? His thoughts flew to the last merman who had attempted to harm Kae.

Demyan.

The murderous Adluo held a knife to Kae's throat while trying to make Shea confess to spying. Demyan saw the bond between them and used Kae, having no moral qualms about hurting an innocent to get what he wanted. He sliced Kae's skin and only left them both alive in order to blackmail Shea's mother, the Aequorean princess, into marrying him. Shea thwarted that plot, and now Demyan held a grudge. Would he try to use Kae against him a second time? The more he considered the possibility, the more certain Shea became.

"Sire, it was Demyan," Shea blurted, interrupting the two mermen. "I know it's him. And he's using Kae to get at me. He knows she and I are friends, from Solstice when his soldiers took us both captive."

"The Adluo pretender is swimming for his life," Lybio said, his tone dismissive. "I doubt he's spared a single thought for you in the last few weeks. He's too busy hiding from Atlantean justice to consider revenge."

King Koios looked thoughtful. "I wouldn't be so sure, Lybio. That Demyan is one determined merman, and if he's found himself somewhere to hole up, you can be assured that his mind is busy weaving new plots to take over the Atlantic, if not our entire world."

Shea heard doubt in Lybio's voice as the older merman spoke, slowly reasoning through the possibilities. "Who would harbor such a criminal when we are seeking him? Certainly not anyone in our own clan. And not the Adluos, since he murdered their entire royal family, including the boy king. He'll find no safe haven in the Pacific, either, after poisoning Prince Azul. That leaves going north…"

"…and the Nerine," Shea finished for him. Lybio had told him not to bring up the Arctic clan, but now it seemed impossible not to. "Could they be hiding him? Or working with him in some way?"

"Anything is possible," King Koios conceded. "But how to go about proving your theory…" The king looked off into the distance for a moment, his eyes seemingly focused on the far wall of the Great Hall before snapping back to his servant. "Lybio, I need you to go personally as my emissary to King Naartok, since you are familiar with his court. While he is not exactly Demyan's type of merman, he may know of a disgruntled faction within his clan."

Shea saw Lybio's momentary hesitation, those few seconds where the merman went perfectly still as if made from stone. Finally, he bowed, his face betraying no emotion. "Yes, Sire."

Shea knew how conflicted Lybio must feel, with his only child out there somewhere, missing, and his king entrusting him with a vital mission. He reached out to touch Lybio's arm. "Don't worry. I'll find her."

"No you won't." King Koios crossed his arms over his chest and lowered his eyebrows at his grandson. "I need you to take the girl's place before the Court of Atlantis. The trial will be held in ten days time, with or without our witnesses. We can not allow Demyan to get away with murder." He looked from Shea to Lybio, narrowing his eyes. "Although…if I send you to visit the Nerine, Lybio, who will make the journey with my grandson?"

Lybio frowned. "Could he not travel with your guards, as my daughter had planned?"

"Not in light of our suspicions about Demyan's scheming," said the king, tapping his forefinger against his chin. "Not all the way from here to Atlantis. If only there were some way to get him closer to the Aegean."

Shea realized he didn't even know where in the world Atlantis was situated. All he knew were the cartoon versions of it being an ancient island city that was lost under the sea, much like the Roman city of Pompeii was lost under a volcanic lava flow. He clenched his fists in frustration at how many times his lack of geographic knowledge had failed him in the last few months. Not wanting to interrupt the king's thought process he elbowed Lybio. "Aegean? Where's that exactly?"

"On the far side of the Atlantic, just after you pass through the Mediterranean Sea," Lybio explained.

"Perhaps it would be safest for him to travel above the surface by ship, in drylander fashion," mused the king. "Agents from Atlantis could meet him on the shores of Santorini and escort him from there. He should make it in time for the last days of the trial."

Shea's ears perked up. He'd heard of Santorini before. Isn't that where Hailey said she was going next week? "Wouldn't an airplane would be faster than a ship, Sire?"

The king looked at Shea and frowned. "Those new metal drylander birds that fly across the sky?" He shook his head. "They fall into the sea all the time. I couldn't ask any of my guards to risk that type of journey. Merfolk do not fly. No, a ship is safer transport for all."

"Airplanes are perfectly safe, proven technology," Shea argued. "They've been around for decades."

Lybio chuckled. "Decades are mere drops in the ocean of time."

Shea continued to press his point. "The number of crashes you see is a tiny percent of the total number of planes in the sky every day. In May I flew with Gramma from Oklahoma to Cape Cod, so it must be safe for merfolk, too."

"You didn't have your gills then," Lybio argued. "They say gills cease to function at such high altitudes. Merfolk can't fly."

Shea glanced at him, realizing that Lybio must not know Martha's secret after all. *Interesting.* He turned back to King Koios. "My neighbors are flying to Greece next week, to Santorini. I could travel with them."

"Humans?" Lybio snorted. "How would they protect you?"

"Protect me from what? You and the king say merfolk don't fly."

King Koios raised both hands. "Enough bickering!" He pointed at Lybio. "I've already given you instruction, Lybio. You must leave at once for the Arctic Ocean, and return with word as quickly as possible. Your wife, Kira, can continue the search for your daughter."

Although Shea could see the frustration etched on his face, Lybio bowed deeply and didn't protest. "Yes, Sire. I shall return to you soon." He swam out of the Great Hall, a swirl of tiny bubbles in his wake.

The king's gaze settled on Shea. "And you. You truly feel these flying contraptions are safe?"

"Safe, and faster than going by ship, too." The more Shea thought about it, the more excited he became at the prospect of traveling to Atlantis. Even though he still worried about Kae, bringing Demyan to justice was the key to finding her, he was sure of it.

Now to head home and enjoy the last two days of John's visit... as if he'd be able to do anything but worry about Kae. What was he going to tell his friend? He'd have to figure something out before he got home.

And then he had to explain to his grandmother he needed a plane ticket to Greece.

Shea's feet were dragging by the time he unlatched the stockade fence and entered the back yard. He smelled bacon sizzling in the kitchen, his stomach gurgling to remind him he skipped dinner last night.

"Shea? Is that you?" His grandmother opened the screen door and Lucky came barreling out of the house, almost knocking him over. "When your dog came home from the beach alone, I wondered what happened. Everything okay?"

He pushed Lucky off him and grabbed the hose to wash the sand from his feet. "Not really. Kae's father came to see me this morning. She's gone missing."

Martha's brow knotted with concern. "Missing? Oh dear. I want to hear the details, but John is sitting here waiting for his breakfast." She let the screen door slam in a not-so-subtle hint that Shea needed to be careful what details he shared. After her revelation yesterday, they'd both decided it would be safer for John if they kept him in the dark about things. The fewer humans on Demyan's target list, the better.

John stood at the door to greet him when he entered the kitchen, giving him a one-armed guy hug. "Dude, I overheard what you told your grandmother about your girlfriend running away. That sucks."

"Yeah, it totally does," Shea agreed. His breath hitched at the concern in John's voice, but he wasn't going to get all weepy. Kae would be okay. Her father would find her and bring her home, and Shea would testify so that Demyan got locked away forever in some underwater dungeon. If his suspicions were correct, it was all Shea's fault she was in this predicament in the first place. He needed to do something to fix it, and felt frustrated he wasn't allowed to help in the search.

Martha placed heaping plates of food on the table and John plunked into his chair, saying, "Don't blame yourself, Shea. It's not your fault."

He looked at John, startled that his friend had read his mind. "What do you know..."

Martha interrupted. "I told him last night that you and Kae fought and broke up, which was why you were such terrible company and went to bed early. I'm sure she's gone off somewhere to pout. In the meantime, your friend here has two more days left on Cape Cod and we should make the most of them."

"But Gramma…"

"No buts, young man. The girl will turn up when she's ready. The best thing you can do now is act like it doesn't matter. When her…friends see you are doing fine, she'll probably turn up lickety split."

Shea saw the logic in his grandmother's words, even if he wasn't exactly sure what "lickety split" meant. If Demyan and his minions thought Kae didn't matter to him, maybe they'd release her faster, or try a new tactic that didn't involve harming the mermaid he loved. It was worth a try.

"Okay, sure." He made himself smile at John and relax as much as he could. "What do you feel like doing today?"

John grinned, obviously relieved he wasn't going to be dealing with a heartbroken friend for the rest of his vacation. "Hailey said something about pirate-themed mini-golf? Sounded like a blast."

The way John said Hailey's name made Shea raise an eyebrow. "You know she's younger than us, right?"

"Doesn't mean she's not cool to hang out with." He put down his fork and crossed his arms over his wide chest. "I thought you said she was one of your best friends here."

"Yeah, she is, but…" Shea searched for the right words. "She's more like my little sister, dude. You can't be crushing on her. It's wrong in so many ways."

John laughed, breaking the tension Shea had felt building. "No problem, dude. Honestly, I wasn't thinking anything along those lines. Don't get me wrong, she's cute, but she's no Jeannie Sanderson or Maria Garcia."

It was Shea's turn to laugh. "I thought you said the cheerleaders were out of our league."

John shook his head, grinning from ear to ear. "Out of your league, perhaps, but not mine. Not after I pitched in the state championship and earned my Varsity letter. Those two are all over me."

"What about Bobby Joe Peters? I thought you told me he and Jeannie started dating after I left Oklahoma?"

John laughed so hard he almost choked in his eggs. "She realized pretty quickly what an ass hat B.J. can be." His eyebrows shot up in alarm as he shot a look at Martha. "I'm so sorry for my language, ma'am."

Martha shook her head. "No worries, young man. When a boy is bad news he deserves whatever names he earns."

Some of the tension drained from Shea's shoulders as he and John caught up more about their friends back in Oklahoma. Had he only been gone two months? It felt more like a lifetime, so much had changed. And so much more was

about to change, but he had to put his worries on hold for two more days. He pushed the food around on his plate, his appetite gone. Like Kae.

Surprisingly, he'd come to terms pretty quickly with the new underwater world at his fingertips. He never felt like he quite "fit in" back in Oklahoma, so the fact that his mother was mermaid royalty was a better explanation than any of the others he'd come up with over the years. Having Kae to help him adjust to his new reality made everything so much better. He touched the transmutare stone at his neck, concentrating on linking with Kae, but there was nothing. Only darkness. Which led him back to the question that kept circling in his mind.

Where could she be?

CHAPTER ELEVEN

The floor beneath her felt hard when Kae shifted her sore hips. She shivered and yanked the thin, scratchy blanket tighter to her chin, keeping her eyes closed, the water much colder than she was used to. Maybe the last few days had all been a bad dream. Maybe when she opened her eyes, Mom would be in the kitchen preparing the morning meal.

Except she was pretty sure it wasn't a dream. Her sore limbs could attest to that.

Slowly she pieced together what she could remember, and worried that there were such large gaps in her memory. The past forty-eight hours were a blur, hazy indistinct images. Travel. Swimming. Places she'd never seen before. Kae routinely traveled as part of the royal entourage with her parents, swimming long distances from the Southern Atlantic all the way to Nantucket Sound, but she'd never made a journey like this.

Vaguely she remembered passing along the outskirts of a few villages – *Yesterday? The day before?* – but most of the swimming was in the open ocean, zooming through the middle depths, far enough below the surface, away from humans and their ships, but high enough from the ocean's floor so as not to be seen by other merfolk. In fact, she hadn't seen a single soul besides Xander since leaving the castle gardens.

She'd never swum so fast for so long in her entire life, let alone gone straight out for almost two full days, barely stopping to eat let alone sleep. When they finally stopped swimming, it was the middle of the second night and pitch dark. Every single part of her hurt – from her shoulders down to her tail fin, and every muscle in between. Even now, she could feel muscles protesting the simple act of sitting up, so she didn't even try.

Xander said he'd explain everything. For the last two days he held her hand constantly as they zoomed through the water on their journey. Last night, he kissed her forehead and told her to rest. She'd been too tired to ask questions and had fallen dead asleep. How long had she slept? She could tell by the coolness of the water she was all alone at the moment. She missed his warm, solid presence by her side. Thinking about it all now, that was the strangest part of the entire journey – how quickly she'd grown close to him, trusting him. When he held her hand, nothing else seemed to matter. Nothing. She swam by his side without feeling fatigue or hunger, without worrying about family or responsibilities.

Her eyes flew open, finding the water around her as black as a cloud of octopus ink. How long had she been asleep? She focused on the silver bracelet encircling her wrist, feeling the cool metal press against her skin even if she couldn't see it in the total darkness. With great effort, she stretched her arms above her head, running her thumb along the silver. Five strands for the earth's five oceans, hammered into the shape of rolling waves.

"So you don't forget me while we're apart…" The words echoed in her head as a face suddenly filled her mind and images came rushing back to her. Shea, with his blond hair and big green eyes. Shea, whose smile lit up his entire face and warmed her like summer sunshine. The only son of the royal princess, heir to the Atlantic throne, and the boy who'd given her a first kiss she would never forget…

Except that she had let it all slip from her mind like sand through her fingers. How had she forgotten about Shea?

He knew she was going on a journey and gave her a gift. He knew they would be apart. But why did she forget all about him? Kae shifted uncomfortably. What did he think about her

swimming away with Xander? Did he know the handsome merman would be her guide on this journey? Kae tried to concentrate, to remember, but that puzzle piece of her memory was still missing.

Xander. The dark-haired hunk remained a mystery to her, despite having spent the last few days alone in his company. He still seemed like an odd mixture of tough guy and lonely little boy, and part of her ached to make his sadness go away. It felt like those dark eyes of his could look right through her, that Xander knew everything about her and everything she was thinking, but she couldn't figure him out. Did she want to figure him out? The thought sent a chill fluttering down her tailfin as more puzzle pieces of memory fell into place. The merman basically kidnapped her...somehow. She was fairly positive she'd never met him before that day in the castle gardens. Yesterday? The day before? The fact that she'd lost track of time made her shiver again. What did he do to her?

They hadn't spoken much along their journey, her gills already working overtime to keep up the fast pace set by the determined merman. But then again, maybe they did talk. She couldn't remember, so how would she know what was said? She sat bolt upright, muscles protesting and tail scraping along the hard rock floor as she shifted her weight. She strained to see but the utter blackness of her surroundings yielded no clues. There were huge blank spots in her mind, parts of her

memory washed away with the tides. She reached up to touch her transmutare medallion to link with her mother but her neck was bare. A chill of fear ran down her spine and left her tail fin quivering in the darkness.

"Where am I?" she wondered aloud. The grinding scrape of metal-on-metal answered her question, a latch being slowly pushed open. Seconds later the outline of a door appeared out of the darkness, an illuminated rectangle on a wall of black, as the door itself swung inward. Kae clutched the thin blanket, not sure what to expect. The mermaid who entered the chamber carried a small, rusty lantern in one hand and a bowl in the other. In the faint glow, Kae could see the girl's skin was dark blue and her long flowing hair was straight and shockingly white. Kae's stomach gurgled and she suddenly realized she was starving. "Is that food?"

The blue mermaid didn't answer, instead placing both the lantern and bowl on the floor and racing out the door, pulling it shut behind her. Kae ignored the sound of metal scraping again and inched closer to the bowl and lantern. She didn't stop to consider the source of the unfamiliar-looking sushi, or that it might have been poisoned, until she'd almost finished it all. Too late to worry about that now, she decided, and devoured the last few bites. If someone wanted her dead, they'd already had enough opportunities while she slept.

Her hunger sated, she turned her attention to her surroundings. The lantern was rusted and old, the handle so worn that Kae feared it might break if she held it at the wrong angle. A soft golden glow came from a single jellyfish trapped inside, bobbing up and down within the glass globe, the tips of its poisoned tentacles pointing directly at Kae.

Holding the lantern and its deadly contents at arm's length, she slowly swam the perimeter of the cramped chamber, inspecting each of the four walls and ceiling. All were solid rock except for the outline of the door, which was also made of rock with no visible hinges or knob on the inside. Where three of the walls were rough hewn and uneven in texture, the wall with the door was flat and smooth to the touch, the door fitting perfectly into its frame. She ran her finger along the rectangular outline, so straight and precise.

The floor was also solid rock, which explained why she'd been so uncomfortable. She could see now that the scratchy blanket she'd been sleeping with was made of flattened reeds of some sort she didn't recognize, crudely woven together. Not at all like the carefully woven linens she'd become used to in her years of living with the royal family.

"Trapped," she said out loud, feeling as if the walls of the chamber were closing in. No windows, no openings – so how was the fresh water circulating through? Or was it? Was there

enough oxygen in the small rock room for her gills to keep pumping?

She started to feel lightheaded and suddenly realized she was breathing the water in and out far too quickly, hyperventilating. She closed her eyes tightly, making an effort to slow her breathing to something resembling normal. She took in a deep mouthful of cold, salty water, exhaling slowly through her gills as she counted to ten and opened her eyes again.

She was still so tired. She needed more sleep, but two questions kept circling her brain.

Where on earth was she?

And why?

CHAPTER TWELVE

Shea handed the two small suitcases to the van driver.

"It's kind of you to share your ride to the airport with us," Martha MacNamara said, smiling at Gloria Thompson. "When Shea told me we were going to be on the same flights all the way to Greece, I couldn't believe it!"

Gloria laughed. "How many flights could there be from Boston to the island of Santorini, right? It's no bother at all."

Shea climbed into the van, passing Chip in the middle row of seats, who stared out the window pointedly ignoring him while his earbuds leaked loud music into the vehicle. Settling into the open seat next to Hailey in the last row, he nodded toward her brother. "What's wrong with him?"

"He's pissed at mom again. So who's taking care of Lucky while you're away? Too bad you couldn't bring him with you, but I guess it's a long flight for a dog and with quarantines and all it would be kinda bad…"

"He's staying with Mrs. McFadden," Shea told her, cutting her off mid-sentence. He could still picture the look on the dog's face when they'd left him with the neighbor, the dog's grey eyes full of worry as if he knew Shea was headed for trouble. Shea shook his head at such a silly thought, and refocused the conversation back on Hailey's brother. "What's Chip got to be upset about? I thought he hated Cape Cod and would be happy to be getting out of here!"

Hailey smirked. "They offered him a job as a lifeguard at that motel over on Shoreline Road, but Mom's making him come to Greece instead. As if there won't be gorgeous girls to flirt with on a Greek island!"

Shea's attention slipped away from Hailey's steady stream of chatter. He pictured Kae and wondered where in the world she could be right now. Five long days passed since she disappeared without a word. Well, she'd said goodbye, but for entirely different reasons. He hadn't slept all week, lying awake at night wondering where she was, if she was okay. Wondering if she was alone, or scared, or hurt. Why hadn't there been any word, any demands made by kidnappers? If Demyan was behind her disappearance, what was he waiting for? His dad, his uncle, and his grandfather were all dead because of

Demyan's machinations. And now Kae might be caught up in those schemes, too. But no one was telling him anything.

Here he was almost a week later, headed to Logan Airport with Hailey's family, ready to journey to Atlantis to testify. He knew he had to go, but he'd rather be out there in the ocean, helping with the search for Kae. Which was the reason Martha insisted on making the journey with him, to make sure he didn't bail and swim off to search the ocean on his own. He thought about sneaking off after John left but then Martha kept him on lock-down all week, not even letting him walk the dog alone.

Shea still wasn't clear about whether King Koios knew his grandmother's mermaid origins. He was the king, right? Shouldn't the king know things like that? Shea also wasn't clear if Martha planned to travel with him after they'd reached the coast of Santorini. Kae's mother Kira visited earlier to explain which beach they needed to be on to meet with the merfolk from Atlantis, but beyond that Shea didn't know what would happen.

"Are you even listening to me? Earth to Shea?" Hailey poked him hard in the ribs, bringing him back into the present. "Honestly, you are such a guy sometimes," she said with a disgusted shake of her head.

Shea laughed. "That's because I *am* a guy, you weirdo." He nudged her shoulder with his own. "Sorry, I'm just a little nervous about flying and all. I've only been in a plane once, you know. I can't believe how cool John was about flying alone. We dropped him at Logan, and he was all 'see you later,' no nerves no anything. I'm glad I've got you and Gramma along for the flight."

"It's no big deal," Hailey assured him, patting his knee like he was a two year old. "People fly all the time. And these flights should be good, I mean, six and a half hours to London, which probably means we get to watch two whole movies plus a meal or two. Then change planes and another three and a half hours to Athens, which means another movie. After that it's a little puddle-jumper plane for the last hour to Thira."

Shea tried to ignore how many hours of flying lay ahead of him and focused on the part that confused him. "I thought we were going to Santorini?"

Hailey laughed. "We are, knucklehead. Thira and Santorini are the same place."

"So why does it have two names?"

"I think it's because there's more than one island. Santorini was the Latin name for the whole place, and it's the biggest island, but there are other, smaller ones too," Hailey explained. "In fact, the whole place is kind of shaped like a giant crescent with the middle sunken below the ocean's surface, as if the islands are just what remains from the tops of mountains. Some theories say that the whole area used to be much bigger, almost another continent, and that's where the lost city of Atlantis used to be."

That got Shea's attention. "Atlantis? What do you mean?"

"Well, I've done a lot an awful lot of reading about Santorini since Mom took the job, and let's just say there's a humungous amount of info and research that points to those legends of a sunken city being true." Hailey lowered her voice to a whisper. "Is that why you're really going to Greece? To visit an underwater kingdom? Is your mom really there on business-business, or is it like *mermaid* business?"

Shea glanced at Chip to make sure he wasn't listening. As far as Shea could tell, Chip couldn't hear anything except the music blaring from his headphones. But. "I don't want to talk about this right now," he whispered back to her, his words sounding harsher than he'd intended.

"Fine." She shrugged and looked out the window. "I'm surprised your girlfriend didn't reappear in time to say goodbye. Her whole disappearing act was such an immature temper tantrum. Or am I completely wrong and she's already on Santorini, meeting up with you once we get there?"

Shea felt his back stiffen. He took a deep breath and exhaled slowly as she continued to tease him.

"You know, I was curious. When you guys kiss, is it like all salty? I mean, Chip always talks about kissing girls with flavored lip gloss and whatnot, but I'm guessing Kae doesn't go for cherry Chapstick, right?"

He unclenched his fist and leveled his gaze on her. "We're about to spend the entire day traveling. Together. Do you really want to pick a fight with me right now?"

Hailey's eyes flew open wide, her words spilling out in a torrent. "What do you mean? I was just teasing, you know. What happened? Did you guys really break up? Did Kae run away from home because of your fight? Like, for real?"

"Not exactly." He'd spent too much time over the last few days thinking about that last time he'd seen her, about the argument they'd had right before she left. And way too much time parsing that Pacific merman's words about Kae. About how *familiar* she seemed with that other dude, whoever he was. That she swam off with her *boyfriend*. Could she have met someone else on the same day they broke up? Did they even break up?

"What do you mean, *not exactly*? How can you…"

He cleared his throat. "Actually, Hailey, I'm not sure what happened."

While they were talking, the driver finished loading the luggage and started the van, heading out of Windmill Point. Martha and Gloria settled in the van's first row, deep in

conversation and Chip turned his iPod up yet another notch. Shea could clearly hear the guitar riffs from the latest Three Days Grace song floating through the van. After teasing him so relentlessly about Kae, Hailey had grown suddenly and uncharacteristically quiet.

Which was just fine with Shea.

CHAPTER THIRTEEN

The sound of scraping metal woke Kae from a fitful sleep. She'd been dreaming she was surrounded by great white sharks, screaming for someone to rescue her as the sharks circled closer and closer. She knew that any minute the beasts were coming in for the kill, and there was nothing she could do.

"Kae? Are you okay?"

At the sound of his voice, Kae's eyes flew open. She immediately had to squint them against the bright light shining in from the hallway, and raised a hand to shield her face. "Shea? Is that you?"

"No, it's me. Xander." He sounded disappointed as he pushed the door open all the way. Her eyes adjusted to the light and she saw the dark-haired merman hovering in the doorway, looking around the cell as if searching for something or someone else. "I heard you screaming for help and swam here as fast as I could. Bad dream?"

She rubbed the sleep from her eyes. "I guess so. I don't really know. I'm having a lot of trouble remembering things."

He crossed the room and hovered by her side. "Don't worry about that. It's probably because of the physical exertion. Long journeys can take their toll. How do you feel now?"

"Better, I think." She sat up and stretched her arms over her head, testing her muscles. They were no longer sore from the long swim. "How many hours have I been asleep? Where...where are we?"

Xander took her hand, giving it a squeeze. A flood of warm feelings instantly filled her, and she relaxed. He reached over and gently stroked the side of her face, sending little shivers of pleasure running through her with his touch. She was suddenly glad that he was here with her, wherever *here* was. "You've been asleep for almost two days, babe. I was beginning to worry that the Nerine sedatives were too strong for you."

Her eyes flew wide with shock as she struggled to pull her hand free. She remembered that bowl of food she'd eaten. "Sedatives? What does that mean? You drugged me?"

He held up his hands in a gesture of surrender. "It was for your own good, to allow your body to heal from the hard journey. I'm just used to measuring doses for larger mermen, like soldiers and such. I had no idea you'd be asleep for so long. I was starting to worry."

"So you're a...healer?"

He smiled, his dark eyes looking sad as he took her hand in his again. "Something like that."

That pulse of warmth flowed through her again and she forgot she was upset with him. But something about what he said tickled her mind. "Nerine," she said, and frowned. "Does that explain why the water is so cold? We're all the way up in the Arctic Ocean?"

Xander nodded and pulled her into a hug, pressing her close as she wrapped her arms around his waist, feeling his rough scales beneath her fingers. When he spoke, her thick curls muffled his soft words. "We are in the Arctic, but you're safe with me, babe. I won't let anyone hurt you."

"Hurt me? Who's going to hurt me?"

"That would be me," said a gravelly voice.

Her head jerked up to see a dark merman at her door, this one frighteningly familiar. She gasped and struggled to untangle herself from Xander's embrace as the menacing merman swam through the opening, a long shining sword hanging at his side. "Prince Demyan!"

He sneered down at her. "Ah, yes, *Prince*. Such an utterly worthless title, don't you agree?" She stared, unable to formulate a response. Demyan didn't seem to notice, caught up as he was in his own self-righteous rant. "It would certainly be *King* Demyan by now, and by all rights should be. I battled and schemed and did everything I needed to in order to earn that title…and it should be mine. Except. Except! Except for Brynn's bastard, your insufferable drylander friend. I should've killed both of you when I had the chance before the Solstice banquet. Before you RUINED everything."

A shiver of fear ran down Kae's spine. She tried to control her body's response, reminding herself that even now, others were searching for this merman to bring him to justice. Her father had assured her that every day the king's men drew closer to finding him. Maybe today would be her ultimate lucky day and soldiers would burst in any minute to arrest the murderer.

She swallowed hard and narrowed her eyes, trying to project more courage than she felt. "Is that why you've brought me here? To this dungeon? To kill me?"

"My dear, if I'd simply wanted to *kill* you, you'd be dead already." Demyan laughed and another shiver snaked across Kae's back. She shook it off and focused on his words. "No, since my first plan failed so spectacularly, I've been forced to come up with alternatives."

"Why do you need me? I won't help with your 'alternative' plan." Her words were sharp, and she could see the surprise on Xander's face, but she plowed on. "I'm not a royal. I can't grant you any kind of power or access to anything. I don't even *know* anything of importance." She looked down at her hands, shocked to realize just how little her life mattered in Neptune's grand scheme of things. She'd already been gone for days and no one seemed to care. No one had come swimming after her. Her only friend now seemed to be Xander, and he was the one who'd brought her here and even admitted he'd drugged her. She felt deflated by this new understanding, and her voice began to falter. "I'm... I'm nobody."

The edges of Demyan's mouth curled as Kae glanced up. She recognized the smile of a sea serpent just before he strikes. "Ah, but you underestimate your *own* importance, my dear mermaid, even if your most obvious quality is your stubborn nature. I myself don't understand the attraction, since I prefer my mermaids to be completely submissive, and I do mean completely." He chuckled and ran one finger down her cheek, eliciting another shiver. "Ah, but that would be another story. For another time, perhaps."

"Leave her alone."

Kae looked at Xander with surprise and saw his fists clenched into tight balls by his sides, his arm muscles tensed. It was the first time he'd spoken since Demyan entered the room. Kae forgot he hovered so close to her, their shoulders almost touching. "You didn't tell me you planned to hurt her."

"Hurt her?" Demyan's chuckle filled the small room as he appraised the other merman. "You don't want me to hurt her? Oh, my my. What an interesting shift of the current." He turned his attention back to Kae. "It would seem my associate here is quite taken with you. Absolutely smitten, I should say." He clapped a hand on Xander's shoulder. "Aren't you, Zan?"

Her eyes flew to the merman she knew as Xander. "Zan? The Adluo sorcerer? Is that who you truly are?" He swallowed hard and finally nodded his assent, his eyes pleading with her for understanding before returning his gaze to the floor. "You lied to me," she whispered, unable to hide her disbelief. She thought back to the warm feelings of trust she'd felt for him, and wondered how much of that had been because of magick. Was he the reason her memories were fuzzy?

"I didn't lie." His eyes remained downcast. "Xander was my nickname at University." It sounded almost like an apology.

Demyan chuckled, the sound grating across her skin like barnacles. "Ah, but you'll always be Zan to me. Ever since that first day I found you in the dolphin stables, covered in someone else's blood." He clapped him on the shoulder again. "We've been through so much together, haven't we? Far too much to let a mere mermaid come between us. Or between me and my rightful place as ruler. Am I right, *Zan*?"

CHAPTER FOURTEEN

Zan didn't dare look Demyan in the eye. He'd seen far too many soldiers slaughtered for such insolence. Especially when Demyan was in this kind of mood. "Of course, Sire," Zan mumbled, his head still down. "I'm yours to command."

Demyan rubbed his hands together, the smile back on his face. "That's what I like to hear. Unfortunately, my source inside the Nerine Court tells me an emissary from King Koios is visiting with King Naartok, looking for this little beauty. Any idea how that clownfish of a king would have a clue as to my whereabouts? Hmm?"

"No, Sire," he said automatically, his mind whirling through possibilities.

"Come now, Zan. You're smarter than that. Tell me how this could have happened."

Zan tried not to look at Kae. "Well, Sire, there really aren't too many possibilities available to you. I'm sure King Koios has scoured every inch of the Atlantic Ocean in the last week, so he knows you are not there. You slew the High Chancellor in front of the crowd, so it's a fair bet you wouldn't be anywhere near Atlantis, and in light of Prince Azul's unfortunate accident, it's also fair guess there would be no safe haven for you anywhere in the Pacific. According to this mermaid, Brynneliana succeeded Theo and already sits on the Southern Ocean's throne as the new Adluo Queen."

He heard Kae gasp and tried not to visibly wince. Yes, he'd used her for information. He was almost positive she didn't remember all the questions she'd answered for him under the influence of magick. Not that he intended to disclose all of his newfound knowledge to Demyan. Especially not the part about how close Kae actually was to the Atlantic heir, or how much the drylander bastard professed to truly care for her. Love. What would a drylander know about loving a mermaid?

If he shared that particular information with Demyan, it would most certainly seal her fate, and Zan preferred Kae alive. As long as she lived, he could still change her heart and make her love him instead of the drylander whelp. Magick could make her follow him, but not love him. That was something he'd have to earn all on his own.

Demyan's sneer brought Zan back to the present. "You want me to believe Koios crossed a mere three oceans off his master list and that left him with the Arctic? Seems like a leap of faith that he could make that connection."

"Perhaps he sent emissaries to both the Indian and the Arctic kings." Zan straightened his shoulders and looked Demyan straight in the eye. "For my part, I interacted with no one but this mermaid on my journey. You sent me to find her and I did. The fact that she was about to leave for Atlantis necessitated a change in the original plan."

Demyan nodded, the wide grin returning to his face. "Quite right. Job well done and all that sort of mung. It's good to have underlings who can think for themselves." Zan bristled at being called an *underling*, but nodded back at him nonetheless. *Better to deal with his insults than his sword.*

"Now then, Zan," Demyan continued, swimming closer to the mermaid. "According to your new plan, I think it's time you paid that drylander scum a visit, asking him to join our little get-together." He tilted his head to one side, staring at Kae. "But how will we convince him that you're already here at the party, my dear?"

"What...what do you mean?" Kae shrunk back all the way to the wall as Demyan advanced, until he hovered before her, scant millimeters from pressing against her body. Next to her, Zan clenched his fists, trying to steady his nerves. He felt

Kae's fear wash over him in waves and it took all of his self-control to keep from striking out at Demyan. He'd promised to keep her safe and yet at the moment he felt powerless to interfere.

Demyan grabbed a handful of blond curls, yanking hard enough to make her cry out in pain. "Perhaps a few locks of your golden hair would convince him? But how would he know it's actually yours?"

She whimpered in response, and Zan felt as if his heart would break. He filled his lungs with cold water and held his breath, waiting for Demyan to make his next move. *If he hurts her, I will kill him*, he promised himself.

"Maybe an actual body part would work best." Demyan released his grip on her hair as he appraised the rest of her. "A finger, perhaps? Or would that sea urchin whelp need the whole hand in order to recognize you?" He made a grab for Kae's wrist, locking his hand around the silver bracelet. He looked down in surprise at the metal. "Well, well, what have we here?"

She tried to pull away, to no avail. "Let go of me."

"Answer the question! Where did you get this piece of finery?" He yanked her wrist again and she cried out in pain.

"It was a gift from the drylander," Zan interjected. Both Demyan and Kae turned to him with surprise. "The mermaid told me when I interrogated her. Certainly the drylander bastard would recognize his token."

"Good work, Zan." Demyan slowly drew his sword from its sheath, still holding Kae's arm with his other hand. "We can send the wrist encircled with silver and then he'll have no doubt which mermaid is here with us."

Zan watched Kae strain to pull her hand away, eyes crazed with fear. Steeling his resolve, he grabbed the hilt of Demyan's sword before he could fully unsheathe it. "Sire, there is a better way."

Demyan's eyes opened wider. "Are you...questioning me?"

"Not at all," Zan lied, forcing a smile onto his face. He kept his hand on the sword hilt, just in case. "Merely pointing out that a more subtle approach might be warranted. One that would ensure the outcome you desire."

A thoughtful look crossed Demyan's face and he released his hold on Kae. She scooted backward into the shadows at the far corner of the small room. "What kind of alternative did you have in mind, exactly?" Although Demyan still had his fingers wrapped around the hilt, Zan realized he needed to release his own grasp so as not to press his luck.

Slowly, he removed his hand from the sword and swam to where Kae quivered against the rock wall. Holding her eyes with his own, he used his magick to calm her. Almost

141

immediately, she ceased shaking. Without flinching or pulling away, she watched as he removed the bracelet from her wrist. Turning back to Demyan, Zan dangled the silver circlet from his fingers. "It may be more effective to send only the token itself, with reassurances that the mermaid remains unharmed. For now. That path leaves more room for future…negotiations, should the drylander not heed your first invitation."

Demyan stared for so long that Zan began to fear he'd made a terrible miscalculation. His mind began to spin with scenarios and possibilities for escape that would save both Kae and himself from harm. The options seemed limited at best without using magick.

All at once, Demyan slammed his sword back into its scabbard and let out a deep, rumbling laugh. Swimming forward, he slapped Zan hard on the back and plucked the bracelet from his fingers. "Now *that's* the Zan I know and love. Always thinking two steps ahead of the game." He bestowed one of his wide, benevolent smiles on Kae. "You are quite safe for now, my dear, thanks to Zan's quick wit. You should be nice to him in return, don't you think? I'll give you two a moment alone so you can thank him properly, before I send Zan off on his next mission." Zan watched him swim from the chamber, leaving the door wide open in his wake. He looked over at Kae, and saw that she too was staring at the open door.

Her eyes darted back to Zan. "We could...you could help me escape."

With a heavy heart, he shook his head. "No, Kae. I can't. There is no escaping Prince Demyan. Trust me on this one. Be thankful you still have all your fingers and fins after defying him like that."

She swallowed hard. "Thank you." He watched as her eyes began to shimmer in a strange way, as if extra seawater were pooling within the eyes themselves. She wiped the back of her hand across her face, clearing away the excess water. "So, what should I be calling you?"

He smiled. "You can call me Xander. I...I like the way it sounds when you say it."

"Okay, *Xander*," she said, emphasizing his name. "What is your plan for me? You've convinced Demyan to spare me pain for the moment – why?"

His smile faltered. "Because. I couldn't bear to watch him torture you, especially not when there was a better way for him to get the drylander's attention."

"And what if there wasn't, Xander? What if the only choice was for him to hurt me?"

It felt like her big emerald eyes were searing straight into his soul. He took a deep breath and blew a stream of tiny bubbles from his gills. "I won't let him hurt you, babe," he promised, meaning every word.

She nodded slowly, her gaze never wavering. "Okay then."

He had no idea how he would fulfill his promise. Despite what he'd said earlier, Demyan was actually the one who always seemed two steps ahead with his plots and schemes. Had he already foreseen Zan's wavering loyalties? If Zan decided to oppose him, Demyan would prove a powerful and dangerous adversary.

King Naartok had crossed Demyan by denying him official sanctuary within the bounds of the Arctic Ocean. Demyan had defied him by joining the group of Nerine who sided with the outlaw Gorgon sea witches, creating a base of operations right under the king's nose, as it were. Zan suspected King Naartok would be among the first casualties of Demyan's new war for world domination.

In his short life, Zan had already witnessed far too much killing and bloodshed. But looking into Kae's eyes, Zan realized that there were some things in this world truly worth fighting for. She was one of them.

"Listen, I need to go now," he said, taking both her hands in his. "And I may be gone for a few days, but you should be safe in this cell. Demyan rarely visits this end of the caverns. I'll even ask the guards to bring you a proper sleeping

mat so you're more comfortable. Just…don't do anything foolish."

Her eyes took on that shimmery quality again as she stared up at him, her eyebrows scrunching together in a look of concern. "Be careful," she whispered. Zan felt his breath catch in his throat as she fluttered upward and kissed him gently on the cheek.

Yeah. Definitely worth fighting for.

CHAPTER FIFTEEN

The hot air swirled with dust as they stood on the tarmac of the Athens airport, waiting for the flight attendant to usher them down the path to Olympic Air Flight 716 to Thira. Shea turned his head to watch as the Aegean Air plane they'd arrived on taxied away from its parking spot, heading back toward the runways for its return flight. A small private jet was just landing, the tires touching down on the runway furthest from the gates, bouncing once before gliding to a halt.

He thought it strange that the boarding gates were all outdoors, and that the "gate" itself was no more than lines painted on the pavement. Not that he had a heck of a lot of experience with planes or airports, but this seemed a far cry from the American airports he'd been in. Hailey elbowed Shea in the side, interrupting his thoughts. "I dare you to step outside the painted area."

Shea looked over at the armed security guards lining the perimeter. They wore full military uniforms, dark sunglasses and berets, and carried large caliber rifles by their sides. There was something sinister about the way they stood, unmoving despite the heat. "You must be out of your mind, Hailey. I know it's been a long day of flying, but let's not get crazy."

"Look at you, chicken of the sea! Those guys wouldn't dare hurt us, we're tourists." She made a move as if to walk toward one of the soldiers and Shea grabbed her hand to pull her back.

"Don't. Okay? Just don't." He squeezed her hand and she looked him in the eyes. "I would hate to lose another friend." On the six-hour flight from Boston to London, Shea had traded places so he could sit with Hailey. He'd shared his concerns about Kae's sudden disappearance, and Hailey agreed it seemed likely that Demyan was the cause.

She lowered her voice and leaned closer to his ear. "I don't think these guys are Adluo guards, so they're not working for the evil prince. They're plain old Greek soldiers, doing their jobs."

He glanced at the one standing closest to them and shrugged. "I don't want to find out the hard way that things aren't what they seem." He squeezed her hand again. "Besides, we only have an hour or so left to hang out together on the flight before Gramma and I have to…leave. Who knows when I'll get to see you again?"

Hailey laughed. "It's not my fault you're swimming off on another adventure."

He shook his head. "No, you dope. I'll be headed back to Windmill Point in a few days, after the hearing. You're the one with the open-ended ticket, and the indefinite plans to stay on Santorini while your mom's working."

"Aww, look at the lovebirds holding hands." Chip was suddenly right next to them, his withering tone dripping with sarcasm. "My wittle sister has her first wittle boyfriend. She goes half-way around the world to hold hands with the boy next door."

"Shut it, Chip." Hailey let go of Shea and punched her brother in the stomach.

He barely flinched. "Is that the best you can do? I totally thought you were stronger than that."

As the argument continued, Shea noticed a few of the guards paying attention. The closest one seemed to stare right at them, although it was hard to tell given the dark sunglasses all the guards wore. An uneasy feeling blossomed in the pit of Shea's stomach and a familiar tingling sensation zipped down his spine. There was magick being used, somewhere close.

"Please," he said in a low voice, stepping between the warring siblings. "Let's not do this here." Hailey caught on to the seriousness in his tone and took a step backward.

"What are you afraid of, MacNamara?" Chip asked with a sneer, oblivious to any potential danger. "Or maybe you're scared I'll tell your girlfriend you were holding hands with my sister. Not a bad idea at that," he added with an evil grin. "Maybe then your hot blonde would give me a chance."

"Leave her out of this," Shea said through clenched teeth. "And please just shut up before…"

"Excuse me." The guard he'd noticed staring now stood directly before him, his eyes hidden by his dark shades. "Your name is MacNamara?"

Shea hesitated, glancing over toward where his grandmother stood chatting with Hailey's mom. Both women seemed oblivious to the soldier's sudden appearance. In fact, none of the other passengers in line seemed to think anything was out of the ordinary, their eyes sweeping right over the well-armed soldier standing directly in their midst. He tried to catch Hailey's eye, but she was staring away from the soldier as if transfixed by the horizon. Frozen in place for the moment, and so was Chip. *Magick*, Shea thought, a wave of panic flooding through him.

The soldier cleared his throat.

"Yes," Shea finally answered.

"This is for you." The soldier thrust his hand forward and dropped a small package at Shea's feet before turning and walking away. Shea bent to pick up the parcel, the brown paper already coming loose around the edges. When he stood, the soldier had blended back into the line of guards, and Shea had no idea which one spoke to him. He looked back at the bundle in his hands, wondering what it held, wondering whether it would be safe to open.

Hailey shook her head, coming out of her daze. "What just happened?"

"I'm not quite sure," Shea said, turning the package over in his hands. There was no tag, no writing, nothing to say whom it was for or where it had come from. Whatever was inside the paper wasn't very heavy, though, and wasn't sending any shivers of magick through him.

"What do you have there, MacNamara?" Chip tried to snatch it from his hands, but Shea blocked the grab.

"Nothing that concerns you, Thompson," Shea told him. "Why don't you go bug somebody else?" Chip snorted in disgust and stalked off to join his mother further down the line.

Hailey rolled her eyes. "Sorry he's such a pain in the butt."

"You and me both." Shea decided he'd better wait until he was somewhere he could open the parcel in private. Just in case.

Hailey stared at the brown bundle. "You know, they say never to accept packages at airports. Especially from strangers. It could be some sort of bomb or something."

What if it is a bomb, set to explode while the plane is in the air? Which argued for Shea opening it up immediately to find out. "Stand closer to my side there, so no one can watch," he told her. Hailey shifted and Shea stripped the brown paper from one end. A wad of seaweed and a piece of yellowed parchment paper fell out into his hand.

"What does the note say?" Hailey craned her neck trying to read the paper over his shoulder as Shea unfolded it. The edges of the paper were torn, and the calligraphy was shaky and old-fashioned looking, as if had been ripped from an antique notebook of some sort.

"Next time I'll send you her hand." He glanced up at Hailey and saw that she'd turned as white as a sheet. He felt a little pale himself as he continued reading out loud. *"Meet at Piraeus by sunset if you want to keep the girl alive."*

"Piraeus is the port of Athens," Hailey said, her voice a little breathless as she rattled on full-tilt. "Someone wants you to meet them at the docks, by the ocean? So it's gotta be one of your merman buddies. But what girl are they talking about? Is it me? Am I in danger?"

Shea had already unwrapped the bundle of seaweed and stared as the silver bracelet shimmered in the bright sunlight. "It's not about you, Hailey. Demyan has Kae."

"We already guessed that," Hailey said, frowning. "What does that have to do with…"

He held up the bracelet, with the five waves of silver still glistening with droplets of seawater. "I gave this to Kae the morning before she disappeared. Remember? I bought it that day you and I went shopping in Hyannis. Whoever kidnapped her sent this as a message."

At that moment, the line began moving forward toward the airplane. "The flight is starting to board," Hailey said, a note of panic in her voice. "What are we going to do?"

Shea glanced around the tarmac, still unable to pick out the soldier who handed him the ominous warning. "If there's a chance to save Kae, I have to go. I'd better tell Gramma I can't get on this plane." He looked up and saw his grandmother already climbing the moveable staircase that had been wheeled up next to the Olympic Air plane.

Hailey followed his eyes. "Too late. She and Mom are sitting in first class for this flight, remember?"

He hesitated. "I can't just leave without telling her. That would set off even more problems."

"The flight only takes an hour," Hailey pointed out. "You could get on board to tell your grandmother, turn around and come back with the plane, and still be at Piraeus before sunset."

Shea drew in a deep breath and exhaled slowly, turning over the alternatives in his mind. "I guess that makes the most sense," he agreed, stumbling forward with the rest of the passengers in the line. The brown paper and seaweed slid from his hands, fluttering to the ground where the dry wind took it all flying across the pavement in the opposite direction. He gripped the letter and bracelet, not sure what to do with either item.

"Maybe you should put that letter away," Hailey suggested. "It's kind of threatening, and you don't want anyone getting the wrong idea. Here, let me hold the bracelet while you fold it up." Shea handed her the silver bangle and folded the piece of parchment into halves until it was small enough to shove into the pocket of his jeans.

When he looked over, Hailey was slipping the bracelet onto her wrist. "What're you doing?"

Her cheeks instantly turned a deep red. "Sorry. It's just so pretty, I wanted to try it on. Besides, it's less conspicuous for me to wear it than you."

Shea frowned. He knew she had a point. It wasn't right to let her wear the gift he'd given Kae, but he also didn't want to attract any more attention. "Fine, you can wear it. For now. When we get on the plane, I want it back."

Hailey squinted and smiled sweetly at him, twisting her wrist back and forth so the bangle caught the light. "I'm telling you, it looks better on me. Shiny, shiny!"

His frown deepened. "I know you don't like her, but this is serious. It means she's really been kidnapped by the bad guys, and her life might be in danger. You read the note. What if they chopped off her whole hand?" His stomach clenched at the thought of anyone causing Kae that much pain. And it was all his fault. Because of his royal family. At least he knew Kae was safe for the moment, and he'd be seeing her soon.

The look on Hailey's face turned more serious and she grabbed his hand again. "I'm sorry. It's not that I hate the girl, but I mean it all seems a little surreal, like an elaborate prank. Like she's going to be waiting at the other end of this flight to jump out and say 'Surprise!' and give you a big, sloppy mermaid kiss."

His cheeks burned as he pictured Kae throwing herself into his arms in front of a crowd of tourists. "That would be awesome, really, but I don't think it's a prank. That Demyan guy is seriously bad news. Murder is nothing to him, and it scares me to think Kae is his prisoner."

Hailey threw an arm around his shoulder and gave him a half-hug. "It's going to be okay. You'll save her in time. You're

like a superhero, with fins instead of a cape. Like Aquaman or something. And hey, you even communicate with fish just like him, even if you can't see the telepathic rings shooting through the water."

Shea laughed in spite of himself, letting some of the guilty feelings fade into the background. They made their way up the stairs into the plane, side by side. "I hate to break it to you, but I'm no Aquaman. Maybe his sidekick."

"Aqualad? No way. He was like the worst sidekick ever, in the history of comic books." Hailey punched his shoulder to emphasize her words. "More importantly, he never got any good lines."

"What, like Robin got any good lines? Gimme a break." They continued arguing about comic book heroes as they found their seats along with the rest of the passengers and the flight crew got ready for departure. Shea was thankful for the distraction, but more determined than ever to save Kae. He might not be a comic book superhero, but he would do whatever he could to save the mermaid he loved.

* * *

Zan watched from the shadows of the Olympic Air hanger, waiting impatiently for the operative to return. Even in the shade, the Athenian air was so hot and arid that Zan felt the moisture wicking away from his skin, his lips already cracking in the heat. How he longed to plunge back into the soothing Mediterranean waters and be done with this dry, dusty place.

But first he needed to make sure Shea got the message.

It hadn't taken him long to find out Shea was traveling to Atlantis now instead of Kae. Demyan had spies everywhere. What did surprise him was that King Koios sent Shea by air instead of by sea. An unanticipated move, but luckily Zan's magick compensated for Demyan's lack of foresight. He'd made it to Athens in time to send a message and set up a confrontation with the drylander.

He pulled the brim of his baseball cap lower, shading his eyes from the bright sun shining through the open hanger doors. A few stray ends of his long hair still stuck out in the back, catching the light and shimmering blue and green. Plenty of humans dyed their hair any number of colors, meaning the color in itself wasn't a huge problem...but there was no way to pass for an airport guard. Instead he used one of Demyan's recruits from the Mediterranean's Daeira clan to deliver the message.

It bothered Zan to think Demyan captured the loyalty of so many mermen, turning them into traitors to their own clans. Most of them were disgruntled soldiers, unhappy with their own little place in their undersea world. Looking for something more out of life. These mermen soaked up Demyan's inflammatory rhetoric as if it were krill to a blue whale, swallowing it whole and without thinking.

Like Demyan, most believed the drylanders were killing the Earth and needed to be stopped. Uniting the oceans was the first step in Demyan's master plan. Once the merfolk united under his rule, complete world domination was next on the madman's agenda.

Zan lived through one palace coup in the Southern Ocean, but barely escaped the second with his life. Because of *Shea*. Kae was now in danger because of Shea, too. His fists clenched by his side.

"I gave him the package as requested."

Startled, Zan whirled around, relieved to recognized the guard in front of him. He'd been so focused inwardly he hadn't heard Demyan's follower, Takis, approaching. The Daeira traitor was dressed as an airport security guard. "You're sure it was the correct drylander?"

The false guard nodded. "Blond, tall, teenager. One of the other drylanders called him 'MacNamara.' He was the only one unaffected by the spell you cast on me. I'm sure it was him."

So far, so good. "Thank you, Takis. I'll be sure to let Demyan know of your loyalty in helping to arrange this meeting."

"Uh, sir?" The guard shuffled his feet. "Is the meeting on Santorini? Because, as I'm sure you're aware, that's right smack in Atlantean territory. There's no safe route in or out of that area to go unseen by the Lord Magistrate's guards."

Zan chuckled. "So kind of you to be concerned for my well being, but the boy is to meet me at Piraeus, well within Daeira-controlled waters." He turned to leave the hanger, more than ready to feel the water caress his dry skin.

"But he boarded the flight."

"What?" Zan whirled to face Takis, unable to hide his surprise. "Did you not deliver the message in time for him to actually *read* it?"

The guard shuffled his feet again, nodding. "He read the letter and gave the silver bracelet to the drylander girl who accompanies him. He laughed with her as they boarded the airplane."

A ferocious anger surged through Zan, uncontrolled magick simmering just below the surface of his skin. The air around him started to swirl, dust rising from the floor of the hanger. Takis backed away nervously, a trickle of blood dripping from the guard's nose. Zan sputtered, barely able to put his thoughts together. "He...he...left? For Santorini? He gave Kae's bracelet to...to a *drylander*?" As Zan repeated the guard's words, he became increasingly agitated by the situation. He'd been so convinced of the simplicity of

Demyan's scheme, it never even occurred to him that Shea would do something different than expected. Zan expected him to *care* about Kae.

How could he ignore the warning in that letter?

The trickle quickly morphed into a red geyser and Takis slumped to the floor, his uniform awash in his own blood. Zan's attention snapped back to the present moment and his stomach churned. He'd lost control and Takis was dead. It happened so fast he had no chance to stop the magick. Staring at the body, his mind catapulted into the past, to that very first time the magick took over and killed Demyan's royal cousins. The very incident that necessitated his years of servitude to Demyan. That was so long ago, he'd forgotten how it started. Over the years he'd come to believe it was truly his fault – that he'd wanted the magick to kill those boys. Demyan made sure he believed it.

Maybe he didn't do it on purpose after all. He never asked the magick to kill Takis, just like he didn't want the young princes to die. The group of boys teased him, threw rocks at him, called him all sorts of evil names... and he got angry. One day he'd had enough and got very, very angry. The magick took advantage, surging through him as a gateway into the world, supercharging the air around him, sucking the life from those closest to feed some unseen power. It must be

similar to the way he used the magick to manipulate storms, but somehow different.

Zan spun on his heel and walked away from the dead body, out into the sunlight, gusts of wind still swirling. Strong emotions surged through him and the magick circled all around, his fingertips almost sparking with power. He closed his eyes and concentrated on regaining control. If he could control the magick, he could harness it to a fuller potential. Perhaps he could figure out a way to use it against Demyan, and get away from him forever. That was indeed a dream worth pursuing. Long ago, Demyan made Zan take a magical vow to never harm anyone of royal blood ever again, or else the harm would backfire onto the sorcerer. The vow kept Demyan safe and kept Zan beholden to the prince's every twisted desire.

After tamping back on the magick, he reopened his eyes and watched as an airplane with the large "Olympic Air" logo across its side increased speed and took off from the ground, quickly gaining altitude. His anger immediately increased, as did the wind, rocking the wings of the small plane as it climbed into the blue sky. Zan realized his anger correlated directly with the wind, and wrapped his mind around controlling the magick, harnessing the brewing storm to do his bidding.

The drylander couldn't be allowed to reach Atlantis. Demyan said he'd spare Kae's life in return for delivering Shea. Zan didn't care what happened to the boy. But he promised to keep Kae safe from Demyan.

And he always kept his promises. Always.

CHAPTER SIXTEEN

The airplane shuddered from side to side as it left the safety of the runway and ascended through the cloudless sky. Shea gripped the hard plastic arms of his seat, wondering if he would ever get used to the sensation of flying. This was his third take-off within the last twenty-four hours. He'd been hoping it would get easier. Because, at the moment, all he could think about was crashing.

This was the smallest plane he'd ever been on in his life, with only two seats on each side of the middle aisle, not all of them filled. The din from the plane's twin turbo prop engines thundered just outside the window next to Hailey, spinning so fast the propellers were merely a blur against the blue sky.

The first two rows up in the front were blocked off by a thin black curtain, hiding the handful of first class passengers from the rest of the cabin. Shea's grandmother was up there somewhere with Mrs. Thompson, while Shea sat with Hailey and Chip. Shea was glad the two women hit it off so well, and even more glad he didn't have to be included in their conversations about curtains and wallpaper patterns.

Only about fifty or so passengers were making the trip to Santorini, a far cry from the huge, over-crowded British Airways flight with which he'd started the day. Hailey patted his arm and leaned her head closer so he could hear her over the roar of the engines. "There's an awful lot of turbulence for such a clear day," she said. "I'm sure it's nothing to worry about. Probably because the plane's so small."

Chip leaned across the aisle, punching Shea in the shoulder. "The card in the back of the seat says this is a Bombardier Dash-8," he said. "Just like the commuter plane that crashed in Buffalo a few years ago. Remember that?"

"Crashed?" Shea hoped he didn't sound as panicky as he felt.

"Killed everyone on board." Chip settled back into his seat, smiling.

Hailey frowned. "Thanks for nothing, Chip. It's probably the wind off the ocean. I mean, wow, look at the waves down there." She pointed out the window, trying to distract Shea.

"Wind. Right." Shea grimaced. He knew firsthand the damage that wind could cause. He'd witnessed tornado destruction back in Oklahoma, when he'd lost his dad and

163

their farm. Wind could be devastating. And deadly. He needed to focus on something else. Maybe curtains and wallpaper weren't such a bad thing to talk about after all. "Tell me again about this lady who hired your mom to decorate? Why is it she can't choose her own curtains?"

Hailey laughed. "Decorating is about more than curtains, you troglodyte. It's about creating a whole look and feel for a home."

The plane gave another shudder and Shea closed his eyes. "And why can't a person decide for themselves how they want their home to feel?"

"Obviously they know what they want. The problem, as my mom says all the time, is knowing how to achieve in reality what you picture in your head."

A deep male voice crackled through the overhead speakers in rapid Greek, followed by English. "Attention, passengers. This is your captain. Please keep seatbelts fastened as we try to steer clear of this turbulence and find a pocket of better air."

"A pocket of better air?" Hailey shook her head. "What does that even mean?"

Chip leaned back across the aisle and grinned. "Maybe this air is broken?" The light streaming through Hailey's window shifted as the plane changed direction and Chip's grin faded. "It looks like he made a ninety degree turn. That seems kind of drastic."

"I'm sure the pilot's done this a million times," Hailey snapped, looking out her window again. "Ooh, look at that lightning over there! It's like a fireworks display!"

Shea resisted the temptation to look out the window. His stomach already felt queasy enough, and now a storm? A slow tingling sensation engulfed his toes. "How close?"

He was surprised when Chip laughed at him. "Don't be a wuss. A lightning strike wouldn't bring an airplane down. Airplanes are designed to absorb lightning and then get rid of the static electricity. Problems only occur when the lightning actually hits an electrical circuit – like, a direct hit – and causes a short circuit. What are the odds of lighting finding the exact spot, right?"

"Oh, look out there now," Hailey interrupted. "Water spouts!"

The blood drained from Shea's face. "Water spouts? Like, tornadoes on the ocean?"

Hailey patted his knee. "This isn't Oklahoma. I'm sure everything's going to be fine." She pulled the plane's information card out of the seat pocket in front of her. "But I guess it never hurts to review a plane's emergency procedures. Looks like the closest exit is two rows back, over the wing. Mom and your Gramma are up there next to the main door."

When she removed her hand from his knee to point at the diagram, Shea felt the tingling course through his legs, zinging from his toes up into his stomach. It was as if some switch in his body flipped into super-high gear. Sweat beaded on his forehead and dripped down his back. The air inside the airplane cabin clung to his body as if it were charged with electricity and Shea was the only magnet on board. He remembered this exact sensation from that day at Plainville High School. The day of the tornado.

"*Magick*," he whispered out loud as a couple of the overhead compartments snapped open, spewing their contents into the aisle and onto his fellow passengers. He wrapped his fingers around his transmutare medallion, taking a deep breath as he felt the magick pulse through his body. He knew without a doubt someone controlled the weather, causing the turbulence on purpose.

"What did you say?" Hailey focused on the information card. The silver bracelet hugged her wrist, glinting in the light from the overhead reading lamp, the sparkle catching Shea's eye. What if the kidnappers thought he wasn't planning to meet them at the Piraeus docks? Was crashing the airplane some kind of twisted Plan B? If Demyan and his henchmen could create a killer microburst tornado in the middle of Oklahoma, was it such a stretch to imagine they could create a storm over open water?

Shea grabbed the plastic card from her hands as the cabin began to convulse violently and the pains shooting down his legs increased in speed. "Where are the exits? Because this plane is going down."

"That's not funny." Hailey voice shook along with the plane. Behind her, Shea saw water spouts on the ocean coming closer. As he watched, several thin spindles of wind and water began to merge together, forming a solid wall of savagely twisting seawater.

The captain's voice came over the speaker again, the English first this time. "Attention. Prepare for a water landing." Shea hoped the torrent of Greek that followed was directed mainly to the crew, because as far as he could tell, everyone else was too busy panicking to follow any directions whatsoever.

He quickly glanced around the cabin at the passengers, all searching under their seats for inflatable life vests and flotation cushions. Random pieces of luggage fell from the overhead bins, adding to the chaos and panic. Where was his grandmother? Were the passengers behind the curtain going through similar preparations?

Wind and water lashed at the plane while the cabin dipped at a decidedly dangerous downward angle, the wind howling against the windows. Duffle bags and packages slid down the center aisle toward the first class curtain, as more items rained down on the passengers from the overhead compartments. Hailey's knuckles turned white as she gripped both plastic armrests, and Shea placed his hand over hers on the armrest they shared. There was nothing he could think of to say that would reassure her — the plane was definitely going down. And it was his fault, he was sure of it.

"We'll be okay, won't we?" Her voice sounded so scared and small that despite his own fears, Shea felt a strong urge to comfort her. But he didn't want to lie.

"I hope so," he told her. "The plane is over water, so at least it's a softer landing."

"Umm, I read that hitting water at high speed is almost like smashing into solid ground," Hailey said, her eyes wide. "If we hit at this angle, the plane will smash into bits!"

"Well then, we have to hope for the best and be ready for the impact," Shea said, twining his fingers with hers and giving them a squeeze. Their heads were inches apart in order to hear each other, so close he could smell the strawberry shampoo she must've used that morning. He tried to concentrate on the fragrance and not the intensity of the pain streaking down his spine. "We can do this, Hailey. You're a strong swimmer."

"Yeah, but my mom's not."

"Gramma is," Shea said firmly. "She'll help your mom, don't worry."

Suddenly, the nose of the plane pulled up, leveling off the cabin. Seconds later, the plane tipped slightly to the right and smashed onto the surface of the water, bucking along through the waves in sickening jolts as pieces from the front of the aircraft ripped free and whizzed by the windows. Shea's body slammed forward with each jolt, straining against the confining seat belt, his head banging into the seat in front of him. After what seemed like a lifetime, the plane stopped moving forward.

And began to settle, sinking slowly into the sea.

CHAPTER SEVENTEEN

The glow from the lantern sputtered and died, and Kae found herself awash in darkness once again. Even without the ability to hear the thoughts of sea creatures, she'd known the jellyfish in the lantern was starving and desperate to escape. There was nothing she could have done to help it without being stung. She was as much a prisoner as that poor creature had been. At least now the jellyfish was free. She hoped the goddess of fate, and Demyan, would be kinder to her. She didn't want to die in this prison cell. But she held out little hope for mercy from the Adluo madman.

At least Xander kept his word about making her more comfortable. That had been the last time anyone visited, when a dark blue Nerine merman delivered the bedroll and blanket. The door hadn't opened since. Her stomach rumbled. How long had it been since her last meal? She frowned, remembering that Xander drugged her food to make her sleep. But at least he'd made sure she was fed. No one else in this place seemed to care if she went hungry. Did anyone even remember her existence?

In the darkened silence, she heard the echoes of whispering voices. Was there someone in the hallway? Pushing her blanket aside, she swam slowly through the darkened cell, arms straight out to feel for the wall so as not to bang her head. Her hands found the stone of the cell wall, and she cupped them around her ear, straining to make out the words as the whispers grew louder...and then faded away.

"Hello? Is someone out there? Anyone? Hello?" She slammed her fists against the stone, trying hard to make enough noise to attract attention. But it was too late. Whoever was swimming down the hallway must be too far away to hear her now. She was alone in the darkness once more.

Kae bit her bottom lip and closed her eyes, willing herself to take a deep breath and remain calm. She uncurled her fists and flattened her hands against the stone wall. Xander promised he wouldn't let Demyan harm her. She needed to trust him.

Except...Xander kidnapped her in the first place. And his name wasn't even really Xander. It was Zan. The sorcerer. And he seemed to have a crush on her. The thought made her shiver.

He'd used magick to make her trust him. To make her follow him. To capture her and bring her to Demyan. And she knew he'd been part of Demyan's scheme back in Nantucket Sound to kill King Koios. It was Zan who bewitched the king's own sister into joining the plot.

An image of that dark hair and even darker eyes filled her mind. She wondered about the haunted look that she had glimpsed behind those black eyes. Was that even real, or was the vulnerability an act to gain her compassion? No, it had to be real. After the way he stood up for her with Demyan, she knew without a doubt he would protect her. From what she'd learned of the Adluos, no one defied Demyan. Ever. And yet Xander had, and had kept her safe. She shook her head again. "I mean *Zan* kept me safe. Jumping jellyfish, I'll never be able to get his name straight in my head."

She blinked. Why was he even in her head?

She tried to picture Shea instead, and wondered what he was doing right at that very moment. At least he was safe, back in Windmill Point. With no access to sunlight and no meals to mark her time, she had no idea whether it was morning or evening on Cape Cod. Would he be walking with Lucky along the beach, watching the sunrise and looking for Kae among the waves? She smiled at the image in her mind, wishing she could be swimming there now, in Nantucket Sound, with Shea by her side. Maybe he'd miss her and come looking. Maybe Shea would come to her rescue.

Or no, wait. She'd told him that she was leaving for Atlantis and wouldn't see him again until September. Did he even know she'd been kidnapped? Xander already left for Windmill Point with her bracelet, proof that Demyan held her hostage. She was live bait, luring Shea north into some kind of trap. What did they want with him, though? It didn't matter what they wanted, or that he'd obviously know it was a trap. He'd come because he loved her.

The image in her mind began to shift, rippling as if someone stirred the surface of the water. Now when she pictured Shea, he was walking on the beach with Hailey instead, hand-in-hand and smiling. Although she knew logically that Shea and Hailey were "just friends," as Shea was so fond of pointing out, she also suspected Hailey wanted more from their friendship. Doubts crept into her mind, like ghosts haunting a shipwreck, making her rethink what was real and what wasn't. Hailey was the opposite of Kae in so many ways, with her dark eyes and darker hair, and her absolute knowledge of all things drylander. She talked fast, could ride a bike without falling, and didn't get confused by words like *Nintendo* or *flip-flops*. Hailey had so much more in common with Shea, both growing up in the human world rather than the underwater world where Kae lived. With Kae out of the picture, Hailey would have her chance.

"Maybe I'm going insane here, all alone in the dark," she said out loud. She shook her head, trying to dispel the troubling thoughts. Hailey would never do that to her. And Shea said he loved her, despite the fact that she was just a servant and he was heir to his grandfather's throne. He shouldn't be in love with her, but she could tell from his kisses that he meant every word. Her fingers strayed to her lips, trying to remember their last kiss.

Shea was the one in real danger. Demyan was using her as bait to lure Shea into his clutches for the exact same reason he shouldn't be in love with her – he was heir to King Koios! Either Demyan planned to use magick to make Shea one of his puppet followers, or…use him as bigger bait to trap an even larger fish, like his mother, the new Queen of the Southern Ocean. Or King Koios himself!

Either way, she needed to escape. There was no way she wanted to be the catalyst for another attempted coup, either in the Atlantic or the Southern Ocean.

The stone under her hands began to shift. Startled, she swam backward in the dark room as a thin outline of light appeared along the wall. Part of her hoped it was the mermaid with food – at the moment, she was so hungry she didn't care if it was drugged or poisoned. But another part of her wondered if she should make a swim for it, rushing past the guard or mermaid servant and zipping into the hallway to escape.

Her fists curled into determined balls. "I have to try," she whispered. She couldn't let Demyan use her to capture Shea. The door swung open silently and she held her breath, not knowing what to expect, or what to hope for.

There was no way she could've anticipated the merman standing in her doorway. She'd recognize his profile anywhere.

"Father!"

Chapter Eighteen

"Hailey, wake up!" Shea shook her arm, willing her to open her eyes. The surface of the water rose steadily outside the window. A trickle of blood oozed from a vertical cut down one side of Hailey's forehead. Shea flicked open the clasp on his safety belt and reached over to unclasp hers.

"Is she okay?" Chip's hand gripped Shea's shoulder hard, the tipped floor of the cabin making him lean in.

"Knocked out, but breathing." Shea looked at Chip. "We need to get out of here."

Chip looked anxious for the first time. "Once the water starts filling the cabin, the plane will sink faster and we won't be able to push the doors open. I read about this one crash, off the coast of South America, where…"

Shea cut him off. "Save it. We need to move now." He looked around the cabin, seeing most of the passengers either knocked out, like Hailey, or still in shock from the crash. Very few were on their feet like Chip. Shea stood and moved into the aisle with him before leaning back over to drag Hailey out of her seat. The cabin crew was nowhere to be seen. "Where are the flight attendants?"

"Up in first class maybe? Isn't that where their little fold-out seats are, near the cockpit?" Chip grabbed Hailey's arm and helped Shea lift her out into the aisle. "Come on, Hail, wake up! We gotta get going!"

"Can you swim?" Shea knew Hailey was a strong swimmer, but had never seen Chip go near the water.

"Varsity diving team back in New York." Chip maneuvered his shoulder under his sister's arm. Other passengers started to rouse, many of them moaning and holding their heads. The storm raged outside, lashing the sides of the airplane with walls of rain and waves. Somewhere in the very back of the cabin, a woman started to scream.

Chip and Shea dragging Hailey between them up the aisle. Shea looked around at the dazed and injured passengers and couldn't help but feel responsible. "We need to help these people," he told Chip. "Someone needs to take charge."

"Yeah, right." Chip shifted Hailey to take more of her weight. The blood flowed from her head wound, leaving a red trail down one cheek. "We're only teenagers, not EMTs.

Who's gonna listen to us? We need to find Mom and your grandmother."

He knew Chip was right, but still Shea worried. So many of these people looked totally unprepared to survive. Just then, the overhead lights flicked off, leaving the cabin in shadows. With his enhanced vision Shea's eyes adjusted to the darkness, but behind him Chip stumbled. A moment later, small pinpricks of light blinked on along the edges of the aisle, emergency lighting to lead the way to their escape.

The bolt of black fabric continued to separate the first class seats from the rest of the cabin, as if reality would be different if you paid more for your seat. Pushing the curtain aside, Shea saw there actually was a difference. A lot more light filtered through first class. The crash landing somehow ripped a large hole in the side of the fuselage, right where the flight attendant station and main door must have been. Shea saw the dark storm clouds swirling and the white-capped waves reaching up toward the opening like eager tongues, as if the water itself wanted to taste the inside of the plane's cabin.

The door to the cockpit remained closed tight, and Shea wondered about the pilots. At least one of them must've lived through the crash to help steady the plane's descent through the harrowing storm. If they hadn't leveled off at the last minute, there would be even more destruction.

Two of the flight attendants sat strapped into their seats, eyes closed, rocking back and forth to the sway of the cabin. A third was helping a woman in the front row who bled profusely from a gash down the side of her face. The man beside her in the aisle seat was slumped over, bleeding. A chunk of stray fuselage protruded from his neck. The first casualty, Shea noted. But would he be the last?

Next to the hole gaping in the side of the plane, the front row of seats was empty. In the second row, Shea's grandmother was unbuckling Mrs. Thompson's safety belt. Martha glanced over at Shea and raised one eyebrow. "Did you feel that?"

"No time to discuss. We need to help these people."

Martha nodded. "The stewardess said there was a self-inflating raft behind that door, but it's stuck." She pointed to a spot next to the gaping hole. "See if it's still in there while I revive Gloria. Chip, hold onto your sister."

Shea let go of Hailey's other arm and wrenched the door open. "Something's in here, Gramma," he called back to her over the sudden roar of the wind. "I don't know how to get it out." The flight attendant appeared by his side, chattering in Greek and motioning for Shea to help her. They removed a hard plastic cover and together dragged what appeared to be a large roll of yellow vinyl toward the hole in the side of the plane. A long rope tethered one end of the roll to the bottom of the closet, unfurling as they moved.

After pushing the yellow rubber out of the hole, the flight attendant yanked on the end of the rope and the boat began to inflate on its own, unrolling itself into a good-sized life raft. She turned to Shea and spoke again in rapid Greek. He held up both hands and shook his head, trying to gesture that he couldn't understand what she was saying. "American."

She took a deep breath and tried again, this time in halting English. "The plane. She is sinking. This raft fits maybe fifty people."

"So many?"

She grabbed his arm. "We need to get out fast."

"Agreed," Shea said, nodding to show he understood the urgency. He hurried to where Chip stood holding Hailey, trying to rouse her. "Chip, get your mom and sister on the boat, then come help me."

"Okay." Chip sounded uncertain as he looked down at his unconscious sibling.

"Now." Shea pushed him toward the door. "Gramma? You've got Mrs. Thompson, right?"

Martha nodded, lifting the dazed woman to her feet. "I'll stay by the door to help the stewardess get the others into the lifeboat."

Shea ripped the curtain from its rings, feeling there was no more need to separate the classes. In the main cabin, several men clustered in the row by the plane's wing, trying to force open the emergency door, which must have jammed upon impact. More were crowded in the aisle nearby, watching and waiting to escape. Others remained in their seats, dazed or unconscious. No one was screaming any more, but the noise level had risen dramatically as everyone struggled to be heard over the increasing noise of the storm.

"There's a life boat at the front of the plane," Shea yelled, trying to make his voice carry over the din. "It's big enough for everyone and already inflated." The men who'd been trying to open the emergency door and the passengers waiting in the aisle all turned and rushed forward, knocking Shea out of the way in their haste. Getting back on his feet, Shea looked around the cabin and decided to start at the front and work his way back. Many of those who were still seated were awake, but seemed confused as to where they were, or what they were supposed to do. He unlatched seatbelt after seatbelt, helping people to their feet and pointing them in the right direction. "Follow the row of lights on the floor," he kept repeating. Many of the passengers had minor head wounds like Hailey, but a few seemed to have broken limbs as well.

As he bent over to unlatch one older woman's belt, she looked into his eyes and asked in accented English, "Are you an angel? Am I dead?"

"No, ma'am, you're not dead," he reassured, putting a hand under her elbow. "But you need to stand up if you can and get off the plane, right now."

"But I don't know how to swim." Her eyes widened as she looked past him to the window where the waves still buffeted the airplane.

Shea smiled. "It'll be okay. What's your name?"

"Teadora," she said, her Greek accent thick. Water began to wash along the floor of the cabin and Shea could see panic in her eyes as the ripples soaked through her leather shoes.

He helped her to her feet. "There's nothing to fear from the water. It'll be okay." He guided her partway down the aisle, and was grateful when Chip took Teadora's wrinkled hand from him. His grandmother stood at the opening, assisting passengers as they stepped through.

He turned to help the next passenger, surprised there were still some who were unconscious.

"Shea, we gotta go," Chip called back to him over the noise of the storm. "The plane is sinking faster."

"Let me get these last few people out of here."

"What people?" Chip looked confused. "How can you even find them in the dark?"

Shea stood over another older guy and shook his shoulder, trying to wake him. Chip's hand wrapped around his upper arm. "No, Shea. We have to leave now. They're gonna cut the rope so the raft doesn't get pulled under!"

The man in the seat started coming around. Shea shrugged off Chip's hand and grabbed the man's shoulders. "Sir, can you stand up?" When he started to rise, Shea glanced at Chip. "Take this guy forward with you. I'll catch up."

"But…"

The water was getting deeper, already halfway to Shea's knees. "Go. I'll be fine. I want to wake those two in the last row and check the restroom." Shea turned away from the other boy and trudged through the steadily rising water to the rear of the plane. When he reached the last row, he checked to make sure Chip had followed his instruction and saw he and the older gentlemen were already at the front of the plane, heading out the opening.

Shea bent down over the remaining two passengers, a middle-aged couple who were holding hands, fingers intertwined even in their unconscious state. From their sunburned noses and the man's brightly colored tropical shirt, Shea guessed that they'd been traveling in Greece on vacation. "Sir? Ma'am? Can you hear me?" He shook their shoulders and saw the woman's eyelids flutter. "Ma'am? You need to wake up. The plane is sinking."

Brown eyes flew open wide. "Sinking? We survived the crash?" She pulled on the man's hand. "Did you hear that, Howard? We survived!" He didn't respond, but slumped forward in his chair. "Howard! Wake up! This is no time to sleep!"

Shea pressed his fingers against the side of the man's thick neck, checking for a pulse like he'd seen them do on countless television shows. He wasn't sure what he was supposed to be feeling for, but the man's skin felt clammy to the touch as he pressed harder, seeking some sign of life.

The woman had let go of the man's hand and began to slap his arm. "Howard! This is no time for jokes. We need to listen to this young man and leave the plane now!" She released her own safety belt and struggled to reach around the man's wide belly. "Help me unbuckle him," she told Shea, panic in her voice.

"I can't find his pulse," Shea said gently. "We need to get you out of here."

"I'm not going anywhere without my Howard," she shrieked, and started pummeling the man's chest in a kind of frenzy. "Wake up, damn you! You're not leaving me here in the middle of the Mediterranean all alone! Wake up!"

"Shea! Get her out of there!" Chip's voice sounded far away over the noise the water was now making as it flowed faster into the cabin. Shea glanced up to see him silhouetted by the opening, gesturing wildly.

"Ma'am, you need to get out of here, right now. The life boat is cutting loose any second." He grabbed her firmly by the arm and pulled her into the aisle, where the water had now reached Shea's knees.

"But my Howard!" She pushed back against Shea's chest as he slogged behind her through the rising water. "You can't leave him there! He's not dead! He can't be dead!"

"I'll go back and get him, I promise," Shea told her. "But you need to get on that life boat!" He was relieved to see Chip coming the last few feet to grab the woman by her arm and drag her forward.

"Promise me! Get my Howard!" She screamed in protest as Chip dragged her forward none too gently.

Chip shot him a disbelieving look. "Shea, come on, man! Leave him! The stewardess already cut the rope!"

"I promised her." Shea took a few steps backward, realizing the water was mid-way up his thighs. "I'll catch up with you in the water, Chip." He turned and pushed his way down the aisle, back to where the last passenger, Howard, was still unconscious. Shea wasn't worried about getting out of the plane himself. He knew he'd be able to breathe underwater even if he sunk to the bottom with the plane. That was the good thing about having gills – never having to say, "I'm drowning."

There was a sudden bang. Shea whipped around to see the rising water had pushed the restroom door inward, slamming open against the small vanity sink inside. The noise also seemed to jolt a reaction out of Howard, whose head lifted partway up before falling back onto his chest.

Shea smiled, relieved to see a sign of life from the guy. "At least there's no one else to rescue. It's just you and me, Howard. And I'm psyched you're still alive. Let's keep you that way."

He reached under the man's armpits and lifted, glad for the sturdy cloth of the brand new Hawaiian-print shirt. He was also thankful for all those years of grueling work on his dad's farm, giving him the strength now to help over 200 pounds of dead weight. Or not-quite-dead-yet weight, as it were.

The water licked at Shea's waist as he wrestled Howard's limp body into the aisle and began the slow process of dragging him toward the opening in the plane's hull. Was the plane filling faster than before? Although it wouldn't be a problem for him to breathe underwater, Shea suddenly realized that the rising water posed more than a little problem for Howard, who had yet to regain consciousness and remained blissfully unaware of his dire situation.

"Come on, Howard," Shea urged as the man's leg got snagged on a piece of fallen luggage. "Help me out here. I'm trying to save your life!" Shea yanked harder and Howard's foot came loose, the pair of them falling backward with a splash, Howard on top and Shea completely underwater.

Shea blew a deep breath out through his gills before getting back on his feet, hoisting the large guy's torso up and as far out of the water as he could. "Okay, Howard, this is it." He glanced forward and saw he still had quite a ways to go, and unfortunately Howard remained out like a light.

The rear of the plane began to tip downward at an increasing angle, making the trek to the opening an uphill battle. Shea clenched his teeth together and pulled against the rush of water splashing down the aisle and gushing under the seats. "Work with me, Howard. We're almost there." With a last final heave, Shea was finally able to see out of the opening. The storm clouds pressed in close around the plane but the driving rain had stopped. The shrieking wind pummeled waves over the rear of the plane, dragging it down, but could no longer reach into the opening, which was now a few feet above the water's surface.

The crowded yellow inflatable was already a short distance from the side of the airplane, tossing with the waves. An eerie quiet had descended on the passengers, who sat wide-eyed as they watched the unbelievable sight of their plane sinking into the sea. Most of them had grabbed their life preservers, but a few were still bleeding. The flight attendant was patching people up as best she could with her first aid kit. Shea saw Hailey, still unconscious, her head resting against her mother's shoulder.

Chip gestured to him. "Shea! Let's go! Dive in!"

"Where's my Howard?" shrieked the woman who'd been seated next to him, breaking the strange silence of the crowd. She was one of the people without a life vest. Another of the passengers held her down in the raft, obviously trying to keep her from overturning the boat.

Shea called down to Chip. "The guy isn't awake yet, but he's still alive. I forgot to put his vest on him, so he'll need your help."

"I hear you." Chips sat on the edge of the boat and tipped himself over backwards into the water without upsetting the balance of the inflatable raft, surfacing among the waves. "I'm ready when you are."

Heaving the body around to the front of the opening, Shea hesitated. Would Chip be able to handle someone this big? He shook his head. There was no other choice. He took a deep breath and pushed Howard as hard as he could, out of the opening and away from the side of the airplane.

Howard landed in the open water with a huge splash. Chip was at his side in an instant, pulling the guy's head above water and tucking his arm over Howard's chest to tow him back to the boat. Shea watched as the passengers on the raft worked together to drag Howard and Chip both back onboard. "Shea, the pilots are still in there," his grandmother yelled. "We couldn't get the cockpit door to open."

"I'll check on it," Shea assured her, turning away from the opening, but not before he heard another passenger protesting.

"He's just a kid! He'll drown if he doesn't get out," he heard some woman say to Martha. He couldn't hear what Martha said in return, but hoped it was something plausible.

In reality, he wasn't concerned about "going down with the ship," because it would be just as easy for him to swim out of it from underwater as it was to jump out. Probably easier. The real problem in Shea's mind was that the storm was the result of magick and he was the intended target. So all of this, the entire crash, was Shea's fault.

And the mermen who caused the crash would be coming to find him.

But…if there was any chance to save that pilot who'd been able to level off the plane at the last minute… that guy was the real hero of the day. *If the plane hit the water nose-first, all of the passengers would've been toast. Including me and Gramma.*

Shea yanked on the door to the cockpit. Locked. He banged his fist as hard as he could and yelled. "Hey! Anyone awake in there?" He pressed his ear to the door and heard faint groaning.

The plane tilted at an even sharper angle as Shea made his way carefully over to the opening. "Gramma," he yelled over the wind. "The cockpit isn't jammed, it's locked but I can hear someone alive inside. Ask the stewardess if there's a key."

He saw Martha confer with the flight attendant, who was shaking her head. Martha yelled back to him. "Try the *transmutare*."

For a minute, Shea thought she was saying something to him in Greek before he realized she meant his mermaid medallion. Kae had told him it had all kinds of magical abilities. Could it also unlock doors? He turned back to the cockpit to find out.

Wrapping one hand around the stone, he grasped the locked doorknob with his other hand. He had no idea what he was doing. He'd never used magick before and didn't have the first clue how to start. Of course, nothing was happening. Shea felt stupid, standing there as if he had all the time in the world when he knew he didn't. The plane rocked at a forty-five degree angle and was going down fast. He closed his eyes and squeezed harder on the stone, concentrated on the magick he could feel pulsing within. He tried to visualize an actual metal key being inserted into the lock and turning. He felt a jolt run through his body, from his medallion through to the doorknob, and heard a click. Could it be that simple? He opened his eyes and found he was suddenly able to turn the knob.

Arm muscles straining, he pushed open the cockpit door and saw the pilot and co-pilot slumped over the instrument console. A third crewmember sprawled on the floor with blood pooled under his head, crushed underneath a fallen panel where the metal hull had ripped. Swallowing back the bile that rose in his throat, Shea stepped gingerly past the dead man to check on the pilots.

When he pressed his hand to one pilot's throat to check for a pulse, the man moaned. "Wake up," Shea urged, quickly moving his hand to the man's arm and giving it a slight shake. "We need to get you out of here." The man groaned in response but didn't move.

Shea glanced over at the other pilot, and saw that the man's eyes were open but unfocused, staring straight over at his co-pilot but obviously seeing nothing. Blood dripped steadily from his nose and mouth. Shea felt the bile rising again and looked away. So much death. He pressed his lips together and drew in a deep breath, refocusing on the one crewman left who still had a chance to get out of this alive.

The cockpit seatbelts were more complicated than the simple lap belts in the passenger cabin. Shea gently pushed the man's torso into a sitting position with his back against the seat, and found the mechanism to unclasp the shoulder harness. Once unhooked, the pilot again slumped forward, but this time Shea caught him before he hit his head on the dashboard. After slipping a life vest over the man's head, Shea hooked his arms under the guy's shoulders and hoisting him up and out of the seat entirely.

He reached the door and saw that the cabin was flooded all the way to the opening in the side of the hull. Seawater poured in through the hole, filling the cabin at an even faster rate than before. There wasn't much time before the last of the air pockets filled – and then the plane would sink like the hunk of twisted metal it truly was.

Shea steadied himself against the cockpit's doorframe and assessed the situation. There was no way he could keep his balance on the angled floor while carrying the pilot and make it through the opening, all while the plane was steadily sinking. If he slipped or dropped the body, they would get tangled in the mess of debris now clogging the cabin. Getting stuck underwater for a while wouldn't bother Shea, but the pilot could drown. Was he willing to take that chance with a man's life?

He glanced back over the dead crewman's body, at the hole in the side of the cockpit's hull, his heart racing a mile a minute. Maybe a better idea would be to wait a few more minutes, and then swim out the hole in the front of the plane as the rest of it sank away from him down into the deep. If he positioned himself near enough to the hole, the pilot wouldn't be underwater for long at all. The opening looked big enough, although the ripped metal had jagged edges. He would have to exercise extreme caution, but there was no stray luggage to tangle with in here. Not yet, at least.

The water reached the door to the cockpit. He made his decision and stepped around the dead guy on the floor, dragging the groaning pilot along with him. The plane tipped further backward again, the angle of the plane's descent increasing, and Shea almost lost his balance. Keeping one arm wrapped around the pilot, he grabbed onto a metal bar bolted to what remained of the cockpit's sidewall and watched as the water rose higher. By the time the water level reached Shea's waist, the pilot was half-floating by his side. He pulled the ripcord on the inflatable life vest and watched it puff right up around the guy's neck and chest. Shea placed his sneaker carefully on the edge of the hole, pulling the groaning man behind him as he stepped through into the open water. He hesitated for a second as he felt the metal hull snag on his jeans, but gave another kick and cleared the opening.

He tried to position his arm around the man in the same cross-chest carry he'd watched Chip use on Howard, but the life vest was in the way. Realizing the vest itself would be enough to keep the pilot's head above water, Shea grabbed onto a loop near the neck and towed him as he swam straight away from the plane. Behind him he could hear all sorts of strange sizzles and pops as saltwater seeped into the cockpit's front electrical panels. He didn't turn to look. He wanted to get as far from the plane as he could while he still had the chance.

Never having learned how to swim in human form, he pumped his legs together as if they were one tail, which wasn't quite as effective with blue jeans instead of scales and fins. His clothing and sneakers were already soaked through, weighing him down and making every kick a huge effort. Using his one free arm to paddle, he strained to put distance between himself and the sinking airplane.

Loud popping noises sounded behind him as the plane made its final descent. Shea could feel the pull of the shattered hull trying to drag him and the unconscious man along with it to the bottom. He kicked as hard as he could, knowing the pilot's life depended on him not succumbing to the vacuum suck created by the plane. Sweat beaded on his forehead from the effort, as he gritted his teeth and kicked with his legs.

A few minutes later, he was just far enough away to be out of the swirling vortex. His leg muscles ached from their efforts, his biceps straining to hold onto the other man's life vest. It'd be so much easier to transform, he thought, but knew right away that would raise too many questions. He needed to keep up appearances.

"Shea!" Chip's voice carried across the open water. "Is that you over there?"

Turning to look, Shea saw the life raft wasn't far away. "Hey! Could use some help over here."

"Is that one of the pilots?" Chip and another passenger used paddles to bring the raft closer.

"Yeah. The other two guys in the cockpit were already dead." He didn't feel the need to go into gruesome detail, not when there were so many listening with injuries of their own. Several hands reached down to grab the still unconscious man, slowly pulling him on board. Shea heaved a huge sigh, relieved the guy's life no longer depended on Shea's swimming ability. As a merman? No problem. But swimming with two legs was not as easy as it looked.

"Your turn, Shea." Chip extended an open hand and Shea grabbed it gratefully, allowing the older boy to pull him up onto the raft. Chip punched his shoulder. "I'm glad you made it out okay. You did good, kiddo."

Shea cocked his head to one side. "This is a new look for you, Chip. An actual smile for a change."

Chip lowered his eyebrows and scowled. "No need to get all sarcastic on me." He nodded toward his sister. "Anyway, I don't have a whole lot to smile about right now. Hailey hasn't woken up yet, our plane totally crashed into the ocean, and six people are already dead."

"Six?" Shea tried to count. "Two in the cockpit, that one guy in first class..."

"One of the flight attendants kicked. A heart attack or something." Chip nodded toward a woman slumped on the far side of the raft. Shea thought she looked asleep, not dead. Even so...

"That's only four."

Chip lowered his voice. Shea could barely hear him over the wind. "Remember those two empty seats we saw in first class? Sucked out the hole in the side of the plane. There are forty of us on the boat. Forty-one, if you count the dead body. Good thing it's a big raft."

Shea looked around at the survivors. A flight attendants was doing her best to patch up the wounded. Most sat quietly with dazed expressions on their faces, rocking back and forth while waves buffeted the boat. Only Hailey, Howard, and the pilot remained unconscious, although Shea thought some of the other passengers looked like they might pass out at any moment. "What now?"

Chip shrugged. "We wait for someone to come looking for us? Airplanes don't just crash without people noticing. Don't you think the pilots would have used the radio to call for help? The flight attendant is sure someone will be searching."

"The pilots may have been too busy trying to control the plane." Shea turned to scan the waves. If the plane crashed because of magick, it was a fair bet sorcerers were searching for survivors, too. Maybe even Demyan himself. These people wouldn't be safe sitting here.

"Hey, look over there!" One of the passengers frantically pointed toward the horizon. "Is that land?"

Shea twisted to see where the guy was pointing. Something definitely loomed behind the storm clouds. He caught his grandmother's eye and she nodded. If there was any chance of saving these people, they needed to be on land, not on open water. He took the paddle from Chip's hands. "So what are we waiting for? Let's get this boat to shore."

Chapter Nineteen

Kae threw her arms around her father's shoulders, hugging him tight. "How did you find me?"

"There's little time." Lybio grabbed her hand, dragging her into the hallway. A petite Nerine mermaid hovered nearby, a glowing lantern in her hand. She gestured for the father and daughter to follow and swam away. Lybio slipped a transmutare medallion around Kae's neck before towing her down the hallway. His powerful tail made quick work of catching up to the blue mermaid.

The corridor's twists and turns confused Kae's sense of direction. At every intersection, the Nerine mermaid held up one blue hand while she peered around the corner, her waving white hair casting strange shadows along the walls. Although they passed countless doors, they had yet to encounter another living soul or hear any other sign of life. Finally, Kae thought she felt the water warming and saw natural light at the end of the hallway. She squeezed her father's hand and he smiled at her. "Almost out," he said softly, confirming her hopes for a quick escape.

They slowed again as they neared the end of the corridor, letting the Nerine advance alone around the last corner and out into the light. Kae held her breath. After several long moments the mermaid came back and nodded her head. "All is clear," she said, her voice unexpectedly light and musical. "Swim straight and true, and don't stop to look behind you." She stroked her hand along Lybio's cheek. "It warms my heart to see you again."

"And I to see you," Lybio said, his voice gravelly. "It's been too long."

She smiled. "The passing years are but small drops in the ocean of time's memory. Take good care of your lovely daughter." With that, she disappeared back into the darkened hallway.

Kae stared at her father, mouth hanging open. Could it be he had even more secrets in his past? His eyebrows lowered as he glared at his daughter, but she noticed a blush on his cheeks. "She's an old friend, nothing more." He grabbed Kae's hand once more. "Let's swim out of here." She nodded and followed him around the corner.

The tunnel ended soon after the turn, the rough rock walls tapering off into a jagged but narrow opening. They slipped out without speaking, but stayed close to the rocky opening as Lybio scanned the area for any sign of danger. Kae blinked rapidly trying to adjust, her eyes unused to the brightness of the Arctic waters in daylight. She looked back to where they'd just emerged and was surprised to discover she couldn't actually see the opening, it blended so well with the surrounding rocks. This is how Demyan is able to hide, she thought. In secret caves not even a mermaid can find.

She'd lost all track of time as well. How long was she underground? How long ago did Xander leave for Nantucket Sound? Did her father know of Demyan's plans?

Lybio squeezed her hand and put a finger against his lips, a signal to stay silent. Kae took a deep breath and turned her head to follow his line of sight. An enormous narwhal swam near the ocean floor, stalking a large Arctic cod. The cod tried to escape by blending with a low crop of rocks, but as the narwhal drew closer it looked as though he drew in a deep breath, sucking the cod and a several rocks straight into its mouth. The cod struggled to swim free of the vacuum before disappearing inside the giant beast.

Kae had heard stories of narwhals, but had never encountered one in person. The whales lived only in the Arctic Ocean, only getting anywhere close to the Atlantic in the summer months with their young calves. Her eyes widened as the narwhal turned to the side and she took in the legendary tusk protruding from the creature's snout. Long and pointed and paler than the rest of his body, the twisting spear winked in the sunlight that filtered down. While the whale was only about fifteen feet long, its spiraling tusk was almost that length again.

Although he was still a good distance from their location, the narwhal positioned himself squarely between the wall of rock and the open ocean. Kae and Lybio would have to swim directly past him in order to escape. Her father bent to put his mouth right next to her ear. "He must be truly old, with flanks so white and that long a tusk. Probably the leader of a large pod. We need to swim with care so as not to alarm them."

"Them?" Kae whispered back. "I only see the one beast." But even as she spoke, several more appeared, smaller in size, some with tusks and some without. Most appeared more black and white in coloring, with mottled darker markings across their bodies. The smallest of the whales were blotchy grey in color, the babies of the group, who themselves were all larger than Kae.

"They like to socialize in summertime." Lybio's voice was barely more than a whisper. "Family groups of ten to twenty are not uncommon all year round, but in the summer the groups congregate and there can be hundreds of narwhals all in one place."

She stared at her father. "How do you know so much about Arctic creatures?"

His lips pressed into a thin line, as if regretting his words. "It matters not. What does matter is that we move slowly and quietly so as not to upset this grouping. You don't want to see a narwhal elder when he gets anxious or upset. Nor do we want to be around them when the younger bulls start to tusk."

"Tusk?" Kae glanced at the long ivory spears protruding from the male snouts. No, she didn't think she wanted to be around for any whale sword play. "Can't we swim upward, and go along the surface to pass them?"

Lybio shook his head. "These creatures are *whales*, remember. Although they are foraging for cod here at the bottom, they need air to breathe, especially the young." As if on cue, two of the smallest whales made for the surface, one of the tusked males following at their side like a bodyguard.

Kae nodded and followed closely as Lybio inched along the edge of the rock wall, trying to keep their progress flowing smoothly, with no sudden movements. Finally, the wall of rock curved away from the pod and Lybio increased the speed of his swimming, once again grabbing Kae's hand and pulling her along. Once they were a good distance from the whale pod, Kae asked, "Were we truly in danger? Are not most whales gentle creatures?"

"Most, but not all." He hesitated, as if wondering whether sharing his knowledge would raise more questions in her mind. A long stream of bubbles blew out from his gills while Kae waited. They covered almost a mile before he continued. "Narwhals are meat eaters, and although their diet is strictly fish, there is no love lost between their species and either the Nerine or the local Inuit drylanders. Both races hunt narwhals for their valuable tusks. An elder like that has most likely seen his share of whale hunts and would not hesitate to end our lives before we could harm his calves."

"End our lives? Are their teeth that impressive?"

Lybio chuckled. "Just the one, actually."

"Which one?"

"You saw it. The large ivory tusks?"

"The horn protruding from the front of their heads? That's a tooth?" She shook her head, wishing Shea were here right now to communicate directly with these fascinating creatures. Which reminded her. "Father, Demyan sent a message to Windmill Point, trying to lure Shea here to the Arctic."

Again Lybio's mouth pressed into a thin line. "Lure him, how? For what purpose?"

Kae felt the heat rushing to her face. Even though she knew her father was well aware of her relationship with the boy, she also knew he didn't approve. "I think Demyan's ultimate purpose is to hold Shea himself captive, as leverage over King Koios. The 'how' is me. The messenger was to threaten my life if Shea doesn't return with him."

He squeezed her hand and said nothing for a long time. When he broke the silence, he said, "I'm glad we got you out of there when we did. The messenger will not find Shea in Nantucket Sound, or in the Atlantic at all, and then your life would have been forfeit."

"Not in Windmill Point? But why?"

"King Koios sent him to Atlantis in your place, to testify at the trial."

"Atlantis? But that journey itself is fraught with danger!" Kae slowed to a halt and pulled her father to a stop beside her. "We must intercept him on his journey before Xander…before the messenger reaches him!"

Lybio smiled and brushed the hair from Kae's face. "Is Xander the handsome young merman I heard tell of in the castle? The one who tricked you into leaving with him? I must meet this merman someday. He must be truly special to make you forget your duties."

Her face grew several degrees hotter, despite the chilled ocean. She looked down at her tail fin, fluttering in the current, wondering if it was Xander's magick alone or if she was indeed attracted to him in some way. Her stomach clenched into a tight knot of disappointed to realize Lybio was more accepting of her running off with a kidnapper than he was of her dating Shea. "Yes, Xander is the one who brought me here. He deceived me about who he truly was."

"Do not think the Atlantic king so inexperienced at these games of intrigue," Lybio said with a small chuckle. "He's been playing longer than the Adluo pretender and can stay a move ahead."

"What do you mean?"

"Shea is safe from Demyan's forces, traveling in the guise of a drylander. He won't be underwater at all until he is safely under the protection of Atlantis's Lord Chancellor himself. It would take a sorcerer to divine Shea's true location."

A fresh wave of fear shot through Kae's body. "A sorcerer? But the messenger *is* a sorcerer. He's Zan, Demyan's master of the Dark Arts. Xander and Zan are one in the same merman. Father, Shea is in trouble!"

Any trace of a smile slipped from Lybio's face. "I've heard tales of this Zan. They say his heart is filled with darkness, his abilities with magick are unprecedented…and unpredictable. He has powers beyond those of any magick user in the whole of the Atlantic."

Kae frowned, feeling a strong need to defend the merman she still thought of in her head as Xander. Maybe he'd lied to her – okay, he'd definitely lied. He'd also tricked her into following him using his magick, and stolen some of her memories...but there was good in him. She'd seen it in his eyes. He could not be the monster in the tales. "His heart is not dark, but merely full of shadows," she protested. "Were he on the right side of the battle, he would be a courageous ally."

Her father gave her a strange look. "But, daughter, he is *not* on the same side as our king. Or your friend Shea. He is Demyan's creature."

"He's not a creature, Father. He's my...friend."

He studied her face a long while before slowly nodding. "Well then. This changes our plans slightly. We will have to swim straight for the Aegean as fast as we can and hope to intercept any confrontation."

"We?"

Her father laid his hand on her shoulder. "Kae, from the tales I've heard of this Zan, he is a powerful sorcerer and can control everything around him. The ocean and the weather, as well as merfolk and drylanders alike. They say he is ruthless and unmerciful, and yet the merman you describe seems to care. About you."

She swallowed down the fear rising in her throat. She knew what he was going to say before the words came out of his mouth.

"Kae, you're the only one who can stop that sorcerer."

"But..." She thought back on the long swim from Cape Cod to the edge of the Arctic. "It took us two days to get here from Nantucket Sound. Atlantis is further still."

"That it is," Lybio agreed. "As you and I don't have the speed granted to the Adluo clan, we'd best get started."

Kae shook her head. "But we don't have time, Father. We need to warn Shea now."

"We can only do our best, little one, and trust in the gods." He laced his fingers with hers and squeezed her hand as they started to swim. "Poseidon brought me to you, and he will help us find the prince."

"You mean Shea."

"I mean the heir to the Atlantic throne," her father said sternly. "Which makes him a prince, a fact you seem to forget more often than you should."

"Father, you don't understand..."

He cut off her sentence, his voice sharp. "I *understand* more than you know. And he *is* a prince, marked by Poseidon himself, the trident blazed across his back for all to see." He paused, exhaling a long breath. When he spoke again his tone was gentle. "I don't want to see you lose your heart to a boy who can't return your love. You deserve to be happy."

"Shea makes me happy," she argued, not willing to acknowledge any truth in his words. She'd been alone in that cell for days with nothing to do but worry. She'd thought down this same path of reasoning more than once. She knew that dating a prince was illogical, but her heart felt differently.

Her father just shook his head and kept swimming.

CHAPTER TWENTY

Only two telescoping aluminum paddles came with the life raft, and Shea wasn't sure they would ever reach land. For every few yards of progress the boat made, another wave reared up to buffet them backward. It was as if the ocean were toying with the survivors, teasing them with the prospect of dry land before pushing them further away. Although the rain stopped, dark clouds surrounded them on all sides, swirling in the howling winds.

Shea handed the paddle to the next volunteer and inched his way across the raft to his grandmother. He kept his voice low, not wanting to cause panic. "It's no use. The waves are too strong, and too well-timed. Someone doesn't want us to reach dry land."

Martha frowned. "I know it may feel like sorcery, but the ocean can be capricious in her own right." She closed her eyes. "I do not feel the presence of a magick user nearby."

"You feel when they're close?"

She opened her eyes. "As can you."

"Hey, sorry to interrupt." Chip put a heavy hand on Shea's shoulder. "But we need to come up with another plan. We'll never make land at this rate, with the wind shifting all the time."

"The storm will blow out eventually," Martha said evenly. "It's already subsiding."

"Yeah, but some of these people can't wait." Chip grimaced. "One lady's femur poked right through her skin a few minutes ago, totally gross! Most of them are seasick and puking...and Hailey hasn't woken up yet. Shea, man, we need to be on land to help these people for real."

Shea looked across the water to the stretch of beach they'd been paddling toward, so close and yet so impossible to reach. An idea occurred to him. "Is there any rope on this raft?"

Chip's gaze moved over to the compartment where the flight attendant found the first aid kit. "I think I saw some with the paddles. Why? What're you thinking?"

What Shea was actually thinking was that if he transformed his shape, he could easily tow the raft through the waves to the shore. But Chip didn't know anything about that side of Shea. Before he could think of anything, Martha spoke. There was an element of command in her voice that Shea had never heard before. Martha simply told Chip to get the rope and he turned to comply without asking another question. She shrugged. "*Syren* training 101. It's like riding a bicycle, I guess."

In seconds, Chip returned with a spool of nylon anchor rope, still in its original shrink-wrap plastic. Shea read the packaging which claimed to be 120 feet of twisted nylon rope, strong enough to anchor 3,700 pounds. A metal carabiner sat attached to the exposed end. "Good enough," he said out loud.

Ripping off the plastic, he handed the end with the clasp to Martha. "Attach this to something secure. There's probably a metal ring on the raft somewhere for just that purpose. Tell Chip to be ready to paddle hard." Before she could even acknowledge his words, Shea sat down on the edge of the boat and removed his sneakers. Holding the rest of the spool tightly in his left hand, he closed his eyes and tipped himself backward into the waves, just as he'd seen Chip do earlier. He would have to trust that Martha could take care of any questions from their fellow passengers.

As he sunk below the surface, he glanced upward, making sure he went far enough under. He took a deep breath of the Mediterranean water, relishing the clean, salty taste for a moment as he plunged deeper. Finally, he took his transmutare stone into his free hand and spoke the words. "*A pedibus usque ad caput mutatio.*" A hot tingling sensation shot through both of his legs, starting right behind his bellybutton and zinging down to the tips of his toes. The water around him warmed as millions of tiny bubbles began to whirl, starting at the soles of his feet and swirling ever faster around his legs, binding them together. He took another deep breath, trying not to freak out. Paralysis was part of the process.

A tightly seething circle churned around his body, the heat moving further and further up his legs. Each second seemed an eternity until the bubbles stopped their frenetic movements and dissipated, rising slowly toward the surface. Even though the whole thing took less than a minute, Shea knew he didn't have any time to spare. The sorcerers might not be here yet, but they were coming. Of that Shea was sure.

Spooling out the rope as he swam, he put a good distance between himself and the raft before surfacing. Even with the wind and waves buffeting the boat, he didn't want to chance any of the passengers spotting the green and gold tail flicking behind him. The land looked to be another hundred yards, so close and yet so far. Looking back to the raft, he lifted his arm high above his head as he crested on a wave, trying to catch Chip and Martha's attention. He saw Martha acknowledge him by raising her own hand. He turned to swim toward shore.

Thirty feet of rope stretched between Shea and the raft, with waves rising and falling between them. He held onto the spool of remaining rope with both hands, pulling forward against the weight of the boat. It felt as though he were tied to an unmovable block of cement. He clenched his jaw and concentrated on pumping as hard as possible, every muscle in his tail straining. His chest and biceps burned with the effort of towing against the tide, until finally he felt something give. Forward movement!

Once Shea got the momentum going in the right direction, the wind and water started working with the paddlers instead of against them. As they neared the shoreline, the waves began to gravitate naturally in the same direction, helping to push the boat toward its intended destination. With each passing minute, the distance grew shorter, but the combination of undulating waves and heavy cloud cover made it difficult to judge. Holding tight to the spool, Shea dove down underwater, and saw that the slope of the bottom angling more sharply toward the surface. Now came the tricky part. How could he finish towing the raft without anyone seeing his tail?

The spool in his hands held almost a hundred more feet of rope. Trusting that the nylon would be strong enough, he swam faster, letting out additional rope as he went until it was all out, the end attached securely to the metal spool. Holding the spool with both hands, he kept swimming. In ten minutes, his tail fin brushed the sandy bottom as foamy waves crashed on the rocky shoreline.

Trees and large rocks loomed just beyond the beach, perfect to secure the raft. Unfortunately, he couldn't cross the open stretch in his present form. Grasping his transmutare stone, he closed his eyes and uttered the words to transform his tail back into legs. When he looked down again, bare toes stuck out below soaking wet blue jeans. Quickly, he stood and pushed his way through the surf and out onto the beach. Pulling the rope with him, he ran to tie the end around the closest tree. The raft bobbing atop the waves, coming closer to land.

Panic gripped him as he realized simply pulling them to shore would capsize everyone on board. As he watched, a monster of a wave swelled behind the raft, catching it in its updraft. The crest of the wave began churning downward with maximum force, but somehow the raft stayed right on the curl, riding the wave like an expert surfer on his favorite board all the way onto shore, sliding smoothly up the sand and rocks. Shea pulled the rope taut and tied it off around the tree, making certain the waves couldn't take the passengers back out to sea.

Passengers patted Chip and another young man on their backs, praising their efforts. His grandmother caught his eye and gestured for him. When he reached her, Martha threw her arms around his neck and hugged him tight. "Well done, boy-o," she said softly in his ear. "You may not get the recognition, but we both know what you did."

He returned the hug. "I think you may have used more than a little mermaid magick yourself, Gramma. Who ever heard of a lifeboat this large acting like a surfboard?"

She chuckled as she stepped back but her demeanor quickly sobered. "Let's help these people off the boat and up to the tree line as fast as we can get them moving. Then you and I have more work ahead of us." He nodded in agreement and turned to help the injured passengers.

CHAPTER TWENTY ONE

The storm clouds slowly dissipated, allowing the sun to finally break through as it made its descent below the horizon. The last of its golden rays played along the surface of the sea, seeping beneath the waves to color the water in a range of brilliant hues.

Zan took little notice of the shimmering beauty surrounding him. He cut swiftly through the now golden waters of the Mediterranean Sea, totally focused on finding the landing site of the Olympic airliner he'd crashed with his magick.

There were times he could pinpoint his storm clouds with such precision that the effects concentrated on a few square meters. When he'd been sent to Oklahoma, in the heart of drylander territory, he'd been able to focus dispassionately and create that kind of targeted storm. Today, however, had not been one of those times. Emotions clouded his judgment and interfered with his magick, creating a much larger, more powerful storm than he'd planned. Okay, he hadn't planned on creating any storm at all. It was supposed to be an easy in and out, grab-the-boy-and-go kind of mission, but once again the drylander screwed up his plans.

The whelp blatantly disregarded his warning note. How could he care so little for Kae's fate as to ignore a threat against her life? How could he give the token of his supposed affection for the beautiful mermaid to that mud-haired drylander girl? If their places were reversed, Zan knew he'd do anything to save Kae. He already stood up to Demyan once. He'd do it again if needed... the water around him warmed as the magick began to swirl. "This is how I get in trouble," he said out loud, closing his eyes. He forced himself to relax, concentrating on each individual breath until the magick subsided. He'd heard before that emotions were dangerous creatures. Especially when tied to unbridled magick.

A magical storm large enough to crash a plane would get noticed by the local authorities of all types. In addition to the Daeira clan, Lord Magistrate Andreaopolous himself would no doubt send investigators to the area, seeking the cause of such an outburst. The drylanders would also send search and rescue team looking for the crash site and survivors. Zan needed to

find Shea and be long gone before any of them arrived on the scene.

Thwarting the drylander rescue team was easy enough. With so much magick in the air, no radio calls for help penetrated the clouds. Air traffic control would have a hard time figuring out what happened or where the plane went down. Zan charged the air around the crash zone with enough electricity to jam any beacons or signals that the downed aircraft might transmit. He knew he couldn't keep it up forever, but certainly long enough to find Shea and take him away.

Strangely, when he reached the site he found little evidence near the water's surface. He'd seen — and caused — plane crashes in the past, and expected to find pieces of fuselage and luggage scattered across a wide swath of open water. He'd watched the bolt of lightning pierce the side, creating a giant hole and thwarting any suggestion of recovery. It should have crashed nose first against the water's surface, breaking into a million little pieces. But he saw none of that. No evidence of drylanders, either living or dead. "Could the plane have already sunk, trapping Shea within along with the rest?" he wondered out loud, deciding it best to look more closely. It mattered not if the boy was alive or dead. Either way, he needed to bring him to Demyan.

With grim determination, he plunged deeper into the waters as the sun dipped below the horizon, casting the ocean back into its original shades of blue.

* * *

"The sun's going down, Shea. We need to start a fire or something." Chip nudged Shea's shoulder trying to get his attention. "Are you listening to me? We're all pretty wet, and people are getting cold."

Shea stood on the shore, scanning a horizon finally clear of storm clouds. Not a ship – or mermaid – in sight. He wasn't sure if that was good or bad. Or both, for that matter. Where was the rescue team searching for crash survivors?

"Why don't you start gathering some wood?" Shea tore his eyes from the setting sun and looked at Chip. Hailey's brother surprised him earlier by stepping up to the challenge of helping the other passengers. Big change of attitude for a surly teen who professed to hate the world. "I'll go tell Gramma and your mom what we're doing and then join you." Chip nodded and gave Shea's shoulder another friendly punch before turning and heading into the trees.

Helping the injured people out of the boat and up to the tree line had been a larger task than Shea had anticipated. Many of those not injured by the crash were severely weakened by seasickness after being thrashed around by the waves. He, Martha, and Chip were among the very few unaffected. He understood why he and his grandmother hadn't been rendered ill, but Chip? "Cast iron stomach, dude," the other boy had said, smacking his belly when Shea asked. "From years of eating New York City takeout of every type and stripe. Nothing makes me vomit."

Which turned out to be a very good thing, since both Howard and Hailey were still unconscious. Although Hailey was easy to move, it had taken both boys to wrestle Howard out of the raft and up the beach, while his wife whined at them the entire time. "Be careful with him! Should his head be dangling like that? Oh, Howard, why don't you just wake up, you big lump of blubber! I can't believe you are this lazy!" Despite her words, Shea saw concern in her face. She was worried. And so was he.

Approached his grandmother now, he saw Hailey still unconscious. Martha wrapped a thin emergency blanket around Hailey's inert form. The compartments on the life raft had been equipped with a number of useful items, like the twenty packets of mylar blankets and several boxes of the type of energy bars that hikers carried for emergencies. For some strange reason, the boat's built-in transmitter beacon wouldn't turn on. One of the flight attendants was attempting to fix it while the other tended the injured pilot and passengers.

"Head injuries can be tricky things," Martha said, smiling as Hailey's mother returned to her side. "Are you feeling better, Gloria? Better out than in, I always say."

The woman let out a rueful laugh. "I guess you're right, but I don't understand what's gotten into me. I've never been seasick before in my life!"

"The waves were pretty big out there," Shea ventured. "And the crash itself was jolting."

"Well, all I can say is thank goodness those pilots were able to land the plane as well as they did." Gloria sat on the ground next to Hailey, stroking her daughter's head and humming to herself, her attention immediately absorbed by her injured child.

Martha tugged Shea's arm and indicated they should walk away and give Gloria some time alone. When they were out of earshot, she turned to him. "What was it you were coming to tell me?"

It took Shea a minute to remember. "Oh, yeah, Chip wants to start a campfire."

"Good idea. Keep everyone warm and help the search and rescue team locate us. I saw safety matches in the first aid kit. Maybe it should be more of a bonfire."

Shea agreed. "I'll see if anyone else is feeling well enough to help. Gramma, what's wrong with Hailey?"

Martha pressed her lips into a tight line before answering. "I think your friend may have suffered some sort of trauma to the brain, like a concussion or maybe even a stroke. We need to find medical help for her as soon as possible."

"Shouldn't there be a rescue team looking for the airplane soon?" Shea glanced again toward the empty horizon. "Too bad there aren't any cell towers nearby. No one can seem to get a signal on their phones to call for help."

"It's a fair bet that the sorcerers who caused the crash are also causing the electrical interference with the cell phones and the emergency transmitter," Martha pointed out. "They would want time to inspect the wreckage before the humans started to show up, but a magical outburst of that magnitude is sure to draw other attention as well."

"Other attention?"

Martha frowned. "Weren't you going to help Chip build a fire?"

"Oh, right!" He turned and jogged up the beach to catch up with Chip. As he glanced back, he saw his grandmother still staring at the horizon.

* * *

Nothing. Zan had searched the sunken wreckage and there was no sign of Shea or the drylander girl the security guard mentioned. In fact, only three human bodies remained within what was left of the aircraft. Where was everyone else?

He was running out of time. After searching every inch of the aircraft and the ocean floor, Zan concluded the passengers must have escaped. Again, the drylander whelp ruined his plans somehow. Swimming toward the surface, Zan tried to recall what he remembered of the surrounding seas. Small islands dotted this area of the Mediterranean, some with names and some without. Plenty of places for the drylanders to make landfall. The waters where the plane crashed bordered both the Mediterranean and Aegean Seas, just in between Daeira and Atlantis territories. Zan hoped by blurring the lines of jurisdiction he'd bought enough time to find and capture Shea.

A circular sweep of the surrounding area would be most logical, working his way outward from the crash site. The passengers – including Shea – didn't go down with the plane, but they didn't disappear into thin air. They had to be somewhere.

Zan needed to find out where.

Chapter Twenty Two

The warm blaze from the fire would've been cheerful under different circumstances. The rising moon overhead and the sound of waves rolling onto the shore mixed with the crackle from the fire to create an idyllic setting.

In reality, most of the people seated near the glowing flames wished they were somewhere else. Anywhere else. No one wanted to be on this island, least of all Shea.

"I don't get it," Chip said to Shea as the pair worked together to heave another large log atop the blaze. "Why haven't there been any search teams or rescue helicopters buzzing around? Someone should've missed us by now – a whole plane disappeared!"

Shea rubbed his hands along his jeans and looked toward the waterline. His grandmother stood at the edge of where the sea and sand met, watching. "I don't know, Chip. Maybe the plane went so far off course that they're looking for us in an entirely different part of the Mediterranean."

"That would seriously suck. Hailey needs help soon, dude."

He patted Chip's arm. "Someone will find us. Have faith." But as Shea turned away from the fire to join Martha by the water, he wished he believed his own words. "Hey, Gramma," he said as he drew near. "Any sign of...anyone?"

Martha shook her head, letting out an exasperated sigh. "I don't know how the Athens air traffic controllers lost the plane completely. You'd think the technology would be better than that these days."

"What about passing ships? Or fishermen?"

"Maybe in the morning." Martha turned away from the water to face Shea. "Did you and Chip find anything while you were gathering firewood?"

"Yeah, we found out it's a pretty small island. I'm surprised there are even as many trees as there are. Most of the wood for the fire is old driftwood from the beach on the north side."

"I don't want you wandering off in the dark," Martha warned. "You're safer if you stick close to the group."

Shea looked at the sick and injured people surrounding the campfire. "But is it safer for the rest of them if I stay? And what about Kae? The letter said to meet at the Piraeus docks by sunset or she would be harmed. That's now."

"What letter?" Martha's steely eyes narrowed, and Shea realized he hadn't mentioned the strange encounter at the Athens airport. Quietly, he filled her in about the bracelet and threatening letter he'd received. His grandmother nodded slowly as she listened. "So this wasn't about you going to Atlantis to testify."

He shook his head. "The king thought that's why Kae was kidnapped in the first place, but it's more likely Demyan planned from the start to use her as bait." He paused, as the wheels turned in his mind.

Martha put a gentle arm around his shoulder. "Kae will be okay. They wouldn't dare harm her if they think they have a chance to…"

"This isn't about her, or even about capturing me. They want to use me as bait to get to King Koios and Mom!" Martha's arm dropped to her side as she stared at him in stunned silence. "Demyan must have a new scheme in the works!"

Martha finally found her voice. "Could he be that deluded? How could he hope to take over the Atlantic Ocean, or recapture the Southern Ocean? The Aequoreans and Adluos are all too familiar with his bloody ways."

"It's fair to say he's more than deluded, Gramma. That guy is positively deranged. He crashed an entire plane of people trying to get me."

She hugged him tight. "It's not your fault, boy-o."

He tried to shrug her off but she refused to let him go. Finally he let out a sigh and relaxed. "I'm not looking to assign blame, Gramma. But we need to get help for these people, and we need to save Kae."

"Absolutely. But I still think you need to stick with the group until morning. You should be safe on dry land for the evening. Better to travel in the light, when you can clearly see what's coming at you." She smiled as she took a step back from him. "Besides, who knows what the morning may bring? The Daeira may solve your sorcerer problem for you. I can't imagine they're too happy right now with unauthorized magick inside their territory."

* * *

Zan visited three deserted islands with nothing to show for his efforts. No sign of life, human or otherwise, amidst those rocky shores. He wondered how far the passengers could swim. Certainly not very far considering their useless drylander legs, so he kept diving to check the ocean floor for any sign. Nothing. Could the aircraft have been equipped with a boat for emergencies? He considered it unlikely that drylanders would have such foresight. From what he knew of them, they didn't possess the same level of intelligence as merfolk.

He skimmed along the surface, searching through the darkness for the next sign of land. An orange glow in the distance caught his eye and he plunged deep to swim in that direction. Surfacing closer, he confirmed his suspicions. The glow was from a fire on the beach. There were definitely humans on the island up ahead.

Now he needed to confirm whether Shea was among them. Did he dare go ashore and search? Did he have any other choice?

Movement in the waters to his left captured his attention. Mermen. It was too late to swim away, that might be misinterpreted. He couldn't take the chance that the mermen approaching might be armed, or part of a larger force. He stayed where he was, hovering at the surface, as two mermen approached and surfaced a few yards to the east of him.

"Greetings, traveler," called one, invoking the formal salutation between strangers, using the universal language. "Great Neptune's blessings upon you."

"And upon you," Zan responded formally. He saw no harm in playing the role of traveler. It worked so well in the Atlantic Summer Court, when he met Kae.

"What brings you through these waters this night?" The second merman had a deeper voice and sounded more suspicious than his partner. His words carried a thick accent, as if he was used to only speaking in his native dialect.

"I travel to Atlantis," Zan lied. "My girlfriend is enrolled for the new semester and I wanted to surprise her with a visit before the new term begins." Better they think him a love-struck guppy than some sort of threat.

The mermen swam closer, and Zan saw they were Daeira, not Atlantean guards, which would explain the accent. Zan knew the guards in Atlantis wouldn't tolerate any imperfection in their ranks and demanded even the lowest ranking servants to be versatile in all languages, especially the universal tongue. These mermen carried older looking spears, and Zan wondered if they were perhaps hunters instead of actual soldiers. The smaller of the two, the one who had invoked the original greeting, spoke first. "Dark magick abounds in these waters. Did you feel it earlier, with that unpredicted storm?"

Zan shook his head. "I crossed over from the Atlantic Ocean just moments before we met. In truth, I was only surfacing to get my bearings from the night sky, as I might be a wee bit lost. The current here does seem a might unpredictable."

"It's from the storm," the other merman continued, his voice growing excited. "We were out here hunting along the border, you know, real careful like so as not to cross into the Aegean, but the storm twisted us all around."

So they're poachers, Zan thought with a smile. *All the better for me.* "Perhaps it was a summer project conducted by University students? Aren't they known for playing with the weather?"

The bigger merman shook his head. "Not like this," he rumbled. "We've hunted in this sector before and never – I mean never – have we felt power like this. Down right scary, it was. And I'm not afraid of no sorcerer, neither. Least aways, none that I've met. This one? Neptune knows, I wouldn't want to meet him in dark waters."

Zan smiled wide, relishing the irony. The pair didn't seem bright enough to pose a threat, and he debated whether to kill them immediately and continue with his search. On the other hand, staying close to them might provide needed cover when the guards from Atlantis showed up to investigate, which would no doubt be soon. "Would it be okay if I were to swim with you two for a while? Like you, I don't fancy the thought of encountering sorcerers in the darkness."

"Sure, sure," agreed the smaller merman. "My name is Yannis, and my friend is Tassos. And you…?"

"Alexandros," Zan said, using the Greek version of his given name. "Though I usually go by Xander."

"Well met, Xander," said Yannis, extending his arm in friendship. Instead of shaking his hand, as was custom in the Atlantic and Southern Oceans, Zan grabbed him by the forearm as Yannis grabbed his arm in a similar fashion, so that the two mermen pulled shoulder to shoulder. Having spent many years in Atlantis, Zan knew this custom of greeting. It was common with the clans in these waters, as well as the Indian Ocean and some parts of the Pacific. The Arctic Ocean was the only place where touching hands or shoulders was not part of the formal greeting. In fact, in the Arctic there was very little touching of any kind, and absolutely none between strangers.

After greeting Yannis, Zan repeated the process with Tassos before asking his next question. "So, where are you camped? I hope it's not too near to this island, as it looks inhabited." He nodded his head toward the fire's glow to the north.

Yannis followed Zan's gaze. "Strange. We hunt these waters quite frequently, and know all the islands in the area. That one is typical of the region, far too small to support a village of drylanders."

His friend Tassos spoke up. "Is there a yacht anchored nearby? Sometimes the drylanders anchor their crafts in shallow waters while they make camp on the sand."

Zan watched the blaze of the fire spark higher. His new friends didn't know about the plane crash. He saw no reason to enlighten them. "I encountered no vessels at anchor. Could there be another explanation?"

Both mermen shook their heads before Yannis spoke. "Come, let us take you to our shelter, where we can be safe from whatever dark sorcerers are out this night."

"And whatever guards be out chasing them," Tassos added with a laugh before Yannis elbowed his stomach. "Ouch! What was that for, Yannis?"

Zan interrupted before Yannis could speak. "Do not worry on my account. I am not a guard in disguise, nor is there any love lost between myself and those in authority."

"Then come, let us away from this spot," Yannis said with a smile. "We can share food and relax in the shelter of our cave, and await morning to venture forth."

Zan took one last look toward the glow of the fire before turning to follow the two poachers. Whatever other skills they might possess, Zan was sure they were good at evading guards, which was the thing that mattered most at the moment.

Besides, there would be plenty of time the following day to check if the drylanders on that island were the ones he sought.

CHAPTER TWENTY THREE

Shea sat alone on the sand watching dawn's rosy fingers unfurl from the horizon, painting the whispers of clouds in ever lighter shades of pinks and oranges as the sun peeked over the water. If he focused on the rising sun, he could almost pretend he was back in Windmill Point, back on his own stretch of Cape Cod beach looking out over a different ocean. His ocean.

He sighed, realizing his feelings of ownership held more truth than he felt comfortable with. Luckily, King Koios still ruled the Atlantic and would for many years to come. No way he would let Demyan or his cohorts mess that up.

After making sure he was alone, he peeled off his shirt and slipped out of his sneakers. He needed to grab this opportunity to seek help while the rest of the survivors slept. Howard had finally regained consciousness during the night

and his wife had woken everyone with her enthusiastic cheers and tears. Hailey still hadn't stirred. She needed a doctor, and fast. If there was any way for Shea to speed the rescue process, he had to try.

The crystal clear saltwater licked at his bare toes. Five feet from the shore lay a steep drop off where he'd plunge well over his head. In up to his knees, he took one last glance over his shoulder before taking the plunge, swimming deep and blowing the delicious saltiness through his gills. He had no idea where he was going, but he couldn't sit idle while his friend slipped away. He needed to find help. He wrapped his fingers around his transmutare and uttered the words to trigger the transformation from human to merman. As the surge of swirling bubbles engulfed his legs, he took a deep breath and held it. He absolutely hated the helpless feeling of paralysis that accompanied every change. Transformation complete, he flexed his tail muscles, the warm water sliding along his scales.

Martha seemed to think Atlantis was due east of the island so Shea swam in the direction of the rising sun. They'd discussed the probability of Atlantis mermen searching these waters for the source of yesterday's magical disturbance. Martha counseled him to approach any strangers with caution – yes, he was in search of help, but somewhere out there was the sorcerer or group of sorcerers who caused the storm and the plane crash. Shea promised to be careful.

Now that the storm had passed, Shea could appreciate the exotic beauty surrounding him, the warm sea so different than his own Atlantic Ocean. The small fish that swam in schools seemed brighter in color, their voices lighter in tone than even the silvery minnows back home. Along the rocky bottom, multi-hued corals grew in gigantic clumps with tiny orange fish darting in and about. A school of hot pink jellyfish bobbing along in a large cluster. Bright red sea stars clung to the sides of rocks, their long spindly arms so different in shape and color than the ones back home near Cape Cod.

But no sign of other mermen.

The rumble of a deeper voice caught his attention, and he turned his head to see a family of large sea turtles, their shells a mottled brown and white, grazing on a patch of barnacles growing on some rocks. As he slowed to watch, the largest of the turtles sucked in one of the red sea stars, crunching it between powerful jaws. Shea recognized them as Loggerhead turtles from pictures in a book on endangered species, and from that animated movie about the lost clown fish. They looked a lot like their cartoon counterparts, with their big eyes and classic patterns on their shells echoed on the leathery skin around their heads. He'd never met one in person, since the waters of Nantucket Sound were a little too chilly for their tastes. Kae had talked about playing with baby loggerheads off the coast of Florida, and he wondered if they were as intelligent as the leatherback turtles he'd met near the Summer Palace, or if they were more like the animated turtles who talked like surfer dudes.

He tried to tune in to their specific thoughts, wondering if these turtles had seen any other mermen in the area. What he heard was two of the female turtles making derisive remarks about his arms. "My arms are not skinny, and I like having hands instead of flippers! Opposable thumbs rock," Shea said out loud, startling them. The entire group turned to stare at him for a long, awkward moment. The largest of the males swam forward until he was face-to-face with Shea, the turtle's enormous black eyes blinking slowly as they considered one another up close. Leathery wrinkles piled deep around the turtle's eyes and along his neck, and Shea wondered how many years this creature had seen.

When he finally spoke, the old turtle's voice sounded slow and ponderous in Shea's head. *You can...hear us?*

"Yes, I can," Shea replied, speaking out loud. He was careful not to make any sudden moves or raise his hands, as the turtle's hard jaw formed a sharp point at the end, almost beak-like. Shea imagined it came in handy for digging at the ocean's bottom but it could probably snap his wrist pretty easily.

This is strange, the turtle said. *It's been a long time since I've had a conversation with a merman. Who are you, young one?*

"My name is Sheachnadh," he told them, using his formal name. He flicked his tail, making the golden scales sparkle in the filtered light. "I'm the grandson of King Koios of the Atlantic Ocean."

Ah, that explains it then. I remember Koios from our last trip out west, the turtle said, bobbing his head up and down as his prodigious flippers stayed straight out to his sides, each as long as Shea's arm and three times as wide. *He also has a similar gift. I am called Tartaruga.*

"My grandfather can talk to sea creatures?" The news startled Shea, but he quickly realized it made sense, accounting for the origins of the seemingly unique ability. Maybe the king could help him learn to control the voices in his head. He'd need to have a long talk with his grandfather when he returned to Cape Cod. Shea refocused on the problem at hand. "I'm in need of assistance," he said to the turtles, his eyes sweeping over the entire group. "Have any of you encountered other merfolk today? I have a friend who is badly injured. She needs help."

Bring the mermaid to us and we'll carry her to Atlantis, the old turtle offered. *We don't usually offer rides, but we'll make an exception for the grandson of Koios.*

Shea frowned. "The problem is...she's not a mermaid. She's human." He heard the stir of surprise and anger rising from the group.

We have no friends among those who would hunt us to the brink of Hades, Tartaruga replied. *These days we have few friends among mermen either, as they hunt us to sell to the humans for meat. Give my regards to your grandfather.* With that, the giant turtle slowly turned and swam away, the rest of his family group following after him.

Shea raised his voice. "There are dark sorcerers abroad in these waters. They caused the harm to the humans and now seek to capture me to use against King Koios. Please, I need your help."

At the mention of the king, Tartaruga stopped swimming and swiveled his considerable head toward Shea. *We saw one sorcerer in our travels, exuding dark magick in his wake. He sought shelter overnight with hunters off in the direction of the setting sun, which is why we travel the opposite line now in such a hurry, as should you.*

"Much thanks for the information, great one. I will follow your wise advice," Shea said, his mind churning. One sorcerer? Could one merman have been responsible for the huge storm that crashed the plane? Somehow that seemed even scarier than the idea of a whole team of sorcerers. Bidding goodbye to the turtles, Shea hurried forward on his

journey east, kicking his tail fin into high gear. At least he knew the sorcerer was behind him.

*   *   *

Zan hovered near the surface, his eyes just above the waterline, watching the island for signs of movement. He'd swum in as close as he dared, at least for now. He had no idea whether this was even the right group of drylanders, and he didn't want to risk attracting more unwanted attention with his magick. The Atlantean soldiers were sure to be somewhere near, and he didn't want to tip his hand too soon. Not until he knew Shea was actually on the island.

The sun had climbed partway into the sky already, the light sparkling as it danced atop the clear, turquoise waters. He breathed in the warm, salty air and a ripple of guilt pass through his body, thinking of Kae still trapped in that cold, Arctic cell. He put her there, gave her to Demyan. He needed to right that particular wrong.

He parted ways with the poachers early in the morning after sharing a meager breakfast in their cave. The pair remained skittish about the prospect of meeting any sorcerers, and tried to talk Zan into returning to the safety of their village. Zan managed to keep a straight face and politely declined their offer, repeating his lie about the girlfriend waiting for him in Atlantis. He didn't want her to worry. In reality, the only mermaid he cared about was trapped in a cell with a madman in charge of her fate. Zan was the one worried. He hoped that word of his magical outburst hadn't made its way to Demyan's ears just yet. He needed to have Shea in hand first in order to justify his out-of-control actions.

Something stirred on the wide sandy beach, and Zan sunk lower in the water as he watched. The drylanders were finally rising from their sleep, and Zan scanned the group for a tall blond teenaged boy. He'd never actually met the boy he'd been sent to retrieve, and only knew his drylander name and a general description, but the boy had few choices, and fewer places to hide. More than thirty drylanders clustered together on the sand, coming and going into the small grove of trees. It was hard to know an exact number since they kept moving about, and humans all tended to look alike. Panning over the group, he saw one of the grey-haired women standing at the water's edge, staring straight out in his direction. He plunged below the surface, wondering how good an old drylander's eyesight could be. Still, he didn't want to take any chances. He swam underwater to his left several yards and then backing away from the island several more before making a slow rise above the water to take another look.

The woman had disappeared from the strand line. Some of the humans were rekindling the fire, and he finally pinpointed the old woman nearby. She spoke with a dark-haired youth, who called to someone in the trees. Another male youth, this one blond, joined them. Could that be the boy he sought? Zan grimaced, trying to decide his next move. What would Demyan want him to do? What would Demyan himself do, were he in this position?

That answer seemed simple. Demyan would kill anyone who got in his way. He'd kill everyone on that island in order to capture Shea. Bile rose in the back of Zan's throat. Though he had little regard for drylanders, he was not a cold killer at heart. Crashing an airplane with magick was one thing. But there was no way Zan could go ashore and simply kill people. The very thought twisted his insides into monstrous knots. He took a slow deep breath and sank below the waves to contemplate his next move. There had to be an alternative that didn't include full-scale bloodshed.

How did things get so complicated?

Chapter Twenty Four

For the first time in her life, Kae wished she were something – anything – other than a mermaid.

It felt like she'd been swimming forever already, and she knew many miles remained ahead of her. She just. Wanted. To. Rest. To use muscles other than those in her tail for a change. Every inch of her fins ached, even more than when Xander brought her north. At least he'd been kind enough to stop and rest along the way. Her father hadn't let them stop once since they started, instead feeding her raw cacao beans as they swam to keep up her energy levels. He said it was an old trick from his University days.

If she were human, no one would expect her to swim halfway around the world. "I'll bet Hailey never has to swim for days on end," she grumbled, struggling to keep up with Lybio's fast pace. They'd been swimming for two days straight without stopping and were very near the western edge of the Atlantic. On the one hand, she was glad they made good time and would soon be close enough to help save Shea. On the other hand, her tail fin was killing her!

Lybio looked at her and frowned, never loosening his grip on her hand or slowing the steady beat of his powerful tail. "Did you say something? Do you wish to stop and rest, little one?"

Guilt flowed through her entire body as her cheeks warmed with embarrassment. She realized how selfish her complaints sounded, when there were lives at stake, maybe even the fate of the oceans. But her tail really did ache...

"I feel terrible even asking to rest for a second, Father, but I'm sore all over." More heat rushing to her cheeks, humiliated to admit how weak she felt, like a guppy trying to keep up with a shark. "Could we stop swimming for just a moment or two?"

"Of course we can rest." He slowed to a halt. "Why didn't you speak up sooner?"

"Well... I know we have to get to Atlantis as fast as possible..."

"Not at the expense of your health. I was too focused to notice the toll this has taken on you." He waved a hand toward some large rocks. "Let's rest here for a little while."

"Thanks." Grateful for the break, she settled herself onto a flat rock and watched her father stretch his own muscles. He looked the same as he ever did, yet she saw him in a whole new light since his appearance in the doorway of her prison cell. She'd always known he worked directly for King Koios, but he was always just "Father" to her. Now he seemed different somehow. She'd discovered earlier in the summer that he had secrets, but how many secrets could there be? His skills with prison breaks aside, Kae decided she needed to ask the main question swishing around in her head for the last hundred miles. "So, who was that blue mermaid and how do you know her? Is she an old girlfriend?"

He narrowed his eyes, his bushy brows lowering. "I'm not sure how that is relevant to relieving your aching tail muscles. Perhaps you should focus your thoughts on stretching your body, rather than your imagination."

"But who is she?"

Lybio sighed. "An old friend, like I said before."

"I didn't think the Nerine made friends with other clans. I thought they weren't even supposed to touch…"

"We were in Atlantis together, and shared classes at the University," Lybio said, rubbing a hand across his eyes.

Kae eyed him skeptically, wondering if that was all they'd "shared," but she said nothing. It felt weird enough thinking of her dad as a University student. Had he ever been that young? When she didn't respond right away, he let out another sigh, as if reading her mind. "Yes, I was your age once. King Koios and I actually attended University together, back in the day. That mermaid you saw in the Arctic caverns is a Nerine princess who was in our circle of friends. Koios and I even spent a few of our school breaks as guests in the Nerine court."

"You hung out with the royals at University?"

"The king and I were boys together, the only ones of our age in the palace. When it came time for University, his father sent me along to watch over Koios, as even then there existed tension between the clans. We did everything together."

Kae scrunched her brow, still having trouble imagining her father as a teenager, let alone hanging around with a bunch of uber-spoiled royals. Did everyone bring a servant with them to University? "So you were what, just a bodyguard?"

"I was his friend. But yes, I had his back, just in case."

"I didn't know you were...best buddies with the king."

"Things change." The look on her father's face was so sad that sudden tears welled behind Kae's eyes. "This is why I try to warn you about Shea, little one. The kingdom will always come first for the royal family. It has to."

She didn't want to go there. Not right now. Besides, her situation was different. Shea was different. Shaking her head slowly, she moved the subject back to her original line of questioning. "So. That blue mermaid? You said she's a princess. Her father's King Naartok?"

"No, King Naartok has no children, and no heir as yet. She's the king's niece, but I fear her father is in league with Demyan. That is how she knew of the caverns where you were being held." Lybio blew out a deep breath, bubbles streaming from his gills. "She took a great risk helping us today, for if she's caught Demyan will surely see that she suffers, royal blood or not. He needs to be stopped once and for all."

A fire lit in Kae's belly. She could help stop Demyan's schemes, and the knowledge filled her with renewed energy. "Come on, Father. I've rested enough. We need to find that sorcerer before Demyan's plan goes any further."

He smiled. "There's a village not far from here, the Outermost Village. It's the last one on this edge of the Atlantic, as the name suggests. We can find dolphins there to take us the rest of the way in a fraction of the time, and be to Atlantis within the day."

Kae smiled as she grabbed her father's hand and gave it a good squeeze. "So what are we waiting for?"

CHAPTER TWENTY FIVE

It took all day to come up with a new plan. One that didn't include killing every living thing on the island.

As he watched the sun carve its path through the brilliant blue sky, Zan hovered near the water's surface and contemplated his options. He examined and discarded each idea in turn until he narrowed it down to just one: sneaking onto the island under the cover of darkness. He'd find the boy and compel him with magick, just as he had with Kae. No muss, no fuss, and no one else bleeding to death. Not if he could help it, anyway.

He'd been observing the humans on and off throughout the morning and afternoon, and was fairly certain he knew which one was the MacNamara boy. Really, there only seemed to be one youth who fit the description Kae provided. That boy spent most of the day with another dark-haired youth, gathering wood and tending to the fire pit at the edge of the beach. Back and forth they went, almost like slaves in their relentless movements, keeping the fire burning and adding hunks of greenery to create billowing black smoke.

Zan knew they were trying to draw attention to their location with the dark clouds of smoke, but he'd cast a circle around the island early that morning to make it invisible to planes flying overhead. The magick would eventually fade and the smoke would certainly be visible if anyone drew near enough, but he hoped the isolation would last until nightfall. A few more hours were all he needed.

His thoughts drifted to the mermaid trapped in the Arctic cell. Her hair felt like gossamer strands of the finest cloth beneath his fingers, the skin of her cheek as soft as the belly of a newborn dolphin. Her lips were full and round, like the colorful wrasse fish he'd seen around the tropical reefs in the Pacific Ocean. Her green eyes sparkled like the glittering jewels on Queen Jessamine's crown…he paused at that thought and frowned.

He'd been there when Demyan killed Queen Jessamine, thrusting his sword through her chest, thick mermaid blood flowing through the marble chamber. Her husband already dead in a suspicious accident that Zan knew Demyan had caused. He and Demyan were visiting the queen to comfort her, but Demyan started taunting her almost immediately. The argument escalated quickly and with one swift motion witnessed only by Zan, Demyan turned his little cousin Theo into both an orphan and the King of the Southern Ocean. A title the poor child didn't hold for very long.

Zan knew no one believed the queen took her own life, and he still wasn't sure if poisoning Theo was part of Demyan's master plan, or a happy coincidence for the ruthless merman. Either way, the final outcome of the Solstice celebration was not as Demyan had expected. He almost took control of both the Atlantic and Southern Oceans in one fell swoop, but ended up swimming for his life. All because of this one young drylander.

From this distance, Zan couldn't understand what Kae saw in the blond boy. He looked a bit shorter and a lot less muscular than the picture her words painted in Zan's mind. Though he seemed intent on helping his fellow drylanders, he hadn't employed his transmutare magick to swim for help, choosing to remain in that useless two-legged form. Fire and smoke seemed to be the only magick he could muster. Regardless of any shortcomings, Zan knew this boy would be a formidable opponent in the fight for the mermaid's affections. A fight he wanted desperately to win.

The sun melted into the horizon, its golden glow seeping and spreading across the surface of the water, rippling along the waves. A smile pulled at Zan's lips. It was almost time. As the sky darkened, he could see the drylanders huddling closer to the fire, not straying far from the bright circle of light it cast onto the sand. He started to swim closer, feeling confident the drylanders wouldn't see him among the shadowy waves.

Not comfortable approaching the beach directly while in his current form, Zan swam to the far side of the small island. In the rocky shallows, he performed the ritual to change his tail into drylander appendages. "Legs," he said out loud, distaste evident in his voice as he gazed at his transformed lower body. "How awkward they seem when compared to the simple beauty of a tail." He rubbed his fingers over one knobby knee, deciding it was a necessary evil. Sizing up his own well-muscled legs against those of the drylanders he'd been observing all day, he grinned with satisfaction. Even in this less-than-perfect form, he compared favorably to the blond boy and his dark-haired counterpart. Gaining the upper hand should prove no problem.

Zan stood and made his way through the waves to the shore, picking his way through the rocks until he stood on dry ground. He bent to brush the excess water from his bare skin, his mind already planning his next move, when he heard a voice from somewhere behind him.

"You forgot to conjure clothing to cover yourself."

He froze, suddenly feeling very exposed, and not just because some female was staring at his bare bottom. Slowly he turned just his head to find that same grey-haired woman, the one who'd been standing on the strand line staring into the waves on and off all day long. *What's she doing on this side of the island? And what does she know of conjuring?*

"I'm not holding a conversation with a naked man," she continued, and Zan suddenly found himself wearing tubes of scratchy blue cloth around his waist and legs. "Those are called blue jeans, and you're welcome."

Zan turned his body to face the woman, pinned by the anger in her piercing blue eyes. Steel grey hair hung down her back in a loose braid, her baggy dress hung down past her knees hiding her form, although he could see she had legs and feet. A drylander. But a drylander who conjured clothing from thin air? His mouth felt unbearably dry all of a sudden. *How can that be?*

"Who are you?"

CHAPTER TWENTY SIX

The guards swimming by his sides made him nervous. It bothered Shea to his very core to be treated as if he were a criminal. As if he were the sorcerer who'd downed the airplane and created such a stir. Every second wasted with their suspicions and protocols meant more time until help reached the crash survivors.

He'd run into the guard patrol soon after leaving the family of turtles. In his naiveté, he'd tried to rush them back to the island where he'd left Gramma and the Thompsons, but the guards followed other orders. Any merfolk found in the vicinity of the crash were to be taken directly to Atlantis for questioning. Trying to argue with that logic resulted in a swollen eye and his hands bound with chains, both of which slowed their progress all the more.

The entire patrol accompanied the prisoner back to the city, reaching the outskirts well before sunset. Even with one eye swollen shut, Shea recognized the same sort of lined path along the ocean floor as the one leading to the summer castle at the bottom of Nantucket Sound. Instead of the posts and antique lanterns he'd seen in the Atlantic, the pathway here was lined with white marble columns that gleamed through crystal clear waters without the help of phosphorescent creatures.

The City of Atlantis itself exceeded even his wildest imaginings. The only underwater place he'd been was the castle in Nantucket Sound, which was amazing in and of itself, but small in scale compared to an entire city. And Atlantis was most definitely a city with a capital "C."

He'd read the myths of how the ancient Greek gods cursed Atlantis and sank it beneath the ocean, and now he could see how those stories might actually be true. Indeed, the buildings and roads looked just like the photographs Hailey had shown him of ancient Greece. Except…these buildings and roads were underwater. All types of colorful fish swam by, shimmering in rainbow hues against the bright white of the marble structures, some of which towered several stories over the sea floor reaching up toward the water's surface. Shea's eyes widened as he tried to take in all the unfamiliar sights and sounds of the sunken city.

Instead of people populating the city, of course, there were mermaids and mermen going in and out of the buildings, stopping to chatter with one another and to stare at the procession of guards escorting Shea. Instead of cars or trucks, he saw wagons harnessed to dolphins carrying goods down the city streets, stopping in front of buildings to unload their barrels and crates, holding up other traffic. Who would have imagined a traffic jam underwater?

He'd never been in a city this large on dry land, or seen this many beings all living in one place. Oklahoma City seemed tiny – miniscule, even, – in comparison to Atlantis. He imagined Hailey's New York City might be something like this, but from the photos he'd seen online, that particular city was mostly dull and grey. Everything here in Atlantis looked freshly polished, sparkling in the last of the day's sunlight.

The merfolk he saw along the route reminded him of the gathering at the Solstice celebration, with every combination of colors he could imagine for skin tone and hair, as well as the brilliant scales along their tails. The mermaids all had brightly colored flowing silk wrapped around their chests, some that matched the color of their hair and others that clashed wildly. Most of the mermen wore some sort of vest, or sashes like those worn by the guards. Very few were bare-chested, as Shea was, and he felt slightly self-conscious, as if he'd been invited to a party and forgotten to dress up.

The smells that wafted through the streets were different too, as though to remind Shea that he was no longer in the Atlantic. The water here tasted and smelled much saltier than back home, which he knew already from earlier in the day. The city itself seemed to add even more to the current, the scents of so many merfolk living in such close proximity added a certain grittiness to the water so that even Shea, a neophyte to this sort of thing, could definitely tell he was swimming through a crowded area.

As he swam through the streets, he watched mermaids hanging lanterns outside each of the buildings, and saw windows light up as the merfolk went home for the evening. Home. It reminded him of the glowing windows of his grandmother's home back in Windmill Point, or Kae's family cottage in Nantucket Sound. Those places suddenly felt so far away from him that the memories made his heart ache.

By the time the guards reached their final checkpoint in a large courtyard, Shea felt completely overwhelmed. The city was so large, the citizenry so diverse, it boggled his mind to realize this world really existed. Knowing about mermaids, even falling in love with a mermaid, was one thing. Or maybe that's two things, Shea reflected. But… Being thrust into a city population of merfolk was quite another story.

He looked up the wide set of marble stairs before him, seeing that they led up into the largest building in the entire city. A dozen thick-looking columns of marble graced the front of the structure, each carved with straight vertical grooves all the way to the top. An elaborately carved beam lay across them, holding up the structure's tall, pointed roof. The giant staircase puzzled him, until he remembered the city wasn't originally built for merfolk but for humans, before the gods sank it beneath the waves and Poseidon took over.

Coming out through the columns swam an elderly merman with long hair and a flowing white beard trailing in his wake. He reminded Shea somewhat of the High Chancellor he'd seen at Summer Solstice, the one Demyan accidentally killed. Like the Chancellor, and unlike the majority of the mermen in Atlantis, he wore neither a sash nor a vest, but a pure white tunic that hung slightly past his waist. Over his heart, Shea saw an elaborate crest embroidered with golden thread.

"Well, well, who have we here?" The old merman eyed Shea with suspicion as he addressed the head of the guards. His gaze took in both the restraints on Shea's wrists and the bruising on his face. "Is this the one who caused the weather disturbance?"

"We're not sure, my Lord." The guard put his hand on Shea's spine and bent him forward. "He seems to bear the Mark of the Trident on his back, but we have no known record of his name and suspect sorcery."

Shea couldn't hold his tongue. "My Lord," he said, looking up with his one good eye to address the white-haired merman. He spoke as quickly as he could, knowing the guard would try to muzzle him. "My name is Sheachnadh, the grandson of King Koios of the Atlantic. My mother is Queen Brynneliana, now ruler of the Southern Ocean. I've come to Atlantis for help…"

The guard pushed him down again, this time holding Shea's neck, his meaty fingers wrapped in a one-handed chokehold, pressing into his windpipe and cutting off his words. "Silence in the presence of the Lord Magistrate. You've come to Atlantis because we've brought you here, jelly-brain."

"Lord Magistrate?" Shea struggled against the guard's strong grasp to raise his head and speak again. He strained to get his words out, his throat fighting to form each syllable. "My grandfather sent me to…meet you…to testify against…Prince Demyan."

The merman at his side pushed him roughly down to the ground, with both hands this time, scraping Shea's nose right against the flat stones lining the floor of the courtyard. Shea tasted iron in the water, and knew the guard had drawn fresh blood. "At least get your lies straight, sorcerer. Prince Demyan is still at large. How can there be a trial without a guilty party?"

"Let him rise, Erastus, and release him from the chains."

The guard released his hold and Shea straightened slowly, the chains biting into his wrists as blood trickled from new wounds. As much as he wanted to retaliate against this big bully of a merman, he was bound and outnumbered. He contented himself with glaring at the guard.

"Sir? Is it safe to release him? I don't understand." Erastus hovered close as if waiting for Shea to try to escape. The magistrate nodded and the guard unbound Shea's hands. He flexed his arm muscles with relief and put a hand to the bridge of his nose to staunch the red flow.

"I've been expecting this boy," the Lord Magistrate explained with a note of amusement. "You have just insulted – and assaulted – the heir to the throne of the Atlantic Ocean."

All color drained from the guard's face. He glanced at Shea, as if seeing him for the first time. The swollen eye. The bleeding nose. "I…I…I don't know what to say." He hung his head, his whole body conveying defeat and despair as he faced his former prisoner. "Forgive me, my Prince. I am yours to command."

Shea stared, unsure what he was supposed to do or say. From the guard's sudden docility, he knew the merman expected to be punished harshly, but he couldn't really blame him for doing his job, even though he acted a little overzealous in the performance of his duty. The old merman seemed to note Shea's dilemma and chuckled. "Do you wish to levy formal charges, my Prince?" Not trusting his voice, Shea shook his head to indicate no. The magistrate dismissed the guards with a curt, "That will be all," and the entire patrol vanished from sight almost instantly, a vast swirl of bubbles trailing in their wake.

The magistrate folded his arms across his chest. "Sorry about the less than cordial welcome. The guards are on edge because of some recent unexplained magical disturbances. And I must admit, my Prince, your appearance here and now is something of a puzzle. You were supposed to be on the beach at my daughter's villa on Santorini two days ago."

"There was a storm," Shea started, and saw the Lord Magistrate narrow his eyes. "King Koios sent me by airplane, and a sudden storm crashed us into the sea."

"A storm, you say."

"Caused by magick," Shea added. "Of that I have no doubt, because I could feel it in the air." He left out the part about his grandmother, as he wasn't sure yet how she fit into this world she had given up so many years ago.

"Perhaps this storm and your aircraft were unfortunate collateral victims of this outburst, this outpouring of magick."

"No, sir. I think we were definitely the targets. I'm fairly certain the reason for the storm was to crash our plane and keep me from reaching Santorini." Saying it out loud made the claim sound a little silly, and highly conceited, as if Shea thought the entire world revolved around him. He could see the doubt on the magistrate's face, but Shea knew there were good reasons for his claim. He pressed his case further. "Sir, Demyan knows of the trial."

The older merman looked at him sharply. "Demyan had his henchmen crash your plane to prevent you from giving testimony?"

"I know he kidnapped a mermaid I care about and is holding her hostage. There was a ransom note. They want me to give myself up to them in exchange for her release."

"To what purpose?"

Shea took a deep breath, deciding it best to lay out all of his suspicions before the magistrate. "I think Demyan has bigger schemes in mind than merely escaping justice for past crimes. I suspect he plots again to take over the Atlantic, and wants to take me prisoner. He'll use me as leverage against my mother and grandfather."

To Shea's surprise, the Lord Magistrate smiled and began to chuckle, finally opening his mouth to laugh out loud. When he had recovered his countenance, he said, "He's swimming for his life. You said it yourself, Demyan knows we are trying him for murder here in the High Court. And yet you ascribe to him such audacity as to be plotting an overthrow of more kingdoms?" The merman shook his head in disbelief, his grey eyes twinkling with merriment. "Sheachnadh, I fear you've read too many of those drylander fairytales. This story you've concocted in your head goes well beyond the boundaries of the possible, swimming into the realm of the fantastical."

Tiny bubbles streamed from his gills as Shea exhaled. He couldn't afford to piss off the Lord Magistrate of Atlantis. Not when one of his best friends lay injured, possibly close to death, on a remote island in the middle of nowhere, while Kae was still being held captive... They'd kidnapped his girlfriend to get to him, and he'd practically ignored that threatening letter. He should never have gotten on that airplane. If Demyan had no qualms about crashing a plane full of people, what harm might he inflict on Kae? Panic roiled his stomach at the thought of her suffering because of him, shivers of fear prickling at the back of his neck.

He clenched his jaw and looked the magistrate in the eye. "Sir, I know it all sounds hard to believe. And yes, I guess hearing myself say it out loud, I have trouble thinking anyone would have an ego large enough to attempt such a coup."

The old merman's eyes twinkled more. "Funny you should mention ego..."

Shea raised his voice over the magistrate, cutting off his words. "What I do know is that Demyan's forces kidnapped the mermaid I love and are holding her prisoner. I also know he crashed my airplane and caused death and suffering. I suspect they're using magick to prevent the rescue team from finding the survivors."

"Are we talking merfolk or drylanders?"

The abrupt change of focus and the merman's blunt tone took Shea by surprise. He hesitated before answering, "All drylanders, except one."

He visibly relaxed and waved his hand dismissively. "Then it's no concern of ours. Let the humans handle that problem. I'll dispatch a unit from the University to clear the area of magical interference, but that is the extent of the help we can offer. As for your mermaid friend, the sooner we convict Demyan, the better off she will be as well."

"But sir," Shea persisted. "One of the girls on that island needs medical attention right away."

"Again, drylanders are of no concern to Atlantis. Bringing Demyan to justice is most important in the here and now. The trial begins at first light." The magistrate put a companionable arm around Shea's shoulders. "Come now. Let us see the healer to get your wounds cleaned up, and then find you suitable raiment and a proper supper."

Shea couldn't believe the Lord Magistrate's disdainful attitude toward the people trapped on the island. They were living beings, who were in danger because of Shea. If he hadn't gotten onto that plane in Athens, there wouldn't have even been a storm and none of them would have been hurt.

Or killed. Demyan and his minions were hunting Shea, and didn't seem to care who got hurt in the process. He hadn't meant to abandon anyone, but swimming for help was the only solution he could think of to find the doctor Hailey so desperately needed. Now this guy was trying to tell him to forget about them? Not going to happen. His hands curled into fists of frustration. He needed to save Hailey, and he needed to save Kae. It was his fault and he was going to solve the problem.

He shrugged the magistrate's arm off his shoulders and tried one last time to make him understand. "Sir, I have to go back and help my friends. Tonight."

The Lord Magistrate shook his head. "I will not stand on the steps of the Supreme Courthouse and discuss this with you any further. If you wish to plead some sort of case, we must continue this discussion inside. Over food, as I am famished." He turned and swam back up the useless staircase.

Shea had no choice but to follow. Swimming in the older merman's wake, his mind swirled. He couldn't bear the thought of coming all this way to return to that island alone. That wouldn't help Hailey get better. It wouldn't help to free Kae. What could he say to make the Magistrate listen? Any arguments regarding his human friends would apparently fall on deaf ears. He tried to think of some reason to help that the Magistrate might find beneficial. Irresistible, even.

They reached the top of the stairs and Shea saw a large open hall before them, infinitely larger than the Great Hall of King Koios. Mermen dressed in tunics similar to the Lord Magistrate's garment clustered together in groups of six or seven, some engaged in heated debate while others laughed and ate in a jovial manner.

The Lord Magistrate looked about with a self-satisfied air and chuckled. "The business of running five kingdoms doesn't stop when the sun goes down. I tell you, we are quite busy enough without sparing precious time on drylander problems as well."

"Running five kingdoms?" Shea was puzzled. "I don't understand, sir. Isn't that what the kings are for?"

"To a certain extent, yes."

"What does that mean? To what extent?" From what his mother explained, he assumed the ruling class did just that – ruled. The Courts of Atlantis helped settle disputes between kingdoms, officiate weddings and ceremonies, and of course teach the next generations at the University.

But actually running the kingdoms?

They finally reached the far end of the large hall, where long tables laden with food lined the back wall. Shea was reminded of the Solstice banquet at his grandfather's castle, and the busy kitchen that created the feast. He wondered at the magical feats it must take to keep so many mouths fed on a daily basis here in Atlantis.

Magick.

The Lord Magistrate was popping another bite of sushi into his mouth when Shea swam close and put a hand on his arm. In a low voice, he said, "Sir? I just thought of another compelling reason for you to help me rescue my friends from that island."

Shaking his head to indicate his lack of enthusiasm, the magistrate swallowed the food in his mouth. "I already explained, young Prince, that the plight of drylanders poses little concern to Atlantis."

"But what about the sorcerer who caused such a storm? Would not a merman with that kind of magical ability be useful here in Atlantis?"

"Well..."

Shea could practically see the wheels turning in the magistrate's head. He pressed his advantage, even though he had no idea if his words held any truth whatsoever. "If we leave now, your guards can capture that sorcerer. Imagine having that kind of magick at your beck and call."

"He must be a powerful wielder of magick," the Lord Magistrate mused, almost to himself. "But any Adluo sorcerer would have to face Atlantean justice," he pointed out half-heartedly.

"And who holds the final say over such sentences from the Court?" Shea was pretty sure he knew the answer to that question even as he asked it.

"Well, as Lord Magistrate, that responsibility falls upon my shoulders," he conceded. He stroked his beard, a faraway look in his eyes. "Perhaps we should further investigate this situation. You say you know how to return to this island?"

Shea nodded his head as relief washed through him. "I can lead you there. How fast can you ready the guards?"

CHAPTER TWENTY SEVEN

From the darkening shadows, Kae knew the sun had dipped below the horizon. She hoped they weren't too late. Although they'd made huge progress since mounting the dolphins at Outermost Village, they hadn't yet reached Atlantis.

The thin leather harness around the dolphin's neck did nothing to increase or slow the creature's speed, serving only to steady the rider, especially when they rose for air. Despite their full-grown size, the dolphins were young and enthusiastic and Kae almost lost her grip during several aerial jumps. As they crested the surface again, her dolphin seemed reluctant to keep up the dizzying pace, stopping to enjoy the shifting sky and the darker purples of twilight.

"I think the animals need to rest, Father," she called as he joined her above water.

Lybio looked at his daughter and pulled up on his reins. "We should stop and let the animals feed." He removed the leather straps from his dolphin's thick neck and indicated for Kae to do the same. The dolphins clicked and nickered to each other and then turned and made similar noises to Lybio before swimming off together.

"I never knew dolphins had to surface so often." She ran her fingers through her hair, trying to untangle some of the knots. The animals swam much faster than she could ever hope to, but jumping through the waves rattled her nerves. And her curls.

Her father smiled. "They're mammals, little one. They have no gills and breathe only air, not water."

"What about the dolphins that pull wagons and such in other parts of the world? Like the wagon that Prince Azul brought from the Pacific Ocean. That was pulled by dolphins."

"Those are special animals, cross-bred at the University in Atlantis especially for the purpose with the addition of gills, very similar to the ones in your own neck," Lybio explained. Kae's hand strayed to her ears, running her fingers along the slits hidden beneath her hair. "However, our king doesn't believe in the subjugation of other intelligent creatures."

"But aren't there stables at both the summer castle and winter palace?"

"For visitors. In the Atlantic, we allow the dolphins to choose whether to help us or not, and come or go as they please. They almost always choose to help when asked. It is in their nature."

"Will they return?" They'd come so close, and yet it felt like they'd never reach their goal. She had no idea if Shea and Xander were even in Atlantis. Her father's great plan to stop the sorcerer fell short of having an actual "plan." The only thing she understood was she needed to find Xander. Or rather, Zan. She frowned and slapped her own forehead. Xander doesn't exist, she reminded herself. Zan pretended to be someone he's not.

"I don't speak fluent dolphin, but they indicated they would return after feeding." His head and shoulders bobbed above the surface as he scanned the horizon. "If I'm remembering correctly, we're half a day's swim from Atlantis without dolphin riding, so we'll be there soon."

Kae followed his gaze. "Father, is that smoke on the horizon, or just clouds?"

He narrowed his eyes. "Hard to say from this distance. Come. Let's take a closer look." He dove beneath the surface. With one last tug at her hair, Kae tossed the curls behind her back and dove to follow.

* * *

"Who are you?"

Her question surprised Zan. She had no fear, facing him with hands on her hips, a stern expression on her face. For someone so obviously ancient, she stood tall and straight, with no deference in her posture. In fact, she actually seemed angry with him.

His stomach clenched into a hard knot. He'd already decided not to harm anyone tonight, except Shea, and only if he had to. This was supposed to be a quick stealth mission, sneak in and grab the boy. He didn't have time to argue with some old woman, mermaid or not. "I asked you first." He cringed at the petulance in his voice. "Who are you, and what are you doing with these drylanders?"

She narrowed her eyes but didn't change her stance. "Your accent is Adluo. Are you here with that monster, Demyan?"

"What do you know of Adluos and monsters, old woman?" He kept his words tough, but on the inside fear snaked down his spine. *Who is she?*

"I know for certain you've been watching the island all day," she replied, crossing her arms over her chest. "What I don't know is if you are the *villain* who caused this situation in the first place." She said the word villain with such animosity that Zan felt it like a slap across the face. "You sorcerers all think you're so brilliant with your magick. You forget that actual people suffer the consequences of your actions."

Zan flinched at her words, his mind picturing the merman lying in the pool of blood at the airport and the bodies trapped in the wreckage of the downed airplane. A few souls might have met their makers, but so what? He needed to free the mermaid he loved. Demyan promised to release her when Zan brought Shea back to the Arctic. He'd do whatever it took. Straightening his back, he looked the old woman in the eye and enunciated carefully. "I never meant to harm anyone. I'm. Following. Orders."

Her laugh sounded hollow. "The excuse of every man and monster back to the dawn of time, from Xerxes to Adolf Hitler to Saddam Hussein. I thought we merfolk were better than that. Are the Adluos nothing more than underwater Nazis?"

Heat flooded his cheeks as she chastised him like a recalcitrant schoolboy. How dare she accuse him – and his clan – of such things! He bit the inside of his cheek, reminding himself to keep his emotions in check. "What do you want of me, old woman?"

"I want you to do the right thing."

"The right thing?" Zan sneered, incredulous at her naiveté. "The right thing for whom? For you? For your precious drylanders? 'Right' is such a subjective word."

"And yet, you know that the path you are swimming is the wrong one. Harming others is not in our nature. It's not what the magick is meant for…"

"You know NOTHING of my nature, OR my circumstances." He narrowed his eyes, the anger rising closer to the surface as the truth of her words bit at him. "I owe Demyan my life."

"And how many others must suffer before your debt is repaid?"

"As many as it takes." The breeze off the water picked up and began to swirl as his emotions took control, the magick seizing a chance to escape. This woman stood in the way of his mission. He raised a hand toward her, not knowing what he intending to do, only that he needed to finish his mission. Grab the dryland bastard and drag him back to Demyan before anything more happened to Kae. She was all that mattered.

"Xander! Wait!"

His eyes flew wide, his body vibrating with warring emotions. He knew that voice, the one that soothed his soul and made him feel like life might be worth living after all. Was the twilight playing cruel tricks on him? The mermaid swimming toward the shore looked just like her, but how could that be? He held his breath, the swirl of magick dissipating almost as quickly as it rose.

"Don't hurt the drylander," she called across the waves. "She's my friend."

Zan's glance darted back to the old woman. "Drylander?"

She shrugged, the defiant anger still written across her face. "It's a long story."

Moments later Kae emerged from the water with a tall, burly merman at her side. He hung back by the water's edge as the mermaid ran forward. Her first words were to the woman. "Mrs. MacNamara? Are you all right?"

"I'm fine, dear." She opened her arms wide to catch Kae as the mermaid threw her arms around her, clinging like a starfish, while Zan's mind spun dizzyingly out of control. MacNamara? As in, Shea MacNamara? But this old woman was no drylander – she was a mermaid!

Kae released the older woman and took a small step back, still not sparing a glance for Zan. "Where is Shea?"

"He swam to get help. Several people were badly injured in the crash, including Hailey. This rude merman friend of yours seeks Shea as well."

Zan's mouth hung open at the information, the last of his anger draining into the sand. Shea wasn't even on the island. His mission was over anyway, because his reason for following orders stood right in front of him, a vision of beauty lighting the twilight. When Kae turned to him, her emerald eyes sparkled in the gathering darkness and it felt like a school of minnows swam circles in his stomach. He reached for her hand and gave it a squeeze to make sure she was real and not some conjured vision. He desperately wanted to pull her into his arms and hug her close, but didn't, unsure if she would welcome a display of affection from him. Instead he focused on gathering facts. "How did you get away?"

"My father saved me." Her head tilted toward the big merman stalking his way up the sand. Zan blanched as he drew near, looming even larger and not in a welcoming sort of way. Before he could react or defend himself, Kae stepped between them and made introductions. "This is my father, Lybio. Father, this is Shea's grandmother, Mrs. MacNamara. And this is Xander. Or rather, I guess his name is really Zan. He's the one I told you about."

The merman nodded respectfully to the old woman before training his frown on Zan. "I take it you know my daughter?" The merman's low voice rumbled menacingly. Zan took a deep breath before attempting to answer, but Kae beat him to it.

"Father, leave him alone. I told you already. He protected me from Demyan."

"He also delivered you to that Arctic dungeon in the first place," he growled, fists clenching by his sides.

The old woman's cackle saved him from the father's wrath. "This is the famous Zan?" She stepped closer and laid a hand on his bicep, her touch sending trickles of power skittering along his skin. "If your magick is as strong as the rumors say, perhaps you can heal my grandson's friend, Hailey, before it's too late."

Kae gasped with fear, the sound twisting a knife in Zan's belly. "Mrs. MacNamara! What's wrong with Hailey?"

"Injured in the plane crash caused by your friend here. A crash that killed six people and injured dozens more. She's unconscious and lies close to death."

The look on Kae's face made Zan want to melt into the sand. She looked so unhappy, and even worse, so disappointed in him. "Why would you do something like that?" Zan opened his mouth to answer, but she held up a hand. "Wait, I know. Because Demyan told you to. Because of me." He stared at her, feeling as miserable as she looked, unable to find words to defend his actions. There was no defense. Water pooled in her eyes, as if her confidence in him had melted. This was his fault.

"Now you have to make it right. Can you help her?" Her eyes pleaded with him and he felt his breath catch in his lungs. He knew he had to do whatever he could to make her happy again. Zan wasn't actually sure whether he could heal a drylander with his magick. But for Kae, he would try.

CHAPTER TWENTY EIGHT

Kae stared at Hailey's motionless body. The rest of the survivors slept while Mrs. MacNamara stole back to the campsite and carried away the unconscious girl. Laying her gently onto the sandy beach, she said, "She hit her head during the crash and hasn't woken since. In the drylander world, it's called a coma. But without medical help, we can't get food or water into her and she's dehydrating rapidly in the summer heat."

Looking at the bandage wrapped around the girl's forehead and the dark circles under her closed eyes, Kae regretted every mean thing she'd ever thought or said about Hailey. Lying there so motionless and barely breathing, she looked young and fragile, hardly a rival for Shea's affection. He tried to tell her so many times that Hailey was just a friend. That they should all be friends. What kind of friend would let this happen? Shea swam to get help not because he loved

277

Hailey, but because he wanted to fix something that was all Kae's fault. He was loyal to his friends.

Waves of guilt crashed over her and more water pooled in her eyes. Lybio put his arm around her shoulders, pulling her close as the first fat teardrops slid down her cheek. She noticed Zan staring at her instead of Hailey. Wiping the moisture from her eyes with the heel of her palm, she stared back. "Can you make her better?"

"I'm not sure. She's a drylander, not a mermaid. I'm not sure how her body will react to my magick."

"You have to try. She can't die because of me."

He snorted. "None of this is your fault, babe. If the mongrel bastard had followed directions, the storm wouldn't have happened in the first place."

She shrugged off her father's comforting arm and stepped closer, lowering her voice. "I know you care for me, Xander. Or Zan. Or whomever you are pretending to be today. You kept me safe and I consider you a friend, by whatever name you want me to call you. Listen when I say this human is also my friend. If you know a way to help her, you need to try."

Without answering, he knelt and put one hand on Hailey's wrist and the other on her shoulder and closed his eyes. Long seconds ticked by in silence as Kae said a silent prayer to Neptune. When Zan reopened his eyes, he shook his head. "I don't think there's anything I can do for her. There's no mermaid blood in her for the magick to connect with, to spark the healing."

"Give her some of mine." Her words tumbled out before she could stop to think or consider what he meant. If there was any way to help, she needed to try. "We have to fix this. You are the most powerful sorcerer in the ocean so if anyone can do it, I know you can." She dropped to her knees on the sand next to Hailey, stroking the hair away from her bandaged forehead, before turning her stare to Zan.

He squirmed under the intensity of her focus. "It's not that simple, babe."

"Why not?"

He rolled his eyes. "Besides the fact she's unconscious? But there may be a way…" He looked up at Mrs. MacNamara. "Can you remove the bandage without causing further damage?"

She produced a small cutting tool from a pocket deep inside her dress. "Scissors, from the first aid kit," she explained. She snipped away the gauze, exposing a long gash on the side of Hailey's forehead that looked angry and red. Released from the pressure of the bandage, fresh blood oozed from the cut, dripping down the side of her head and staining the sand.

"May I have the sharp tool?" Zan held out his hand before his dark eyes turned on Kae. "Are you sure you want to try this?"

She took a deep breath and nodded, her mouth suddenly too dry to speak. She didn't know what he planned... but she trusted him. The realization shocked her. He was, after all, the one who stole her away. He caused the crash that injured Hailey. But deep inside, she knew he'd never cause her harm. She nodded again and he scooted closer until their legs pressed together. Awareness pricked her skin at every point where they connected, electricity shooting through her body making the tiny hairs on her arms stand straight.

Long fingers wrapped around her wrist and held it over Hailey's body, her hand tingling under his touch until it felt numb. With great precision, he drew the sharp point of the scissors across her palm, opening a long red welt that ran almost the length of her hand. Above her, she heard her father's sharp intake of breath. She smiled to reassure him. "Don't worry, I can't even feel it."

"I used a simple spell to numb your hand. I don't want to cause any more pain, babe."

She ignored the way his words twisted her insides and focused on her hand, watching the thick, red blood ooze from the cut. When there was a red pool in the palm of her hand, he spoke again. "Kae. I need you to relax and trust me."

She looked into his dark eyes and felt that familiar tug on her heart, but without the pulse of warm feelings she associated with Zan. "You're not using your magick on me," she said, surprised by the sudden realization. She knew now that those warm pulses were his magick at work, making her like and trust him. But he didn't have the magick turned on and she still trusted him. Still considered him a friend.

He raised his eyebrows. "I didn't know you could tell," he said, sounding embarrassed. He held her gaze. "And no, I'm not. I have to focus my magick on healing. I need you to trust me on your own."

"I do," she said, her voice barely above a whisper as she stared into his eyes. She felt him pulling on her numbed hand, but he never broke eye contact, even as he started chanting in Latin. When she finally looked down at Hailey again, she was surprised to see that her cut palm was lined up against the open wound, Kae's blood seeping over Hailey's forehead, but not as much as she would have thought. *My blood must be going right into Hailey's body*, she realized. *He's going to try to use it to heal her from the inside.* She glanced back at Zan. "Have you done anything like this before?"

He shook his head and rested his other hand against her cheek. "You're brave, Kae, to help your friend like this. Brave and very beautiful. I'm so sorry I messed things up."

"You're fixing them now," she reminded him, a faint smile playing on her lips. Her head began to feel light, as if she might float off into the sky and join the stars over the ocean. The air around her seemed thick and hard to breathe. "Zan? I don't feel so well." Her entire body began tingling, just like her hand had done when Zan had cast his numbing spell, as everything faded to black.

Her father's voice echoed in her ears like he was somewhere far away. "Stay with us, little one. That's enough blood, sorcerer!" His huge hands grabbed her shoulders and dragged her backward, away from Hailey.

"No, I need to help," she mumbled, trying to pull out of his grasp and falling to her side. The sand felt soft beneath her cheek, her body floating on a cloud of sea foam. Wait, that couldn't be right. She was on land, not at sea. The ground started to spin underneath her as though her cloud of foam rode a wave crashing onto the shore. Her eyes were still open even though everything was dark, so dark. Suddenly Zan's face was very close, his breath warming her cheek, his strong hand cradling the back of her neck.

"You did well, Kae. Now get some sleep and heal yourself." She felt a tingle rush through her as his lips brushed against hers and his breath filled her mouth, as if he were filling her with his own heat. It wasn't quite a kiss, but it felt as though he were giving himself to her nonetheless. She stared into his dark eyes a moment longer before drifting off on a billowing cloud of sleep. The last thing she was certain of was her father's worried voice.

"Let's hope Poseidon spares this girl's life, sorcerer. Else yours won't last much longer."

Kae she thought she heard Zan answer. "My life isn't worth living without her."

That can't be right, she thought as sleep carried her away. *He can't be in love with Hailey. He doesn't even know her.*

CHAPTER TWENTY NINE

Ever so gently, Zan laid Kae's head onto the sand and withdrew his hand from the back of her neck. She felt so light and fragile, her face so pale, he worried that he'd let her give away too much of her blood. His lips moved in silent prayer that his magick would speed her healing.

"Praying for guidance? Let's hope Poseidon spares this girl's life, sorcerer. Else yours won't last much longer." The hulking merman glared across her sleeping body.

Zan heaved a heavy sigh without taking his eyes off Kae. "My life isn't worth living without her."

Her father looked momentarily shocked, but his features quickly resolved into a scowl. "Then you'd best pray hard. Now go. Help the human girl."

Reluctantly, Zan returned to the drylander's side. Fresh blood smeared her forehead, but most had seeped into the wound already. He wrapped one hand around her wrist, and pinched the skin on her forehead to close the wound. As he muttered Latin incantations, the skin fused together. Once the cut was sealed, he directed the MacNamara woman to wipe away the rest of the blood.

Without the bandages and blood, she looked like a small child who'd fallen asleep after a long day. She was pretty in a dark-haired sort of way, if nothing like Kae's blonde beauty. The dark circles ringing her eyes began to lessen, and her breathing seemed deeper, more normal.

He gripped her shoulder with one hand and her wrist again with the other. Closing his eyes, he reached out with his magick and felt the mermaid blood coursing through the girl's body. Kae's blood. The drylander's body sucked in the mermaid blood as if it were nectar from the gods, which made sense to Zan, given whose blood it was.

He'd been so focused on healing the drylander that he hadn't noticed the energy draining from Kae until it was almost too late. Lucky her father had paid attention to his daughter's wellbeing.

Beneath his hands, the drylander's body start to stir. Color returned to pink her cheeks, and her dark eyelashes fluttered for several long moments until they finally raised. Dark brown eyes, the deep color of rich garden loam, stared up at him as she blinked those long eyelashes. "Where am I? Why is it so dark?"

The old woman leaned over her, covering her rosy cheeks with both hands. "Hailey? You're awake! Oh, thank the gods, you're okay!"

"Gramma MacNamara?" Hailey stared at the woman before returning her gaze to Zan's face. "Then, who are you? What happened? And where am I?" Her voice sounded weak but the questions kept flowing. "What happened to the airplane? Was it able to land safely? Why do you have such gorgeous dark eyes? Where's my mom? Is Chip all right? Where's Shea?"

"Hush." Zan laid two fingers over her lips to stem the tide of words with a gentle pulse of magick. Mrs. MacNamara answered the most pertinent of the questions.

"Hailey, the plane crashed into the ocean. You hit your head and have been asleep for a few days. Your mom and brother are fine." She patted the girl's arm. "You're very lucky Kae and Zan were able to help you."

Hailey's eyes locked again with Zan's. As he watched, tiny specks of green began to bloom within the deep brown of her irises, growing like tiny seedlings in garden dirt. Green, like the color of Kae's emerald eyes. He removed his fingers from her lips but she remained calm and quiet, still staring up at him. "Thank you," she whispered, her voice sending prickles

286

up the back of his neck, unnerving him. Hers now held some of the same musical qualities that made Kae's voice so unique.

"I...I...need to check on Kae, and make sure she's okay, too," he stammered, unable to tear his eyes from her face, watching the transformation take place. Her solid brown eyes were now clearly flecked with large patches of emerald, but still retained the warmth of the darker color. He'd never seen anything like it and wondered what it meant.

Kae's eyelids fluttered as if she were dreaming, her long blonde lashes caressing her still pale cheeks as her father smoothed the curls away from her face. Zan felt a rush of panic, realizing how close he came to losing her again, this time to no fault of Demyan.

He'd meant what he said earlier. Even though he'd only just met the mermaid, his life wouldn't be worth living without Kae in the world. He could tell the father felt the same way about his daughter, and respected him all the more for it. He knelt beside her still form. "How is she?"

The merman frowned at the question. "I think she's starting to come around. No thanks to you. Your tricks back there almost killed her."

Zan bit back a protest. He didn't know if Lybio would appreciate knowing Zan breathed some of his own magick into Kae to speed her healing. He inhaled the damp night air and clamped his mouth firmly shut until his lungs burned with the effort. When he finally exhaled, he realized he wasn't angry. He didn't care what Lybio thought. The only important thing was Kae. She would recover. She would live.

He also realized he was suddenly exhausted. Expending so much magick in such a concentrated effort left him drained. He'd been tired in the past after big outbursts of magick, so it wasn't all that unusual. On the other hand, he'd never in all of his seventeen years felt so satisfied with the results of his work. Even though saving the life of a drylander girl was of no importance to him, it seemed to mean a great deal to Kae. What made her happy was enough to make him happy. He knew without another doubt that he would do anything and everything to please her.

"Xander?"

He smiled at Kae's use of his nickname. His smile widened when he realized her emerald eyes were open and looking up at him. Not at her father. Not at her friend, the drylander. Looking at him. "Hey, there, welcome back," he said gently, reaching for her hand. Her skin felt cold to the touch as he rubbed his thumb in a circle on her palm. "And it's Zan, remember? Glad you decided to rejoin us."

"Hailey?" she asked, not turning her gaze from him.

His lips quirked into a smile. "She's fine. Eyes open and asking questions as fast as she can." Kae had mentioned the drylander's annoying habit during their swim from the Atlantic to the Arctic. A journey that seemed so long ago. Almost like another lifetime. So much had happened since then. Life before Kae was a distant memory.

He'd never opened up to anyone before her, never felt he deserved any friendship for his own sake. Other merfolk feared his power, and gave their respect. Demyan called him by the name 'friend' because he wanted to use Zan's power to further his twisted agenda. But real friendship? Never. Kae was his first friend. The only true friend he'd ever known.

Her next words shocked him to his core. "Zan, you must leave."

"Leave? Why?" The sudden ache in his heart was more than he could bear. He froze where he was, her hand slipping from his grasp. "You want me to leave?"

"When Prince Demyan finds out all you've done, he'll come after you for punishment." Her voice was soft but her eyes were clear, holding him firmly with her gaze. "Swim away and hide yourself."

He stared into her face unable to process what she was saying. He'd just saved that drylander. He'd given some of his own magick to help Kae recover. And yet, now she wanted to be rid of him as quickly as possible? "I don't understand. I thought we were…friends."

Water filled her eyes, making them shimmer in the moonlight. "We are. And I don't want to see you hurt."

A small fire of hope kindled in his chest. She cared about him. He still had a chance. He took a deep breath to steady his nerves, enfolding her small hand in both of his. "There is nowhere I could ever hide from Demyan. His spies are everywhere, in every ocean. I am as safe right here as anywhere."

"But…"

"I'm not leaving your side, Kae. He'll come after you as well."

"The boy speaks truth," Lybio said, his rumbling voice startling Zan. He'd kind of forgotten the big merman was even there. "None of us are safe as long as Prince Demyan is at large."

A menacing laugh echoed across the water. "You're certainly right about that."

Zan's eyes went wide. He knew that voice. Looking to where the waves crashed upon the shore, he saw their little band was no longer alone on this stretch of beach. Prince Demyan and a dozen of his soldiers were rising from the surf.

CHAPTER THIRTY

Hearing the voice from her nightmares, Kae pushed herself onto her elbows, hoping against hope she'd dreamed it.

Even in the darkness, she could see she hadn't imagined anything.

Prince Demyan stalked up the beach, his legs moving stiffly as if not quite sure how to maneuver properly. For someone who hated drylanders as much as Demyan, he probably didn't get ashore very often.

In the scabbard hanging from his waist Kae saw rubies gleaming on the handle of a sword, the same weapon she'd seen him wield at Solstice when he slew the Atlantean High Chancellor. The blue-skinned soldiers on either side of Demyan held spears and swords in their hands, walking just as stiffly but pointing their deadly weapons at her father and Zan with grim purpose. Why were the Nerine so far from their own territory?

"Zan, Zan, Zan." The sneer in Demyan's voice as he repeated the name grated Kae's ears. "I should have guessed I'd find you tucked away on some romantic island hideaway with your mermaid plaything."

Anger flared through her at his suggestive tone. She opened her mouth to retort, but Zan suddenly squeezed her hand with such force her eyes darted to him instead. He shook his head ever so slightly, indicating for her to remain silent, before dropping her hand. As much as she wanted to tell off Prince Demyan, she knew Zan was right. She pressed her lips slowly back together. Mermaid plaything? As if!

Both Zan and her father were rising to their feet, facing Demyan and the Nerine soldiers. Zan spoke first. "How did you find me?"

The smile on Demyan's face made Kae's stomach twist. "How many sorcerers are capable of creating storms like yours, Zan? Hmm? You are the most powerful wielder of magick I've ever known, and yet you think no one will notice when you stir up half the Mediterranean all by your little self?"

"The boy was on a plane, headed for Atlantis. I had to stop him."

"And where is he now?"

Lybio answered quickly, the sheer anger in his voice shocking Kae. "Dead. The crash killed him. Your boy did his job too well."

She felt the tears stinging her eyes even as her father spoke. She knew the words were lies — Mrs. MacNamara herself had said Shea survived the crash, and that he swam off to get help from Atlantis. But the mere thought of Shea dying made her heart feel as if it might explode inside her chest.

Demyan saw her tears and laughed out loud at her grief. "Oh that's a good one, Zan. So caught up in your mermaid fantasies that you decided to kill your rival? Is that any way to win hearts and minds?" His face hardened, the laughter suddenly gone. "I ordered you to bring him to me. What is so difficult about following orders?" He took a step toward Kae and put his hand on the sword's hilt. "And what did I promise if you failed on your mission?"

Before her father could say another word, Zan planted himself in front of Kae. Her vision filled with tensed muscles rippling along Zan's back and legs. "Leave her alone, Demyan." His fists clenched at his sides, but he had no sword to defend himself. Only his magick.

"So we're on a first name basis now, are we?" The sneering laughter returned to Demyan's voice. "What happened to '*my Prince,*' or '*my Lord,*' or even '*Sire*'? Need I remind you that you are my creature to command, little Zan? That you owe me your life?"

"I've paid my debt to you many times over," Zan growled. The breeze swirled sand around the beach and up into the air. Kae felt the touch of magick all around her, and something inside her seemed to warm and blossom.

"Tsk, tsk, tsk." Demyan took few steps back from Zan as he spoke. "Careful now with your anger. You wouldn't want to make your little friend bleed out all over the beach, would you?"

Zan whirled to check on Kae, panic written all over his face as their eyes locked. Demyan snapped quick commands to his Nerine soldiers. Blue mermen rushed forward to grab Lybio's arms while others pointed swords at the women. Lybio struggled against his captors until the soldier guarding Kae pressed his sword against her flesh hard enough to make her cry in pain. Cursing darkly, Lybio finally stilled. Two of the blue mermen had grabbed Zan's arms, pulling him backward and forcing him to his knees. One pressed the shaft of his spear against the back of Zan's neck, crushing his face down into the sand.

The situation under control, Demyan stepped forward again, slowly pulling his sword from the scabbard. Kae couldn't take her eyes off the rubies glinting between Demyan's fingers.

"Now where were we?" An evil gleam lit Demyan's eyes. "Oh, right. We were discussing debts and promises. My promise to you was if you failed, I would hurt your little mermaid. Now I can clearly see that keeping her alive is useful to me, but there are other ways I can hurt her." Demyan spun suddenly to face Lybio, and thrust his sword deep into the larger merman. When he pulled the sword from the body, Lybio crumpled to the sand.

"Father, no!" Ignoring the Nerine soldiers, she ran to her father's side, pressing her hands to his belly to staunch the flow of blood. "You monster!" she screamed at Demyan as she watched her father's life ebbing away. "You won't get away with this!"

The madman chuckled and pushed the bloodied blade back into its scabbard. "But my dear, I already have."

"Not quite, Prince Demyan." More mermen emerged from the waves, some sort of soldiers by the look of their weapons, but none of them with the blue skin of the Nerines who came with Demyan. The one who spoke wore a white tunic with gold decorations that sparkled in the moonlight. "Guards, seize the prince! Seize them all!"

The guards rushed onto the beach to overpower Demyan and another urgent yell caught her attention. "Kae! Are you okay?" Shea appeared at her side, his big green eyes the most beautiful things she'd seen in forever. He threw his arms around her, enveloping her in a warm embrace. As much as she longed to return the hug, her hands still pressed against her father's wound. He quickly realized something was wrong and pulled back. One of his eyes was darkly bruised and swollen shut, and a cut along the bridge of his nose oozed a trickle of fresh blood. What happened to his perfect face?

"Father…Demyan's sword…your face…He's dying." Kae knew she was babbling, but couldn't seem to get her words to work properly or form a coherent sentence. She saw Shea take in the situation, saw her same helplessness mirrored in his eyes.

"Let me save him!" Zan was pleading with his captors, struggling against the guards who pulled him from the sand. The Atlanteans pushed Zan into line alongside Demyan and the Nerine. "I can heal that merman if you let me."

There was no time for arguments. Kae turned to Shea. "Tell them to let Zan go," she begged. "He can fix Father with his magick, just like he saved Hailey's life."

"He healed Hailey?" Shea's one good eye filled with confusion. "But that's Demyan's pet sorcerer. He's the one who crashed our plane in the first place!"

"And then he saved her," Kae repeated firmly. "Get him over here right now."

Precious minutes ebbed away while Shea argued with the merman in the white tunic, convincing him to release the sorcerer. Finally, Zan knelt by Kae's side, one of the guards standing a hair's breadth away. The rest of the guards bound the hands of the other prisoners, but Kae couldn't care less about any of them. Her only concern was saving her father.

"Don't move your hands from the wound," Zan warned as he took a closer look at Lybio. She noticed tiny cuts covering Zan's face, from when the Nerine soldiers had ground him into the sand. He wrapped one hand around Lybio's wrist and put the other on his shoulder, much as he had done earlier with Hailey. Closing his eyes he spoke so softly she had to strain to hear him. "He's lost a lot of blood and we need to work fast. I need you to help me, Kae. Concentrate. Picture the wound in your mind, and see the skin closing the hole, fusing back together."

"How is that going to help? She's not a doctor," Shea argued. Kae hadn't realized he was standing so close behind her.

"Shea, let Zan work," Kae told him without turning around to look at him. "Why don't you go check on Hailey and your Gramma?" He exhaled sharply, but listened to her and walked away. She glanced up at Zan and saw him staring after Shea. "I'm sorry about his behavior. He's just worried."

Zan shrugged. "I can't do this alone, Kae. Concentrate on your father's wound."

She closed her eyes and tried to do as he asked, not sure how her visualization would help Zan but willing to do whatever it took. Again she felt the warmth inside her as it blossomed. She could feel magick pulsing from Zan's hands into her father's still body. She tried to picture the hole in her father's stomach getting smaller, with Zan's magick closing the wound until there was just a seam along his skin, like two pieces of cloth being sewn together.

"Good, that's good, Kae," Zan murmured. "Hold that thought in your head and keep your hands where they are, but open your eyes now. I need to raise your father to close the exit wound."

"Maybe the guard can help you," Kae suggested, looking behind him for the Atlantean who was supposed to be keeping watch over Zan, but they were all alone.

"We can do this together, Kae. You and me." She watched carefully, keeping her hands in position as Zan pulled Lybio's shoulder up, tipping him onto his side. From her angle, she couldn't see her father's back, but watched Zan's face as his eyebrows knit together. Removing the hand from her father's wrist, he placed it along Lybio's back.

She was afraid of the answer, but had to ask. "Will he heal?"

Despite his eyes being closed in concentration, Zan nodded. "I think so. He lost a lot of blood, but you reached him in time to help."

"*We* reached him in time," she reminded him. He opened his eyes and looked at her. His dark eyes looked so sad, so wistful.

"I wish I'd met you earlier," he said, his voice so low she almost missed his words. "My life might have turned out different, if only someone like you believed in me from the start."

What could she say? She did believe in him, and she cared for him...but seeing Shea again confirmed her deepest feelings, and what she knew in her heart. She loved Shea, not Zan. She reached across and put a gentle hand on Zan's cheek. "I will always be your friend."

The barest of smiles tugged his lips and she felt a warm pulse flow through her hand. More magick? She frowned and let her hand drop back to her father's stomach before she realized what happened. "Zan, your face! The cuts are gone!"

"You must have healed them." His words were distracted as he examined Lybio's exit wound. "There. The skin sealed. I think he'll make a full recovery." Gently he rolled Lybio onto his back and put his hand over the merman's heart. "Beating normally."

Kae frowned again, undeterred by his change of topic. "I'm not a Healer, Zan. How could my touch make your cuts disappear?"

"The same way you healed your father." He pulled her hands away from her father's skin to reveal a thin vertical scar in the middle of his belly.

She stared into his dark eyes, unflinching. "You did that. I felt your magick pulsing through his body."

Zan stared back at her. "The magick is in you too, babe. Because of you, he will open his eyes again soon, and make a full recovery."

"How? How is that even possible?" Her mind whirled. She'd never had any inklings of magick before. Sure, she had an untrained syren voice, and liked to coax the seedlings in the king's garden, but magick? Never in a million years.

He cleared his throat, sounding nervous. "I let you give the drylander too much of your blood. You got very weak and…I panicked. I gave you some of my magick to help you heal."

She breathed a sigh of relief. At least this explanation made sense. "You healed me with magick and I transferred some directly to my father."

Zan shook his head. "No, Kae. I *gave* you some of my magick. It's a part of you now."

"You…what?" She didn't see how that could be possible, but Zan seemed to be convinced of what he was telling her. "You had no right!"

"No right? No right to save you?"

"No right to *change* me," she snapped. "Zan, we're friends. I will always love you. But I'm *in love* with Shea. You can't bind me to you with magick to change my mind."

"That wasn't my intent."

"No? Then what was your plan?"

He lowered his head. "I didn't want to lose you. I couldn't let you slip away, not when I could help you."

That gave her pause, the anger extinguishing as quickly as it had sparked. "Maybe I'm overreacting. I mean, how long can a little borrowed magick last, right?"

"I'm afraid there's more to confess. When you gave your blood to the drylander? Something happened to her as well. You gave a part of yourself to Hailey."

"I…we…Hailey?" Kae glanced to where Hailey was sitting up, chatting with Shea and his grandmother. Even from where she was sitting, Kae could hear the musical lilt in Hailey's voice, a sound that hadn't ever been there before. "Could the changes in her be from hitting her head in the crash?"

Slowly, he shook his head, his voice low as he patted her arm. "It's your blood. Her body absorbed so much of it, it's changing her. You should go talk to your friend and see for yourself. I'll stay here and keep watch over your father."

Kae walked up the beach, her mind reeling with Zan's revelations. He'd gifted her with magick, some of his own powerful magick, no less. And apparently she'd given some piece of herself to Hailey. The three of their lives had become twisted together, intertwined by fate and magick. What did it mean for her future? Would the magick grow inside her or slowly dissipate over time? Would she be able to control it or would it control her? She shuddered at the idea of losing herself into a swirl of magical energy, but at the same time a distinct thrill ran down her spine at the thought of actually wielding such power.

Shea saw her coming and jumped to meet her. "Your father?"

Kae pushed her darker thoughts aside and smiled. "He'll be fine. Zan's magick sealed the wound completely." She left out the part about Zan's magick being inside her as well.

"That's great news!" He enveloped her with his warmth, hugging her close. She leaned into his body, her own arms snaking around his waist. He felt so familiar. Like she was home.

"Kae, come sit with me! I want to talk to you!" Hailey's voice practically shimmered with excitement. She was sitting with her legs crisscrossed and seemed as alert and full of life as ever before, despite having been unconscious the last few days.

She disentangled from his embrace. "I'd better go say hello."

He nodded in understanding. "Did you see which way Gramma went? She disappeared all of a sudden. Was she helping with your dad?" She indicated no, and he frowned. "Maybe she's headed back to the campsite? I guess I should find her before the Atlanteans leave. You know that you and I need to go with them, right? To give testimony back in Atlantis?"

She tried to smile but there was ice forming in the pit of her belly. Testify? Against Demyan, gladly. But against Zan? Could she help convict a friend? Not noticing her sudden distraction, Shea kissed her cheek and took off along the beach, presumably to find his grandmother.

Hailey threw her arms wide and called again to Kae. "Come give me a hug!"

A glint of silver on Hailey's wrist caught Kae's eye and she froze mid-step. "Is that my silver bracelet?"

Hailey's laughter sounded like tinkling wind chimes. "I was holding it for you. I told Shea it looked better on me than on him." She slipped it off and slid the bracelet onto Kae's wrist when she came closer. "But it looks even better on you.

You are such a wonderful person. I can totally see why Shea loves you."

Her smile looked so happy and so genuine, Kae couldn't help but smile back. "Thanks, Hailey. I'm so glad you're feeling better." She dropped to her knees next to her and gave her a hug before looking at her face. Her lower jaw dropped. "Hailey, your eyes..."

Hailey grinned, the emerald patches in her irises twinkling in the moonlight. "Shea told me they'd changed color. Weird, huh? I must've hit my head even harder than I thought. I'll tell you what, though, I feel like I can see better in the dark than I used to."

"Really? How strange," Kae said, not sure whether to tell Hailey the truth of the situation.

Hailey lowered her voice. "Please tell me who all these strangers are, and where are Gramma MacNamara and Shea? I'm so glad they captured that Demyan guy who tried to kill your dad, though. I saw you and that other guy healing him, I hope he's better. Did you see the buff guys with the blue skin? What's up with them? And is it just me or is everyone looking at me in a funny way? I mean, really, I'm not the one with the blue skin!"

Kae's smile widened. *Same old Hailey. Thank the gods.*

CHAPTER THIRTY ONE

"Gramma, wait!" Shea ran to catch up with Martha. For a woman who was well over a hundred, she moved quickly. He finally reached her and fell in step beside her. "Where are you going?"

"Dawn will be breaking soon, Sheachnadh. I need to return to the campsite and make sure Hailey's mother and brother don't panic when they find her missing."

Which made perfectly good sense to Shea. But he'd also seen the way she'd covered her face and avoided the Lord Magistrate's eyes. For some reason, she didn't want to talk with the other merfolk. "Gramma, you don't need to run off. They've captured Demyan now and he's going to Atlantis for trial. You can come with me to testify."

She shook her head. "No, dear, I can't. I made my choices long ago."

"What are you talking about?"

Martha looked back in the direction they'd come. "That magistrate has no love of drylanders."

Shea grimaced, recalling his struggle to get the merman's help. "I figured that one out for myself. In the end, I convinced him to bring help only because I told him the sorcerer would be here at the island. Actually, I'd no idea we'd find Zan here – or Demyan for that matter! I just wanted to help Hailey."

"And that's the problem right there. She's your friend first, a human second. The Lord Magistrate doesn't make those types of distinctions." She sighed and continued walking to the campsite. "I didn't think through the possible consequences of accompanying you on this trip. There was no way I could ever swim into Atlantis. Not with that particular merman in charge. Not after the choices I've made with my life."

Shea felt stunned. "So…you really *know* the Lord Magistrate?" Martha nodded but didn't elaborate, leaving Shea to wonder what happened between them to make her hide from him all these years later. "You know I still have to go back with them," he reminded her.

"And I'll be waiting for you on Santorini with the Thompsons." She patted his cheek. "Now that Zan lifted the magick surrounding the island, rescue teams should be here within hours." Martha suddenly stopped in her tracks and Shea almost knocked her over. "And one more thing, dear. You need to keep a close eye on Kae, and I'll keep an eye on Hailey."

"Gramma, what are you talking about? I just talked to Kae. She's fine, now that her dad is recovering." Shea remembered the change in Hailey's eyes, and the way her smile made his stomach clench. Even her laughter sounded a little different, making his pulse race almost as much as Kae's voice did. Maybe his grandmother was right. Something was different about her now that he couldn't quite put his finger on. "It's Hailey who needs watching. She's the one who seems changed by this whole experience."

"It's not the experience. It's the magick."

Shea narrowed his eyes. "The what?"

"Zan's magick. Sometimes magick can do strange things, especially when it's that powerful. It's almost like it has a mind of its own." Her words sounded ominous, sending a shiver down his back. "Just be careful, Sheachnadh, and keep an eye on Kae."

He swallowed, feeling his stomach clench into a knot. "What about Hailey?"

"When she's able to walk, accompany her back to the campsite, and take your leave of the Thompson family. I will come up with an explanation that satisfies." Martha didn't

slow her pace, marching steadily onward, down the beach. Shea's own feet slowed to a halt as he watched her go, his mind spinning with her reaction to the Lord Magistrate and the warnings about magick. What did his grandmother know about magick?

By the time Shea returned to where the merfolk gathered, early morning brightness lightened the horizon. The Lord Magistrate was still taking statements from the Nerine soldiers, but Demyan and half the Atlantean guards were no longer on the beach. Shea hailed a familiar-looking merman as he approached.

"Erastus, what did they do with Prince Demyan?"

The Atlantean guard turned toward his voice, a deep frown creasing his face. He blanched when he saw who was asking the question. "Forgive me, my Prince," he said, bowing low before answering. "The Lord Magistrate sent Prince Demyan back to the City already. He thought it best to keep the rogue prince separated from his sorcerer."

Shea thanked the merman for the information and then made a show of wincing as he rubbed his swollen eye. Erastus bowed and moved away as quickly as possible, still apparently fearing repercussions from his earlier bullying treatment. Shea grinned to himself, hoping the guard would think twice before using his fists on another prisoner.

Hailey stood next to Kae near where her father rested, but seemed to be deep in conversation with Zan. Shea knelt in the sand next to Kae. "Has Lybio woken up yet?"

She locked her emerald gaze on him and a familiar electricity surged through his body. With great effort he resisted the strong need to wrap his arms around her, hold her tight and kiss her until he couldn't breathe. And then maybe kiss her some more, never letting her go. He'd come way too close to losing her forever. Her life had been endangered because of her relationship with him. Demyan would never have bothered with her if she were just another servant girl.

Was he selfish enough to let her suffer because of him? Would she be better off without him? He didn't want to think about a life without her, but did she feel the same? Maybe she realized the whole thing was his fault and was ready to call it quits. He'd put everyone's life in danger – Kae, her father, and a whole plane-load of innocent people – all because of the stupid birthmark on his back. How he wished he could go back to being plain old Shea MacNamara from Oklahoma.

Except then he never would have met Kae.

His hand found hers and squeezed, trying to convey with one simple gesture all the complex emotions threatening to overwhelm him. She leaned her head closer until their foreheads touched. They breathed the same air for long moments, feeling the electricity crackle between them. He stared into her eyes and tried to figure out a way to make everything better. Nothing came to mind except how much he loved her. He couldn't walk away, even if that would be the best thing for both of them. He took one last deep breath and pulled away from her, gesturing at her father with his free hand. "How is he?"

"Don't worry. Zan says he'll wake up any minute now. His magick is pretty amazing."

"You're the one who's amazing. Escaping from Demyan and swimming all the way here to foil his plans. I'm so sorry you got tangled up in this whole mess. Dating the heir to the throne isn't as easy as you thought."

She put a finger against his lips. "Don't. Don't apologize for who you are. Remember, I understood who you were before you did."

"But did you? Did you know things like this might happen?" He dropped her hand and sat back on his heels. Now that he was really looking, she seemed different, too. Stronger, more self-assured. Which made a whole lot of sense, given what she'd been through in the last few weeks.

Her simple laughter was music to his ears. "Well, maybe I didn't expect to be held prisoner in the Arctic Ocean, but yeah. I knew it wouldn't be an easy swim through the oyster fields. Or a pie walk, as you would say."

Shea smiled. "You mean a cake walk?"

Her grin grew wider. "Yeah, that must be it. Cake walk. We need to go on one of those, it sounds interesting. And squishy."

He leaned back in to kiss her, regardless of whether her father woke up and saw them or not, but a voice from behind interrupted. "My Prince? There are still matters to discuss before dawn fully breaks and this island is swarming with more drylanders." Shea turned to see the Lord Magistrate tapping his foot impatiently like any self-important man in the world above water would.

Slowly Shea released Kae's hand and rose to his feet. "What sort of matters, Lord Magistrate? I brought you to the island. Your guards captured Prince Demyan and his sorcerer. Kae and I will come to Atlantis and testify at Demyan's trial about these and past crimes. We just need to wait until her father awakens so she can see for herself that he's fully recovered."

"There's the matter of what to do with the sorcerer." The magistrate tilted his head toward Zan, still chatting with Hailey. Four Atlantean guards stood nearby, apparently awaiting some word from the magistrate.

Kae shot to her feet, hands clenched into fists. "But he helped us! He protected me from that madman, Demyan. He doesn't deserve to go to prison!"

Shea glanced at her, and saw the passion of her conviction written across her face. Shea trusted her instincts. If she truly believed in Zan, there must be good in him.

But.

This was the same merman whose rage had sent an entire plane load of humans crashing into the sea.

The same merman who caused the death of his father. And his uncle. And the grandfather he never even got the chance to meet.

Zan had to pay for his crimes.

The Lord Magistrate crossed his arms against his chest, obviously quite a bit more skeptical about Zan's intentions than the mermaid. "Young lady. That sorcerer was instrumental in the deaths of King Anaxima and Queen Jessamine of the Southern Ocean, as well as being part of the plot to poison their young son, Theosisto, one of the Pacific princes, and your own King Koios. These crimes against the Adluo and Aequorean royal families can not go unpunished."

"Don't forget those people he just killed in the plane crash," Shea added. Okay, so the guy saved Kae's life. And Hailey's. And Lybio's.

But.

The Magistrate waved off Shea's words. "Drylander events hold no bearing in the courts of Atlantis. Royal assassinations, however, are most pertinent. As is the death of the High Chancellor himself."

Kae's cheeks flushed with anger. "I was present for the Chancellor's death. Prince Demyan slew the High Chancellor. As for the others, Zan was like a slave to Prince Demyan, only following orders. He does not have an evil heart."

"And what would the serving girl suggest?"

Shea found the merman's attitude exceedingly patronizing on many levels. Humans don't count? His grandmother warned him of the Lord Magistrate's feelings about drylanders. But he dismissed Kae's opinion solely because of her class status. He could fix that. Moving closer to Kae, he draped an arm across her shoulders. "Sir, I think you should take my girlfriend's assessments more seriously. Because of me, she was held captive by the rogue prince. If she says Zan saved her, you need to take her words seriously."

The merman's eyebrows shot so high they disappeared in the tufts of his white hair. "My Prince, I didn't realize...you didn't mention...." He narrowed his eyes at Kae for a moment, as if seeing her in a whole new light. Clearing his throat, he faced Shea once more. "I'm sure the Courts can find grounds for some modicum of leniency, given the nature of the help the sorcerer has rendered to...your royal family. Perhaps you would be willing to help paint a fuller picture of his situation at his hearing?"

313

Shea felt his stomach clench uncomfortably at the word "leniency." With every fiber of his being, Shea wanted Zan to pay for all the pain he'd caused. But he also owed him a debt for saving Kae's life. And for saving his friend Hailey. His arm tightened around Kae. "We would both be happy to speak at his trial, to help the court understand the extenuating circumstances of Zan's crimes."

Kae didn't seem to buy the Lord Magistrate's placating words. She wanted firm promises, apparently. "He saved my life and the life of my father. Zan doesn't deserve Atlantean jail."

"And my father and grandfather didn't deserve to die," Shea whispered in her ear. "Even if they were merely human."

Kae's eyes flew wide, seeming stunned. "Poseidon's beard! How could I have forgotten your dad? Oh, Shea, I'm so sorry. I'm a jellybrained cuttlefish if there ever was one. But you have to understand that I would've died up there in the Arctic if it weren't for Zan."

Shea bit his tongue. He wanted to remind her that she wouldn't have even been in the Arctic in the first place if it weren't for the wonderful Zan. As he gazed into her shining green eyes, he decided to let go of the argument. Zan was in custody. The courts of Atlantis would decide his fate. He let out a sigh and smiled at her instead of fighting.

The Lord Magistrate chuckled. "I see you have your hands full with this one. A sorceress in training perhaps, to sway your mind so easily with mere words."

Shea narrowed his eyes at the magistrate, who threw up his hands in a mock gesture of surrender. "I apologize for the jest, my Prince."

Playing the royal card for the second time, Shea waved his hand to dismiss the rude merman. "There are things we need to attend to here. We will join you in Atlantis."

The merman bowed at the waist, the gesture of submission belied by the surly tone of his voice. "As you wish."

"And, Lord Magistrate?"

He swiveled to look back at Shea.

"Tell your guards to be more gentle with Zan than they were with me." With the tips of his fingers, Shea gently massaged the skin around his still swollen eye. "We certainly don't need matching souvenirs from Atlantis."

The Lord Magistrate bowed again and started walking without saying another word.

Kae threw her arms around Shea's neck. "Oh, Shea! You were wonderful with that nasty merman. Thank you so, so much for sticking up for me."

His arms slipped around her waist as if it were the most natural place for them to be. "Don't mention it. Or, on second thought, do. Feel free to thank me with lots and lots of hugs and kisses, of course, and any baked goods you might have lying around."

She drew her head back to look in his eyes. "Baked goods?"

He sighed. "Cookies, cupcakes, brownies...stuff like that. It's, you know, a drylander thing."

She smiled and leaned her forehead against his. "You're my *thing*, as you say."

"Sounds good to me." He tilted his chin up and caught her mouth with his, savoring that salty-sweet taste that he knew he'd never get enough of. "I love you, Kae," he said when their lips finally parted.

"And I'm *in love* with you," she said, emerald eyes twinkling in the pink light of dawn.

"Is there a difference?" he asked, not really caring about anything but the next taste of her soft, sweet lips.

"Oh, yes," she whispered before his mouth claimed hers.

ACKNOWLEDGEMENTS

First I'd like to say a general and heartfelt thank you to the many readers and friends who purchase and enjoy my YA novels, and everyone who encouraged me to tell more tales about Shea and his world beneath the waves. You all helped make this series possible. I'm so glad to have this second chance to bring my undersea dreams to life thanks to Wicked Wale Publishing and Kate Conway. Kate, you rock!

Special thank yous are in order for my husband, for giving me the time to write and the support when I needed it (which is always), and to Sean and Brian and Andy for all your understanding, ideas, and encouragement, and for not rolling your eyes every time I find another mermaid gadget to add to my collection. Okay, I know you roll your eyes, but I love you guys.

And a heartfelt thank you and couple of gigantic hugs go out to my mom and dad, to whom I dedicated this book. I can't tell you how much it meant to me that you both liked the first book so very much. I love you both, and miss you every day, Mom.

About the Author

Katie O'Sullivan lives on the shores of Cape Cod and dreams of mermaids. Together with her family and their big dogs, she enjoys long walks on familiar beaches as well as visits to new places.

A graduate of Colgate University with a degree in English Literature, Katie has been writing stories since second grade. She reads omnivorously, and writes romance and adventure for young adults, and something steamier for the young at heart.

Please visit her blog or find her on Facebook for the latest information on upcoming events, book signings, and news.

Website: www.katie-osullivan.com

Blog: http://katieosullivan.blogspot.com

Facebook:

https://www.facebook.com/AuthorKatieOSullivan

Twitter: https://twitter.com/OkatieO

319

Coming July 2016

Turn the page to read a sample chapter from:

DECEPTION

SON OF A MERMAID BOOK THREE

By Katie O'Sullivan

DECEPTION

CHAPTER ONE

Even if it had been a dream, Shea MacNamara couldn't imagine feeling more out of place, like he'd stepped back through the pages of a history book... but with a slightly twisted version of history. He glanced around the cavernous amphitheater, marveling yet again at the ancient Greek architecture built solid enough to withstand the ravages of time. The stone benches curved smoothly around the semi-circle, each row higher than the last, each with a perfect view of the stage at the heart of the courtroom. A row of four magistrates in flowing white tunics sat on high marble stools behind tall, imposing lecterns. A single Doric column rose three feet high from the exact center of the stage.

The marble structure looked like it could've been torn straight from the pages of his friend Hailey's *Guide Book to*

Ancient Greece. Except for the shimmering school of fish circling the upper deck of the grandstand, and, of course, all the brightly clad merfolk seated on the benches circling the arena. Each row reached closer and closer toward the sky...a sky that hung somewhere unseen beyond the surface of the Aegean Sea, while the arena itself sat nestled several thousand feet below the waves at the heart of the underwater city of Atlantis.

A sharp elbow to the ribs refocused his attention, and he glanced at the mermaid by his side. He raised one eyebrow as his lips curled upward, wondering for probably the millionth time how he'd ever gotten so lucky. Kae was easily the most beautiful mermaid he'd ever met. And now that he'd been in Atlantis for a while, he could say it with a whole lot more conviction than before. After all, she was the very first mermaid he'd spoken to...and that was before he even *believed* in mermaids.

Since the start of the fall semester, he'd met plenty of pretty young mermaids around campus and in his classes. Even mermaids several grades ahead of him suddenly needed to retake introductory classes, vying for the desks closest to Shea's or the seats nearest him in the grand lecture halls. The experience was a far cry from the previous fall, during his freshman year at Plainville High School, when none of the girls even gave him the time of day. Of course, back then he'd been just another Oklahoma farmboy. Now he was the son of the Queen of the Southern Ocean, heir to the King of the Atlantic and one of the most eligible bachelors on campus.

Even if he was still merely fifteen, and only learned how to swim in June.

"Quit daydreaming, you clownfish. Pay attention." Kae's flowing blond curls tickled his neck when she leaned closer to whisper in his ear. He felt a familiar tingle run through his body when she rested her hand on top of his, squeezing tight. "The magistrates have called for the defendant to be brought forth."

Shea tipped his head closer, resting his forehead against hers, staring deeply into her emerald eyes. "Stay calm. Just breathe." A steady stream of bubbles blew out of her gills, and her grip loosened. "He can't hurt you or your family. Not ever again."

The mermaid nodded, closing her eyes and gulping the saltwater. "It just feels like we've been waiting forever for the start of this trial. Delay after delay after delay."

He struggled to find words that might soothe her. "I know it seems like a tactic of some sort, but I'm sure the court wants to make sure everything is carried out to the letter of the law. You know, cross all the Ts, dot every I, that sort of thing."

"Forget the alphabet, for Neptune's sake!" Kae opened her eyes, the barely contained anger simmering in their green depths. "My dad healed, but think of all the others who lay dead in Demyan's wake. And think of poor Zan, locked up in that tiny dungeon cell this whole time! The fall equinox already passed and Winter Solstice isn't that far away. I want this, no, *need this*, to be over soon."

She gave his hand another squeeze and he felt a surge of angry emotion. He hated that Demyan's defenders used every tactic available to delay and postpone this trial, including the intimidation of witnesses. Some of those witnesses disappeared without warning, causing further delays. Here it was October already, and the trial was just getting underway. He worried about Kae's safety, and agreed whole heartedly that the sooner the trial ended, the better for everyone.

"He's not going to be swimming out of here without punishment," Shea reassured her. "And you shouldn't be afraid to testify. Just tell the truth." Her blond curls bobbed up and down and her grip eased up once again.

Since both he and Kae were on the witness list, they sat in one of the first few rows, close enough to see the subtle smirk on Demyan's face when guards led him into the courtroom. Metal cuffs encircled both wrists, a bright chain dangling between them and dragging along the stone floor. One of the guards led the clanking prisoner to the center of the platform and the short column. Shea hadn't noticed the metal clasp or the lock the guard used now to attach the chain atop the pillar. He shuddered, remembering that brief time when he himself wore similar heavy chains, upon his first arrival in Atlantis.

"What does he have to smile about?" Kae hissed in Shea's ear, distracting him from his memories. "You'd think he's been enjoying his time in the dungeons."

Shea frowned. "Atlantis doesn't keep merfolk with royal blood in the regular dungeons. He's been locked up in that tower complex on the south end of the campus. I certainly don't think it's a four-star hotel but…"

"Royal…blood…" Kae spluttered, her green eyes flashing as her voice rose above a whisper. "Are you kidding me? All the chaos he's created, yet he's still afforded the luxuries of the ruling class? That's ludicrous!"

"Hey, I don't write the laws." He forgot to keep his voice down. "Besides, why didn't your jailbird buddy fill you in on those details? What is it you guys spend so much time talking about?"

The momentary look of shock on Kae's face was quickly replaced with anger. "You're jealous of Zan? Are you making a joke? All the talk around school is not whether we'll break up, but how long it will be before you dump me for one of the Pacific princesses who follow you everywhere." She gestured toward the upper reaches of the grandstands. A bevy of beautiful mermaids dressed in colorful scarves tinged with golden thread gathered in the upper reaches where they giggled and whispered.

"They're not here to see me. They're here because Demyan killed their cousin, Prince Azul." He scowled, feeling uncomfortable. Sure, he'd heard the same rumors, but he didn't think Kae took such gossip seriously. His roommates, on the other hand, took perverse pleasure in keeping track of the latest betting odds, informing Shea on a daily basis.

One of the magistrates banged a stone gavel three times against his rostrum. His bushy grey eyebrows lowered as he yelled, "Order in the court!" He paused for a moment for the crowd noise to die.

Shea shrugged and mouthed the word "Sorry," before taking Kae's hand in both of his. The mermaid closed her eyes and took a deep breath before nodding her head to acknowledge his apology. When she opened her eyes again, Shea saw anxiety mixed with fear.

While Demyan might have plotted to take over the Atlantic and poison his grandfather, he hadn't succeeded. But Demyan did kidnap Kae and make her watch as he shoved a sword through her father's chest, taking him to the brink of death. Her father lived only because of Zan's magick.

The magistrate cleared his throat before continuing. "This courtroom is now in session. Stay if you wish to hear and be heard. We begin this day the trial of Prince Demyan of the Adluo clan, being formally accused with four counts of regicide and one of attempted regicide, two counts of parricide, and one count of hericide, as well as various and numerous wartime atrocities committed during the prolonged conflict between the Adluo and Aequorean clans."

Kae elbowed Shea's side again, her voice now so low he could barely make out the words. "What are they babbling on about? What are all those 'cides'? What about trying to poison King Koios, and killing the University's High Chancellor, and kidnapping me, for Neptune's sake?"

"Hush," he whispered back, pressing a finger against her lips. "They've got it all covered. I'll explain the formal charges later."

"But…"

The second magistrate banged his gavel three times. "What says the defendant, Prince Demyan of the Adluo clan? How do you plead your case to the Court?"

Demyan smiled back at them silently. A blue-skinned merman rose from a bench in the front row and swam forward. A shock of white hair flowed behind him, and even without seeing his eyes, Shea figured he must be from the

Nerine clan. The blue merman bowed his head to each of the four magistrates before he spoke.

"My Lord pleads his innocence, your Honors, and has employed me as counsel to speak on his behalf. Prince Demyan regrets any harm caused by his actions, and insists he merely performed his sworn duties as Prince Regent to his cousin, King Theosisto, the true mastermind behind the plot to overthrow the Atlantic Ocean. Prince Demyan denies any accusations of wrongdoing in the eyes of the Atlantean Court, and most sincerely hopes you will see fit to understand and excuse the most grave of wartime realities, that soldiers must follow the orders they are given."

"What a crock of whale blubber," hissed Kae. Shea frowned and put a finger to his lips, trying to indicate the need to control herself before they got thrown out of the amphitheater. He knew from experience talking back to Atlantean guards led to harsh consequences, and imagined that held true in the courtroom as well.

The second magistrate nodded before speaking again. "The defendant's plea is duly noted by the Court. Let it be known to all that the Court always takes declarations of wartime into account when deciding the fates of soldiers called to serve. But officially, we need to hear the defendant's plea from his own lips."

Every eye found Demyan, chained but uncowed in the center of the stage. He stared straight ahead, chin held high, and actually smiled at the magistrates lined before him. "Not."

The same magistrate leaned forward over his podium. "Not what?"

"Not Guilty."

A wave of murmurs raced along the benches. Shea felt Kae's body tense, but she didn't make a sound, her lips pressed into a thin, tight line.

The third magistrate rose and banged his stone gavel three times. The spectators hushed immediately. "Who speaks for the prosecution? Who will make the case of guilt against Prince Demyan?"

Shea's eyes flew wide with surprise when the Lord Magistrate himself rose from the bench in the front row. He hadn't seen much of the merman in the last few weeks. Which was just fine with Shea. At the beginning of the semester, the Lord Magistrate called upon him to attend luncheons and dinners in his elaborate underwater palace, under the guise of introducing him to Atlantean society. Shea got the distinct impression of being used for political maneuvering, but didn't understand the intricacies of whatever plan the magistrate was formulating.

330

The older merman always touted Shea's connections to both the Atlantic and Southern Oceans, and made sure to emphasize Poseidon's trident on the boy's back. At the same time, he tried to obfuscate the fact that Shea's father had been a drylander. He made Shea feel uncomfortable in his own scales, as if having mixed-blood heritage were a shameful secret to be swept under the table.

"If it should please the Court, the position of prosecution counsel has fallen to me. In light of the heights the defendant's crimes have risen, as well as the defendant's status as a member of the Adluo royal family, it would seem only just to have the highest level of prosecution making the case against him."

"Very well," the third magistrate said with a curt nod. "So long as we have your word that your arguments will be more legal than political in nature."

"My very word indeed," said the Lord Magistrate with a chuckle. He bowed deeply to each of the four merman behind their podiums. "And may I say it is quite an honor to once again stand before all of you, my respected friends and colleagues. I have been too long away from the simple matters of the Court, too caught up in the complex business of running our world. I look forward to making my arguments before you."

Shea thought he saw the fourth magistrate grimace before carefully wiping the expression from his face. He wondered if he imagined the look. Peering more closely at the last magistrate, he wondered if the merman had a problem with the Lord Magistrate, either his class-centered way of looking at the world or his xenophobic tendencies that were really not much better than Demyan's philosophies. Then again, maybe he was just projecting his own dislike of the Lord Magistrate onto others, wishing someone else saw the guy as the same puffed up blowfish Shea pictured him.

Another elbow to the ribs, and a small whisper directly in his ear. "What're you smiling about?"

"Tell you later," he whispered back, watching the proceedings unfold like a carefully orchestrated performance. The prosecution and defense hovered on opposite sides of the circular stage with Demyan in the middle, chained to the column. The first magistrate on the podium called out a litany of names, and one or the other counsel would confirm that the merman or mermaid was indeed being called as a witness. Shea's ears perked up when his own name was called, and noticed that the Lord Magistrate hesitated slightly before claiming him as a witness against Demyan.

When Kae's name was called soon after, Shea was surprised to hear both sides claim her as a witness. It seemed to take the panel of magistrates by surprise as well.

The fourth magistrate at the end of the row finally spoke, his graveled voice measured in its cadence. "Who is this mermaid named Kae? How is it you can both claim her to be on your side? This seems rather unprecedented."

"She is a serving girl from the Aequorean royal house," the Lord Magistrate explained with a dismissive wave of his hand. "A direct witness to several of the events of the Solstice holiday, but we have more reliable, upper class witnesses to those same events, such as the Aequorean heir. If the defense wishes her on their list, I will lodge no objections."

"What if I object?" Kae's voice rang loudly through the open courtroom.

All eyes turned to stare at the blonde mermaid. The magistrate on the end spoke again. "Are you the mermaid in question?"

Kae nodded. "I want to see… the accused convicted of his crimes. I don't want to defend him."

The Lord Magistrate interrupted. "This is not about what you want or don't want, young lady. This is about seeing Atlantean justice served."

The magistrate on the end of the row cleared his throat loudly enough to make the Lord Magistrate turn to face him. "May I finish speaking?" When the prosecutor bowed, the magistrate turned his attention back to Kae. "You make it sound as though this is more personal to you than as just a servant who witnessed a crime."

"It is personal to me, your Honor, to see justice prevail in this case."

The merman steepled his fingers as he leaned back in his chair. "Very well. While the law prohibits us from striking your name from the defense, you can be assured of having your full say." He turned to his colleagues seated with him. "The mermaid will remain as a witness for both sides in this case."

Nods of agreement met his words, except from the Lord Magistrate. He seemed ruffled by the exchange, but chose to move on to the next item on his agenda.

"Your Honors, it has been brought to my attention that several of my key witnesses may not be able to attend these proceedings, including and most importantly the new Adluo queen. Queen Brynneliana is currently traveling to the Australian coast to broker peace talks between the princes of the Pacific and the Indian Oceans, over the disputed territories once ruled by the recently deceased Prince Azul. Yet another lingering side effect of the tragic Solstice events."

Shea felt a lump rise in his throat. He hadn't realized just how much he'd been looking forward to seeing his mother again. Hearing the news this way made it all the harder.

It felt like ages ago his mom was crowned queen of the Southern Ocean and yet again had to leave him alone. He wanted to share so many stories with her, stuff that had happened over the last few months, and he had a few questions to ask...

He tried to remind himself it wasn't her fault. She had duties to her clans – to both the Aequoreans and Adluos now – that needed to be fulfilled. This was the whole reason he'd grown up without knowing her, apparently. Now that he knew the secrets of his heritage, he thought he'd be able to spend more time getting to know his own mom.

Except it hadn't turned out that way. Not yet, at least.

The week after Solstice proved awkward for both of them, as his mother tried to explain why she'd stayed away for fifteen years. That she truly loved both him and his father. She cried every time she mentioned her husband. His mother and father sacrificed their chance at happiness together for his safety. She wanted him to grow up in a normal, human environment, she said, until they determined if his mermaid blood would prevail. If he developed gills. He knew from his grandmother that it wasn't always a sure thing, but the trident birthmark on his back should've been a clue that the gods had a plan for Shea.

Unfortunately, that plan didn't include more time getting acquainted with his mother. After waiting fifteen years

to meet his mother, their reunion ended after only a few days. Now four more months passed, only to hear she wasn't able to make the journey to Atlantis.

Kae sensed his despair. "Cheer up," she whispered close to his ear. "Winter Solstice will be here before you know it. We'll swim out of here after final exams and head straight to the Southern Ocean. You'll have a whole month to spend with your mother, the Queen."

He closed his eyes, bubbles streaming from his gills. He knew she was right. But it still hurt. He missed out on having a mother in his life for fifteen years, even though his dad had always been around. And now his father was gone too. So much had changed in the last few months. He wondered if he'd ever really get used to life under the sea. Somehow, he doubted anything would ever feel normal again.

CPSIA information can be obtained
at www.ICGtesting.com
Printed in the USA
LVOW12s0929061116

511834LV00001B/93/P